NORTH
KOREA

WITHDRAWN

SOUTH
KOREA

Shanghai

HONG KONG
(DETAIL) 1970s

MAINLAND
CHINA

NEW
TERRITORIES

Sai Kung
Peninsula

Taipei

Kowloon

TAIWAN

Lantau Island

Central
Hong Kong Island

PHILIPPINES

N
W E
S

Letters in the
JADE
DRAGON
BOX

Other Books by
GALE SEARS

The *Autumn Sky* trilogy
Autumn Sky
Until the Dawn
Upon the Mountains

Christmas for a Dollar

The Route

The Silence of God

Letters in the

JADE DRAGON BOX

a historical novel

GALE SEARS

DESERET
BOOK

SALT LAKE CITY, UTAH

© 2011 Gale Sears

This book is a work of fiction. The characters, places, and incidents in it are the product of the author's imagination or are represented fictitiously.

Visit us at DeseretBook.com

Library of Congress Cataloging-in-Publication Data

Sears, Gale, author.
  Letters in the jade dragon box / Gale Sears.
    pages cm
  Includes bibliographical references.
  ISBN 978-1-60641-248-0 (hardbound : alk. paper)
  1. Mormons—China—Hong Kong—Fiction.   2. Hong Kong (China)—Fiction.
I. Title.
  PS3619.E256L48 2011
  813'.6—dc22

2011025960

Printed in the United States of America
Publishers Printing, Salt Lake City, UT

10   9   8   7   6   5   4   3   2   1

To Grant and Luana Heaton,
for their love of China—indeed,
for all the people of the Southern Far East Mission.

And to Shawn, whose mission called him home.

Acknowledgments

I extend my deep gratitude to the many people who helped bring about this book.

To Grant and Luana Heaton for inviting me into their home and sharing stories and insights about the wonderful people of Hong Kong as well as the genesis of The Church of Jesus Christ of Latter-day Saints in China.

Thanks to Matt Christensen, Chris Hughes, and Daisy and Gary Ma, for their help with the Chinese characters and calligraphy.

To Sandy Brown (Hu Yao-hwa), for her extensive perusal of the manuscript, concise suggestions for improvement, and help with the pronunciation for the audio book.

To Levi Sim, Ma Khe-ni, and Richard Turley Jr. for offering gems of information about the remarkable country of China with its rich history, and good people.

ACKNOWLEDGMENTS

To Shaunna Chymboryk and Sandy Brown for being my first readers.

To my husband, George, for supporting me in many ways during a difficult time.

And finally, to the amazing team at Deseret Book, who make me believe that all things are possible.

Chapter 1

September 9, 1976

IT BEGINS WITH A DEATH. Thousands of people mourn. Thousands of people celebrate. Hundreds of thousands of people precede him to the grave—a grave he dug for them in China's sacred soil.

● ● ●

For Chen Wen-shan, the day began normally with a breakfast of cornflakes and a scowl from her great-uncle. But at school, things changed. Her friend Song Li-ying was absent, which had never happened in their school years together, and her teacher Mrs. Yang broke one of her own classroom rules by looking at the clock every five minutes. And at three o'clock, the school's intercom system came screeching to life, interrupting the physics lesson. The principal's voice, normally brusque and strong, hesitated. "Word—word has reached Hong Kong that just after midnight last night, the Chairman of China, Mao Tse-tung—died."

Snap. The intercom went off.

Wen-shan sat very still, her hand pressed flat on her work papers. No one moved or made a sound. All eyes were on Mrs. Yang as though she would explain everything.

Mao Tse-tung is dead? What does that mean?

Someone's pencil rolled off their desk and clinked onto the linoleum floor. The teacher's mouth opened, but no words came out. The intercom scratched to life again and everyone jumped—even Mrs. Yang.

"School will close early today. Classes cancelled."

Snap. The intercom went off.

One young man stood abruptly and left the classroom, forgetting his books and his jacket.

Wen-shan looked around and saw mass movement as her classmates stood. She stood with them. She gathered her books and papers into her schoolbag. Mrs. Yang stared at her watch and Wen-shan could see her jaw working to control her emotions. No one spoke to the teacher as they exited.

Wen-shan reached the outside of the school and ran. Eight blocks to her house and she ran all the way. As she neared home, she saw Song Li-ying framed by the half-moon arch of the courtyard wall. She stood by the front gate, waving a paper. She didn't talk or call out, only waved her paper.

"Li Li, what is it?"

The paper waved again.

Wen-shan stopped to open the gate, but Li-ying shoved the

note forward—a section ripped from the paper. Wen-shan read it.

"Yes, I know. Chairman Mao is dead. They told us at school."

Her friend blinked as though the sun was too bright. "The Stone Boy is dead," she whispered.

Wen-shan's heart beat faster. *The Stone Boy is dead.*

"Where were you today?" Wen-shan asked as she shoved open the gate. The girls moved into the courtyard.

"Father found out the news early this morning. He thought it safer if I stayed home."

Wen-shan glanced to the bungalows on the left and right of the yard, but none of her neighbors seemed to be home. She continued down the curving path to the bungalow she shared with her great-uncle. She knew he wouldn't be home. He was at the furniture store taking care of things for the British owner.

Wen-shan moved up the steps to the small porch and un-locked the front door. Li-ying hesitated on the landing. "Come in, Li Li. He's not here to frighten you."

The girls removed their shoes and entered the cool interior of the house. It was dim and smelled lightly of sandalwood in-cense. Wen-shan put her schoolbag in her room and went to the kitchen for a snack. She found almond cookies, took a handful, and gave three to Li-ying.

"I think we should go down to the main street and see what's happening."

Li-ying agreed and the two girls ran several blocks to the main street. They saw many people talking excitedly together—some were crying, some pressing hands to their heads in prayer and looking at the sky. There were firecrackers everywhere. Long red ropes of firecrackers hung from third-story balconies, popping and cracking, the fire climbing the bundles like a ladder. The noise was terrible and wonderful. The smoke rose, explosions shredding the delicate red paper. The friends tried to catch the paper as it floated lazily through the air, landing on the heads of the celebrators, the taxi cycles, and the rough street. So much paper. The little children kicked it into great piles.

"Wen-shan, look at that!"

Wen-shan followed her friend's gaze. Mrs. Wong, from the Golden Door Bakery, was handing out good-fortune buns. The two raced to stand in line.

"All Hong Kong is full of joy today!" Mrs. Wong cried as she held out the steaming basket. "Take one! No charge."

Li-ying and Wen-shan looked at each other with wide eyes. This *must* be a spectacular day. Mrs. Wong had never given away any of her bakery goods for free. Wen-shan remembered that her friend Jun-jai always called Mrs. Wong "the crafty businesswoman." *"Ah, that Mrs. Wong—she could sell fish to the mermaids."* That was what he always said.

Wen-shan shoved the soft steamed bun into her mouth and hummed with delight as she tasted the sweet filling. Just as she was reaching for another bun, she saw the tall, lanky body of her friend Wei Jun-jai moving down the street. He held his transistor radio to his ear.

Wen-shan grabbed Li-ying's hand. "Come on! Let's catch up to Jun-jai. He might have news."

Firecrackers popped at their feet, and they squealed with delight.

"Jun-jai! Stop! Wait for us!"

Jun-jai turned his head from side to side as though he had heard his name, but with all the noise he couldn't be sure. He shrugged and continued his travels. Wen-shan shoved past several people to catch him.

"Hey!" a man in a business suit complained. "Hey, little chubby girl, stop trying to push people out of your way."

Wen-shan grew sullen at his words. "Stop being a Capitalist Roader!" she yelled back at him as she headed for the intersection where Jun-jai had stopped.

The man spat out a rude remark, and Li-ying grabbed Wen-shan's arm. "Wen-shan, you must not say terrible things like that to people."

"Well, he said a terrible thing to me."

"But you are only fifteen. You must be respectful of your elders."

"Old-school thinking."

Li-ying stopped; her beautiful dark eyes were full of anger. "Not old-school thinking. I have been taught manners, that's all."

"Jun-jai!" Wen-shan called again. "Wait!" She started forward. "Hurry, we're losing him!"

"I don't care. I'm going home." Li-ying turned away.

Wen-shan swallowed her pride. It slid down her throat like bitter gingerroot. "Wait! Wait! I'm sorry. Really, I am. It's just that he called me a chubby girl. It made me angry. You don't know what that feels like. You are like a willow branch."

Li-ying glared at her. "Yes, but I get insulted too, for my glasses and my crooked teeth. Does that mean I have to call my tormentors terrible Communist names?"

"Well, I . . ."

"Especially on a day like today?"

"Hey! Wen-shan. Li-ying. Were you calling me?" Jun-jai

waved as he walked forward. He maneuvered around two elders who were arguing about the day's events.

Wen-shan waved back. "Yes. We didn't think you heard us." She thought Jun-jai looked very hip in his American-cut pants and white buttoned shirt. He had the sleeves rolled up, and she thought that his wristwatch made him seem older than sixteen—more like eighteen. She was glad they had been friends since childhood, because if they met today, she doubted he would have even given her a glance.

As he approached, Li-ying tried to hide behind her friend. Wen-shan pulled her to her side. They smiled at Jun-jai.

"We wondered if you've heard any more news about Chairman Mao's death. Do we know what he died of?"

Li-ying shook her head. "Wen-shan, how can you talk about death so offhandedly?"

"That's not offhanded. That's practical."

Jun-jai turned off his radio. "Not much news. All we know for sure is that he's gone to meet his ancestors."

"I wonder what they will think of him?" Wen-shan's attention was diverted by the harsh words between the two elders. "What's their problem?"

Jun-jai turned to listen. "The one is saying the celebrations are too dangerous. There are many communists in the city who will cause problems." He turned back. "Like the agitation in '67."

Wen-shan snorted. "Hong Kong is not their domain."

Li-ying grimaced.

"Ah! Li-ying, you of all people should be glad the Stone Boy is dead. Wasn't your family run out of China because of him?"

Jun-jai spoke up. "'Ching Duke of Ch'i had a thousand teams of horses; but the people, on his death day, found nought in him to praise.'"

Wen-shan laughed at Jun-jai, and he laughed with her. "Ah! Jun-jai, the great student of Confucius!"

The tension was broken and a smile brushed the corner of Li-ying's mouth. "Just like your uncle, Wen-shan. He is also a great student of Confucius, yes?"

Wen-shan stopped laughing. A car sped by, and she watched it, pretending not to have heard.

"How is your uncle?" Jun-jai asked.

Wen-shan cleared her throat to blunt her irritation. "Fine, I suppose. I don't talk to him much."

"I always like talking to him. He is very wise."

"Hmm. A wise man who never speaks." She watched another car pass. "So, where were you going, Jun-jai?"

"To my auntie's. She is having a big dinner to celebrate. Would you like to come?" He looked at Li-ying. "You're invited too."

"Oh . . . oh, very kind of you, Wei Jun-jai," Li-ying stammered, "but I must return soon to my home. We also are having a family dinner to celebrate."

He nodded and looked back at Wen-shan. "Does your uncle expect you?"

She chose her words carefully. "I don't believe so. He is visiting at the home of his British friend. He probably won't be home until late."

"Then, if you'd like, come with me. You can telephone him from my auntie's house."

"I will not be imposing on your auntie's generosity?"

"No, of course not, especially not on a special day like today."

At that moment Wen-shan was not jealous of Song Li-ying and her large family. At that moment she was glad for her old uncle who rarely talked to her except to quote Confucius or some odd Christian scripture. She bowed her head several times. "I would be greatly honored to come to the dinner. Thank you for inviting me, Jun-jai."

Firecrackers crackled nearby, and the girls squealed and jumped. They laughed and clapped their hands with excitement, thinking that September 9 was a very good day.

Li-ying took her friend's hand. "I must be going now. I have to stop at the market and buy lychees for my grandfather."

"Good fortune to your family," Jun-jai said. He bowed, and Li-ying bowed quickly to cover her blushing face.

"Good fortune to your family," she replied. She smiled at Wen-shan. "Have a good time."

"Yes, I will. My heart celebrates with all Hong Kong."

"And Taiwan," Li-ying said. "The national flag must be flying high."

Wen-shan nodded. "Yes, and no black armbands like on the day Chiang Kai-shek died."

"Don't be so sure," Jun-jai interjected. "People will wear them out of show if nothing else, and some will truly mourn. They have chanted Chairman Mao's name for a long time."

Wen-shan shrugged. "Well, you may be right. I don't know that much about it. I just know that I want to celebrate."

"Yes, we should be on our way," Jun-jai encouraged.

They waved to Li-ying as she moved off into the crowd.

Wen-shan smiled with satisfaction. An entire afternoon with her friend Jun-jai, eating good food and celebrating with other happy people. For a moment her conscience twisted as she thought of her old uncle, but he was busy at the furniture store and would not miss her. He never missed her.

• • •

Auntie Ting was a bundle of energy, scurrying from kitchen to table as she set out bowls of noodles, plates of vegetables, steamed buns, heaping bowls of rice, platters of sweet glazed chicken, deep-fried fish, and spicy pork knuckles. There were a lucky thirteen people at her table and she beamed at each one as though she hadn't just spent the day cooking. Wen-shan liked her face.

"Welcome! Welcome!" Auntie Ting said on a sigh as she plopped dramatically into her chair. "So glad you could all be here, and so glad for Jun-jai's friend, Chen Wen-shan, to join us." Wen-shan blushed. "She makes number thirteen at our table. Lucky thirteen!"

The old auntie sitting to Wen-shan's right turned to stare and smile, and Wen-shan tried not to notice the gaps where her teeth should have been.

"Are *we* lucky or is *she* lucky?" the old auntie asked as she raised her eyebrows at Jun-jai.

Wen-shan's embarrassment was interrupted by someone passing her a platter of bok choy. At Auntie Ting's insistence, she filled her bowl with all the delicious food and was content to eat and listen instead of joining in on any of the conversations. Jun-jai and his brother were talking about President Nixon's visit to China in 1972—both agreeing that Nixon had been a pawn in the hand of Mao Tse-tung. Auntie Ting complained about the cost of meat. The toothless auntie on Wen-shan's right was telling ghost stories to a young nephew, and despite her age, the auntie's voice was rich and expressive, and Wen-shan was capti-vated. The woman finished one story about a man sleeping on the bones of a skeleton and turned to catch Wen-shan listening.

"Did you like that?"

Wen-shan nodded.

"I can tell you one about an emperor and some angry peasants, if you'd like."

"Yes, please," Wen-shan and the nephew said together.

The auntie took a drink of tea and began. "Emperor Chan Lee was taking a trip to the province of Guangxi. He rode on his strong black horse and had many fierce guards behind him."

When Wen-shan heard the words *province of Guangxi*, her stomach clenched. Guilin, in the province of Guangxi, was her birthplace and the source of many of her nightmares. She tried to concentrate on other things, but the old woman's voice wrapped the story in such mystery that Wen-shan could not stop listening.

"Chan Lee was a ruthless emperor, and many innocent people died from his sword and because of his evil programs. As Chan Lee rode along, the Spirit Wind came and whispered in his ear to turn back. The Spirit Wind warned him that many people stood waiting for him on the Hundred Flower Bridge. They were going to take revenge for the wrongs Chan Lee had done to their families.

"Chan Lee laughed at the words of the Spirit Wind. He raised his sword high in the morning light. 'I have killed many strong men with my sword, and I have my fierce guards behind me,' he said. 'Do you think I fear a few starving peasants?' He rode on through the mountain pass. The path grew shadowed as the sun hid its face behind the high peaks.

"The Spirit Wind now came howling through the pass, shouting into Chan Lee's ears to turn back! The Spirit Wind warned him that there were even more people waiting for him on the Hundred Flower Bridge and that the river below was dark and angry. Chan Lee lost his temper and slashed at the Spirit Wind with his sword. 'Leave me alone, you cursed spirit! I am the great Emperor Chan Lee! I have a fierce guard behind me! I have a mighty sword. I would not fear a thousand starving peasants!'

"Immediately the cold Spirit Wind was gone, and in its place a thick gray fog swirled. Chan Lee moved forward, but his fierce guards hesitated. 'I command you onward, you cowards!' Chan Lee snapped as he plunged into the fog. His strong black horse squealed with fear and threw Chan Lee from his back. The emperor's fierce guards ran away. Chan Lee was swallowed by the fog, where he wandered alone for many hours, muttering and cursing his men. He vowed that he would hang them all when he returned to the palace."

Wen-shan became aware that all other conversations had stopped as everyone turned their attention to the auntie's story.

"Finally, the Hundred Flower Bridge appeared before him, and a thousand ragged peasants stood at its threshold. The Emperor Chan Lee drew his sword. A poor man stepped forward. 'You do not frighten us, Chan Lee.' He moved forward again and the others followed.

"'You had better fear me!' yelled Chan Lee. 'I am the great Emperor Chan Lee, and I have a terrible sword.'

"The crowd pushed forward. Chan Lee stumbled back toward the river. 'Come any closer and you will feel the sharp edge of my sword,' he warned.

"A woman rushed toward him, and Chan Lee swung his heavy sword and sliced through her neck, but her head did not leave her body, and the woman laughed. 'You cannot kill me twice, Chan Lee. I am Nu Gui, and I have a fierce army behind *me*! Here is Yuan Gui, and You Hun Ye Gui, and Diao Si Gui, and we have fingers of ice.'

"The great emperor screamed in terror as he swung his sword through the bodies of mist. The ghost army advanced, forcing Chan Lee into the dark river. Now he felt the clammy hands of Shui Gui dragging him into the pitiless depths. Chan Lee drank the black water of death, and his great sword fell from his hand and sank into the mud. Nu Gui stood alone by the now-peaceful river. She sang a song of home as she disappeared into the morning sunlight."

The old auntie looked around solemnly at the listeners, and then a slow smile touched her mouth. Jun-jai started the applause and everyone joined in immediately. Jun-jai leaned over to whisper in Wen-shan's ear, "She is very wise, that one."

"Why?" Wen-shan questioned.

"Did you think that story was really about the imaginary Emperor Chan Lee?"

Wen-shan didn't know what he was talking about, but she didn't want to appear stupid, so she just nodded her head and said, "Ah, she is quite wise. Tell me more."

"Well, she certainly knows how to tell two stories at once. Cruel leaders will one day have to answer for their crimes, no matter how well they think they can swim."

"What does that mean?"

But Jun-jai could not finish his explanation because he was interrupted by his brother standing to leave. Many family members stood to make their polite farewells, and Wen-shan stood with them. Auntie Ting brought Wen-shan her sweater and gave her a bag of almond cookies. "For your walk home."

Wen-shan took the crisp white bag and bowed several times. "Thank you so much for allowing me to be a part of the celebration."

"Oh, most welcome. Lucky thirteen!"

Wen-shan smiled. "You are a very excellent cook."

"Ah, that? Just a little family get-together."

Jun-jai walked up to give his auntie a hug. "Yes, you should see this home during a festival—there is no room to move."

Auntie Ting slapped his arm. "Ah! You are so American with your teasing."

"Thank you for the compliment, Auntie."

Wen-shan bowed to Jun-jai. "And thank you, Jun-jai, for inviting me to dinner."

Auntie Ting opened the door, and Wen-shan moved out into the narrow apartment hallway.

"Should Jun-jai go with you?" Auntie Ting questioned. "It is getting dark."

"Oh, no, I'll be fine. I walk around at night by myself all the time." Auntie Ting gave her a questioning look. "Really, I'll be fine. There will be many people out tonight." Wen-shan walked off down the hallway with the crisp paper of her cookie bag crackling with each step.

When she stepped out onto the street, she turned to the west to find the sun had already set. A moist, cool wind brushed against her neck and made her shiver.

"I have only half a mile to home," she told herself.

She walked fast, but the ghosts of Nu Gui and Shui Gui floated along behind her. It was almost dark when she saw the wall of her courtyard. She gave a small chirp of gladness and ran. Her almond cookies might have turned to dust, but she didn't care. She reached the gate, threw it open, and ran through the garden. There was light coming from the front window, so she knew the door would be unlocked.

She flew out of her shoes and yanked open the door. Taking

big gulps of air, she quickly closed the door and laid her head against the wood.

"Wen-shan?"

Her great-uncle's voice made her jump.

He was coming from his room to scold her.

She went quickly to her room, stripping the picture of Zhong Kui, the vanquisher of ghosts, from the wall as she went. "I'm fine, Uncle," she called. "I have just returned from the dinner with Wei Jun-jai's family. I'm very tired. I'll talk to you in the morning." She knew it was improper not to report in, but she was tired.

Her bedroom door shut as his opened.

Ah, no scolding tonight.

Notes

A brief history of Hong Kong: In the 1700s, the British East India Trading Company traded goods with China. One of the more profitable items traded was opium. British merchants controlled many of China's port cities. There was a war between China and Britain over the opium trade. Britain prevailed, and in 1842, Hong Kong (which means *fragrant harbor*) became a colony of the British Empire. First contained to Hong Kong Island, the colony's boundaries were eventually extended to include the Kowloon Peninsula and the New Territories in 1898.

Chinese naming system: The last name is written first, followed by the generational name and then the given name. Mao's two-part name consists of *Tse,* which means "to shine on" and *tung,* which means "the East."

Stone Boy: In order to not tempt fate with too grand a name, peasant mothers often gave their children a rough, or common, name. Such was the case for Mao Tse-tung. His rough name was *Shisan yazi* or "Boy of Stone."

September 9, 1976: The death date of Mao Tse-tung.

Capitalist Roader: Anyone thought to lean toward capitalism, or be on the capitalist road, was called this derogatory name.

Confucius: Born in 551 BC on the Shantung peninsula of China, Confucius was

China's first professional teacher and moral philosopher, and is known today as Asia's greatest moral and social thinker. Many of his thoughts and teachings were collected in a booklet known as the Analects.

Chiang Kai-shek: Born in 1887 in the Zhejiang province, China, Chiang was a professional military man and a Nationalist chief of staff. He was anti-Soviet and deeply averse to the Soviet socialist dogma of class struggle (dividing society into classes and making them fight each other). In 1927, he became Chairman of the Nationalist Party. He fled to Taiwan when the Communists took over in 1949. He continued to rule the Nationalist Party until his death on April 5, 1975.

Ghost stories: Ghosts play a substantial role in Chinese culture. Ghosts take many forms depending on the way in which the person died. The term for ghost is *Gui* (pronounced *Gweye*).

> **Qweilo:** White ghost. Sometimes a person of Caucasian descent is called a *qweilo* or "white man."
> **Nu Gui:** The ghost of a woman who had committed suicide due to some injustice.
> **Yuan Gui:** The ghost of someone who died a wrongful death.
> **You Hun Ye Gui:** A wandering ghost of someone who died far away from his home or family.
> **Diao Si Gui:** The ghost of someone who had been hanged.
> **Shui Gui:** The spirit of someone who drowned and continues living in the water.
> **Zhong Kui:** The vanquisher of ghosts and evil beings. Portraits of him are hung in Chinese houses to scare away evil spirits and demons.

Ghost dramas: An ancient dramatic genre which is characterized by tales of revenge by dead victims' spirits on those who had persecuted them. In China, there is a strong tradition of using historical allusion to voice opposition. In 1963, Mao banned all ghost dramas. To him, those ghost avengers were uncomfortably close to the class enemies who had perished under his rule.

The old auntie's ghost story includes many inferences to Mao Tse-tung. The Hundred Flower Bridge is a reference to one of Mao's campaigns that he called "Let a Hundred Flowers Bloom." Party leaders and intellectuals were supposed to express their opinions about communism and Chairman Mao's leadership, but in truth, it was a means for Mao to uncover and silence dissidents. The fact that Emperor Chan Lee drowns in the story is telling because Mao Tse-tung prided himself on being a strong swimmer. And the thousand avenging ghosts in the story represent a fraction of the millions of people who perished under Mao's rule.

Chapter 2

W EN-SHAN DRESSED IN HER school uniform and
went to eat her breakfast of cornflakes. Her uncle was
not in the house. She looked out the front window and saw him
clipping the hydrangea bushes and talking to their neighbor,
Mr. Yee. Mr. Yee was not her favorite neighbor. In fact, Wen-
shan did not like the renters occupying either of the side bungalows.

Mr. Yee worked for the British bank, and Wen-shan figured he was arrogant because of his high position. Mr. and
Mrs. Tuan, in the bungalow opposite Mr. Yee's, had two bratty
children—a boy, Yan, and a daughter, Ya Ya. The youngsters
irritated her with their obnoxious questions: *Why do they
call it a monsoon? Where does the sky end? Don't you like dim
sum for breakfast? Can you stand on one foot for a long time?*
Besides, Mrs. Tuan was nosy—always peering out her window

or standing at the front gate to watch the world and criticize any impropriety. The small-eyed woman had also warned Zhao Tai-lu about Wen-shan's fondness for rock-and-roll music, which caused her uncle to ban it from the house. This, more than anything else, sealed Wen-shan's opinion of the toadlike woman.

Wen-shan ate another bite of cornflakes and watched a young man wobble past the gate on a rusty red bicycle. He was trying to keep the bike steady as he looked at something in his hand. He moved out of sight, but before Wen-shan lifted another bite of cereal to her mouth, he was back, this time walking the bike and looking exhausted. He rang the bell at their gate.

Uncle Zhao and Mr. Yee stopped their conversation and looked over at the sweaty young man. He was fishing for something in his jacket pocket. Wen-shan watched as her uncle set down the clippers and moved to the gate. She couldn't hear what either party was saying, but the young man handed her uncle a card of some sort and Uncle Zhao handed him a coin. The young man bowed several times, put the coin in his pocket, and rode away.

Her uncle stood staring at the card, and Wen-shan instinctively looked over to the Tuans' house. As she suspected, Mrs. Tuan was suddenly out sweeping her porch. Wen-shan wanted to hear how Mrs. Tuan would try to coax information from her tight-lipped uncle, so she set her bowl on the coffee table and went outside.

"Good morning, Uncle," Wen-shan said.

He looked at her and nodded.

"Look! Look!" Mrs. Tuan chirped. "Your uncle has received a special message."

A smile ticked the corner of Wen-shan's mouth. "A special message? Really?"

"Oh, must be special message. Come by messenger bike."

Sweep. Sweep.

"I wonder what it could be?" Wen-shan said, emphasizing the word *wonder*.

"Yes, yes. Nice white paper for envelope. Very official."

On the garden side of the front wall stood a small bamboo storage shed. Her uncle headed there to put away the garden tools, and Mrs. Tuan looked anxious.

Sweep. Sweep. Sweep.

"You are not going to read your message?"

Her uncle came back from the shed.

"No." He turned to Wen-shan. "You have school."

Mrs. Tuan must have decided her porch was clean enough already, because she moved quickly into the house and snapped the door shut.

Wen-shan was disappointed. Even though she loved seeing Mrs. Tuan's attempts at snooping blighted, she really wanted to know what the message was all about.

"Uncle . . ."

"School." He passed her and opened the door.

"But, Uncle . . ."

"You will find out what it says when you get home from school."

Wen-shan came inside and her uncle shut the door.

"Bowl. Sink."

Wen-shan snatched her cereal bowl from the coffee table and took it to the kitchen.

"Can I at least see the envelope?" she asked curtly.

"'The superior man is satisfied and composed; the common man is always full of distress,'" her uncle said, quoting Confucius.

Wen-shan held back her frustration. "I just want to see the envelope, and then I'll run quickly to school."

"Since it has your name on it, along with mine, you have every right." He held out the envelope.

"My name?" She took the card. "Who's it from?"

"The Department of Art and Antiquities."

Wen-shan was speechless as she stared at the English writing on the envelope. *The Department of Art and Antiquities.* And in the center of the envelope were two names: *Zhao Tai-lu* and *Chen Wen-shan.*

"Now, have you seen the envelope?"

"Yes."

"Then your promise was to go quickly to school."

Wen-shan looked dazedly up at her uncle, who held out his hand for the card.

Reluctantly she relinquished it, and went to get her school-bag. Her mind was filled with questions, but her uncle had already gone to his bedroom to get ready for work. So, she trudged off to school, unrequited. She would have to wait not only until after school, but until her uncle returned from the furniture store. By then she would most likely have exploded from curiosity.

●　●　●

Song Li-ying caught Wen-shan's eye during history class and motioned with her head toward the door. Wen-shan looked over, as did all the other students and the teacher. In the doorway stood Uncle Zhao, his hat in his hand and his head slightly bowed.

Wen-shan felt heat rise into her face as a few classmates

mumbled inquiries about the older gentleman and what he wanted. Her teacher rose from his seat and went to greet the visitor. They shared a few unheard comments, and the teacher turned to look at her.

"Chen Wen-shan, please collect your belongings. You will be going with your uncle."

Wen-shan did as she was told, gave a look to Li-ying, and exited with her uncle. They walked silently in the dim hallway. Wen-shan knew she must wait for her uncle to speak first, but patience was not one of her virtues.

"Is it about the card?"

"Yes."

"Did you read it?"

"Yes."

They reached the front doors of the school and moved outside. Her uncle stopped on the steps and handed her the envelope. She pushed back the opened flap and removed the note card. On the front of the card in embossed black letters was the title of the agency. *The Department of Art and Antiquities.* She opened the card to find a note written in carefully penned English.

Dear Mr. Zhao Tai-lu,

My name is George Riley Smythe. I am the curator for the Hong Kong Museum of Art. I extend an invitation to you and your great-niece, Chen Wenshan, to present yourselves at my home at your earliest convenience. It involves a matter which will be of interest to your feelings.

Regards,

Mr. George R. Smythe

Wen-shan flipped the card over to find Mr. Smythe's address and telephone number.

"Did you telephone?"

"Yes."

"And we're going there?"

"Yes. Right now."

Her uncle started walking.

"We're going to Kowloon to meet with Mr. Smythe?"

"Yes."

"About a matter which will be of interest to our feelings?"

"Yes."

"But I'm in my school clothes."

"No matter. We have to hurry. I told him we would be there by five o'clock."

"Uncle—"

"Hurry, hurry. We have to travel to the harbor and catch the ferry."

Wen-shan was almost running to keep up with her uncle's long strides.

"But I have my schoolbag."

"No complaining or talking, just walk."

Wen-shan reset her bag on her shoulder and pushed ahead. She had many thoughts to occupy her mind as she and her uncle made their way to Bonham Road. The road would eventually lead to the harbor and the Star Ferry, and then to what? Who was Mr. George Riley Smythe, and how did he know their names? How did he know *her* name? The card was very mysterious. What connection did she and her great-uncle have with this museum curator? He was a stranger. And why were they going to his house and not to an office at the museum?

They arrived at the ferry dock and Wen-shan's uncle

purchased two tickets. There was a little chop in the water of Victoria Harbor, but Wen-shan didn't give it a second thought. She had taken the Star Ferry from Hong Kong Island to Kowloon, Hong Kong, many times—times when the water was smooth and sparkling, and other times when the wind whipped it into whitecaps.

After a few minutes' wait, Wen-shan and her uncle boarded the ferry and found seats inside the upper cabin. While he read his Chinese newspaper, she looked out the window and let her mind drift. As the ferry turned, she had a view of a portion of the central business district with scooters, buses, and people all moving in an endless flow. Bamboo scaffolding was everywhere, surrounding new construction like birdcages. Progress. One of her teachers called it a necessary blight. Wen-shan shrugged. *Well, people have to live and work somewhere.*

She thought of her uncle's house. It sat on the lower slopes of Victoria Peak with lush vegetation surrounding it and a modicum of lingering quiet. But Central Hong Kong was expanding rapidly, pushing more and more structures up the mountainside. The solid stone buildings of the early British takeover were giving way to concrete, steel, and glass. Wen-shan remembered a time when she could stand at their front gate and see an unobstructed view of the harbor. Now she could catch only a glimpse of the blue water through gaps between the finished and partially finished skyscrapers of downtown. Progress.

"Uncle?"

A rattle of paper.

"Uncle?"

"Yes?"

"When you get off the ferry at Kowloon, do you feel funny?"

He scowled at her. "What do you mean?"

Now the question seemed foolish and she didn't want to ask it.

"What do you mean, Wen-shan?"

She swallowed. "I mean . . . well . . . you step onto land that is connected to mainland China."

"So?"

"Mainland China. Where you were born; where I was born."

The paper rattled again. "Silly question."

"You don't ever think about it?"

"No."

Wen-shan felt her uncle's cold rebuke and turned her face to the window. After a few minutes of uncomfortable silence, she stood and maneuvered past him. "I'm going out on the deck."

As she stood at the railing, looking at Kowloon, Wen-shan chided herself. She should have known better than to try to get her uncle to say anything about China. He spoke to her very little as it was, and never about the great land that stretched out beyond Kowloon and the New Territories. She searched her own meager memories, but most of those were only slivers of images that made her stomach hurt or came as nightmares. Perhaps it was the same with her uncle.

A child stood with her mother at the railing. She giggled as the ocean breeze tugged at her lightweight coat and tousled her dark hair. Wen-shan moved farther forward on the deck. She needed space to think about Mr. George Riley Smythe and his unusual invitation. She'd never been in the home of a British gentleman and wondered how different it would be from a Chinese home. She was nervous about making some mistake in etiquette. The only other British person she knew well was

Mr. Pierpont, the owner of the furniture store where her uncle worked, and he was well-tempered and always smiling. Perhaps Mr. Smythe would be like that.

The boat's mournful horn sounded as they neared the dock, and Wen-shan quickly returned to her seat to fetch her school-bag. Her uncle had put away his paper and was just standing when she reached him.

"We must not be late," he said.

"No, of course not."

They moved with the crowd down the stairwell, off the ferry, and out onto the crowded streets of Kowloon.

NOTE

Kowloon, Hong Kong: Located on the Chinese mainland, the city sits opposite Hong Kong Island.

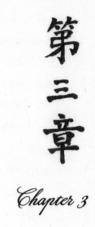

Chapter 3

WEN-SHAN AND HER UNCLE stood in front of a wrought iron gate, peering in at the large stone house and shaded yard. They checked and rechecked the address before finally deciding it was the residence of Mr. George Riley Smythe. The property was adjacent to King's Park, which Wen-shan found very appropriate. She was angry at her uncle for making her come to such a fancy place in her school uniform. Besides, her shoulders hurt from having to carry her heavy bag. They had walked all the way from the ferry station, making several wrong turns before finally arriving at their destination, so Wen-shan was tired, hot, and cranky.

"Well, are we going in?"

Her uncle had his hand on the gate latch, but wasn't moving.

"Not yet. Too early."

At one minute to five, he opened the gate, and they began

their walk down the straight stone path to the front door. They reached the front stoop, and Wen-shan noticed that her uncle's hand trembled slightly when he reached to ring the doorbell.

"Do we take off our shoes?" Wen-shan asked. She didn't see any shoes sitting on the stoop.

"I don't know."

As they were looking around for someplace to leave their shoes, the door opened and they were greeted by a tall, silver-haired man in a business suit.

"Mr. Zhao? Miss Chen?"

They nodded.

"Welcome! Welcome! Come in. I am Mr. George Riley Smythe." The man took her uncle's hand and bowed. He then turned and bowed to her.

Wen-shan was shocked that Mr. Smythe would answer his own door. With a home like this she expected to be greeted by a servant.

They followed the tall man into his home and saw shoes sitting in the entryway. They immediately took theirs off and set them carefully on the rug.

"If you will come this way," Mr. Smythe said. He led them through a spacious living room containing a large sofa and leather chairs. Chinese bureaus, ornate lamps, and expensive-looking statues and bric-a-brac from many Asian cultures filled the space. Wen-shan barely saw a portion of the room before they were led out into a hallway. After passing several rooms, Mr. Smythe stopped in front of a door.

"Here we are!" he said brightly, opening the door and taking them inside.

This room was an office. Two walls were lined with shelves containing hundreds of books. The large window at the back of the room was open, and a fresh breeze moved the gauzy curtains that hung on either side.

Wen-shan loved how the golden afternoon sunlight poured into the room and shimmered on the pale walls.

Her uncle gave her a look that said "quit staring at things," and she dropped the smile from her face.

"Please, sit down," Mr. Smythe instructed.

Wen-shan and her uncle bowed and sat down carefully on the beautiful teakwood chairs.

"In a moment I'll have my cook, Mrs. Delany, bring us some tea and sandwiches, but first we have a little business to discuss." He sat down in the chair on the other side of the desk. "I'm sorry that my wife is not here to meet you, but she's gone off to the New Territories to hike around the mountains for a few days with friends." He chuckled. "Not my idea of fun, I can tell you." Mr. Smythe leaned forward with his arms on his desk. "Now, I will soon tell you the reason you are here, but first I must ask a few questions. Would that be all right?"

Uncle Zhao nodded.

"Very good." He took out a notebook and pen, and Wen-shan saw her uncle sit straighter.

"Where were you born?"

"Guangxi province."

"The town?"

Her uncle shifted in his seat. "Near Guilin. A small town on the road to the Dragon Back Terraces."

Mr. Smythe wrote in his notebook. "Did you ever live in Guilin?"

"Yes. Our family moved to Guilin when my brother was four and I was two."

"And as an adult, when did you leave?"

Wen-shan wondered how her uncle would avoid such a direct question.

He brought his hands together and laid them in his lap. "I have been in Hong Kong many years, Mr. Smythe."

"Many years?"

"Yes, many, many years."

"Did you wear a black armband when Chiang Kai-shek died?"

Another hesitation.

"Yes."

The answer seemed to satisfy Mr. Smythe, but Wen-shan was confused. The questions didn't seem to make any sense.

Mr. Smythe's voice took on a tone of ease and lightness. "Mrs. Smythe and I have spent many years collecting treasures from mainland China."

Wen-shan could not keep up with Mr. Smythe's disjointed conversation. There seemed to be hidden meaning in the words, but she had no idea how to make sense of them. She glanced over at her uncle; he was looking earnestly at Mr. Smythe, while keeping his hands calmly folded in his lap.

Mr. Smythe stood. "If you will excuse me a moment, I would like to show you one of the treasures we've collected." He went out the door, leaving Wen-shan to gawk. Her uncle remained silent.

Wen-shan turned to look at the door. "He is a very odd man, isn't he?" she whispered.

"Do not judge something until you have seen the entire picture."

A mantel clock sat on one of the bookshelves, and Wen-shan heard it ticking in the silence of the room. Her stomach grumbled, and her uncle cast her a critical look.

"I'm hungry." Her stomach grumbled again. "I can't help it."

The door opened and Wen-shan and her uncle looked over.

Into the room came an old man who, if standing straight, Wen-shan knew would have been shorter than she was. He was wearing the long dress of the scholar.

He lifted his wrinkled face, and when he saw Zhao Tai-lu, he smiled.

"Ah, ah, ah," Uncle Zhao moaned as he stumbled forward to take the old man's hands. "Ah, Master Quan . . . Master Quan." He bowed low several times and Master Quan patted his hand.

Wen-shan looked at Mr. Smythe, who was standing in the doorway, smiling broadly. Her attention returned to her uncle, who continued to say Master Quan's name. He seemed to be on the verge of tears. It was very odd behavior.

"How . . . how is this possible? How are you here? Guilin is far."

Master Quan chuckled. "In my old age I grew wings." He studied Tai-lu's face. "And you? How did you escape?"

Her uncle smiled. "I grew fins."

Mr. Smythe brought a chair and set it for Master Quan. "Please, sit."

As her great-uncle led the venerable gentleman forward, Wen-shan stood.

"Master Quan, this is my great-niece Chen Wen-shan."

Wen-shan bowed low and Master Quan bowed also. His eyes crinkled with delight as he took her hand. "This one looks like her mother."

Wen-shan stepped back. "How do you know my mother?"

Mr. Smythe was at his desk. "Sit, everyone, and I, with the help of Master Quan, will try to explain."

Wen-shan felt as though someone had poured icy water through her veins. She sat without knowing that she'd done so. She was barely aware that Mr. Smythe was talking.

"It is better that you do not know the details of how Mrs. Smythe and I smuggled this treasure out of China." He smiled at Master Quan.

The old gentleman tapped the side of his head with his finger. "They are very smart people, and they have lots of moles digging, digging, digging information for them."

Mr. Smythe chuckled. "We do. In my capacity as curator of arts and antiquities, I have many contacts and some influence."

Master Quan chuckled at that.

Wen-shan's legs were jumping, and she put her hands on her knees and pressed down. "Excuse me, sir. May I ask how Master Quan knows my mother?"

Her uncle's face clouded, but Wen-shan didn't care. No one had spoken of her mother for ten years and now a stranger came who carried a story of her on his lips.

Mr. Smythe nodded. "Zhao Tai-lu, I believe it is your story to tell."

Her uncle looked at the floor. Wen-shan knew he did not want to tell the story, but that he could not disrespect the curator of the Hong Kong Museum of Art. Reluctantly, he began.

"Master Quan was an art teacher at the university in Guilin. He was my brother's favorite teacher. Mine as well."

Wen-shan sat forward. "Your brother? You mean my grandfather?"

"Yes, your grandfather, Zhao Tai-lang."

"The Zhao brothers were very talented artists," Master Quan said. "But this one decided to go into the military. He wanted to be in Chiang Kai-shek's army."

Wen-shan stood to quiet her jumping legs. "You said I look like my mother, Master Quan. When did you last see her? Why hasn't she written me for ten years?"

"Wen-shan, sit down."

"No, Uncle! I want to know. I want to know about my mother!"

Mr. Smythe's mellow British voice washed over the tension. "Of course, that is the most important thing. That is why Master Quan and I have been searching for you."

"What do you mean?"

"Mrs. Smythe and I brought Master Quan out of Guilin almost a year ago. Over the years, he has helped us to save many art pieces from destruction."

Master Quan shook his head. "Not as many as I wanted."

"And then came the inevitable time when his life was in danger. That's when we gave him a pair of wings to fly to safety."

Wen-shan tried to stay calm. "What does this have to do with me and my uncle? I want to know if my mother is alive."

Master Quan looked directly at her. "When I left Guilin, she and your grandfather were alive."

Her uncle interrupted. "I apologize for my niece's impatience."

"It's perfectly understandable," Mr. Smythe said calmly. "Wen-shan, your grandfather and mother could not write to you."

"What do you mean?"

Master Quan looked at her sadly. "In Mao's China, it is not possible."

Mr. Smythe concurred. "There has been little post in or out of China for a long time."

Wen-shan lowered her head to keep back her emotion.

"But that does not mean that they did not think of you," Master Quan said softly.

"How do you know that?"

Master Quan smiled. "I think it is time for us to show the treasure I brought for them. A treasure out of Guilin."

Mr. Smythe stood and moved to a cupboard located on the bottom of one of the bookcases. As he knelt down to lift something out of the cupboard, a breath of wind fluttered one of the curtains across his arm. As he stood, the soft white fabric slid away, revealing a wooden box in his hands. He brought it carefully and set it on his desk.

Wen-shan stepped forward and her uncle stood.

The box was large; the length of it was longer than both Mr. Smythe's hands, fingertip to fingertip, and the width was only slightly smaller. The depth was Wen-shan's hand, fingertip to wrist. There were metal latches on either side that connected the lid to the base.

Her uncle moved next to her and reached out. "It is my brother's brush box." He ran his fingers along the aged brown wood, worn and polished by the hands of ten generations.

"Look, Uncle, look at the top," Wen-shan whispered.

Embedded in the lid of the box was a green jade carving. As Wen-shan stared at the swirls and cutouts of the relief, a magnificent dragon emerged, coiling through the clouds.

"Your grandfather wanted you to have this, Chen Wen-shan," Master Quan said.

"Me?"

"Yes. He and your mother kept it hidden from the Communists despite great peril."

Wen-shan turned to look at the scholar.

"He asked me, if I had the chance to escape, to bring the

box to Hong Kong. He said I must bring it here and find you and your uncle."

"That was very dangerous for you, Master Quan."

"Yes, but here I am, and here is the box. Hong Kong is a big place, but one month ago we finally find you."

"A month ago?" Wen-shan frowned.

Mr. Smythe picked up the narrative. "Your grandfather instructed Master Quan not to give you the box until Mao Tse-tung was dead—until it was safe."

"Safe? I don't understand."

"Your grandfather does not know Hong Kong; he only knows Guilin, and there is much fear in Guilin."

Master Quan laid his hands over his heart. "He did not want you to suffer at the hand of Mao Tse-tung. But now, Chairman Mao has gone to his ancestors, and the box is yours—yours and your great-uncle's."

Her uncle bowed. "Thank you, Master Quan, for risking so much to bring us this treasure."

Wen-shan noted the reverence in her uncle's voice.

Master Quan smiled. "Ah, but I think there is greater treasure *inside* box. Open it."

"Have you seen what's inside?" Wen-shan asked.

"I have not seen, but your grandfather told me. Open it. It's all right."

The excitement in Master Quan's voice made Wen-shan's heart beat faster. She looked over at her uncle and he nodded. She undid the latches and put her hands on either side of the lid. Wen-shan felt the touch of the cool wood and imagined her mother's hand resting there. She lifted the lid and set it on the desktop. Many silk scrolls and tubes of parchment lay tightly packed together, and each article had a ribbon tied around it.

Wen-shan was aware of Master Quan beside her. He reached out slowly and touched one of the silk scrolls. "These are your grandfather's paintings and calligraphy."

"May I see one?"

"Of course. They belong to you and your uncle," Mr. Smythe said.

"Uncle?"

He was silent and she could not read his expression. Nevertheless, he had not said no, so Wen-shan untied the ribbon and unrolled the scroll. A misty watercolor image formed in front of her. Through the pale green vegetation of spring and forests of swaying bamboo, the ancient dragon-spine peaks of Guilin lifted to the sky. A path skirted the Li River and disappeared into the cool shadows of the bamboo. Wen-shan felt like she was walking on that path, walking on paths she could not remember.

"It is one of the most perfect paintings I have ever seen," Mr. Smythe said reverently. "Truly, Miss Chen, your grandfather is a master."

Wen-shan could not find her voice. She turned as she felt movement behind her, and she saw her uncle cover his face and collapse into his chair.

Mr. Smythe was at his side in a moment. "Mr. Zhao, are you all right?"

Her uncle did not answer.

Master Quan spoke in his place. "It is many years to be without a brother."

"Of course. Of course," Mr. Smythe said solicitously. "Quite understandable. I will call Mrs. Delany to bring the tea and sandwiches. That will help."

"Mr. Smythe," Tai-lu said weakly, uncovering his face. "It is very kind of you, but I feel that Wen-shan and I should be going home. We have much to consider."

"Yes, Mr. Zhao. I understand perfectly." Mr. Smythe straightened and moved to the door. "I will have my driver take you to the dock."

Tai-lu nodded. "Yes, that would be helpful."

After Mr. Smythe left, Wen-shan slowly rolled up the scroll and tied the ribbon.

Master Quan reached for one of the parchments. "May I?"

"Of course," Wen-shan said.

"These are letters from your mother."

A chill ran down the skin on Wen-shan's arms.

"They are numbered. See these little tags?"

Wen-shan nodded.

"Your mother felt it important for you to read them in order."

"Yes. I see. Thank you, Master Quan."

He handed over the letter and Wen-shan shivered. She felt as though a ghost had passed between them, and she looked quickly to the golden light still pouring in through the window.

As she put the letter into the box and replaced the lid, Mr. Smythe returned.

"The driver is bringing the car."

Zhao Tai-lu stood and moved to the desk. He bowed. "Thank you, Mr. Smythe." He bowed again. "Thank you for all you have done."

He turned to Master Quan and bowed deeply. "Because of your great kindness and courage, you have brought honor to your family, Master Quan." He laid his hand on the box. "This is a great gift."

Master Quan bowed. "Fortune smiled."

Wen-shan bowed to the scholar. "I hope someday you will come and tell us the story of your escape, Master Quan."

Her uncle nodded. "Yes, you are invited anytime, Master Quan." He lifted the box, and Wen-shan could tell it was heavy.

Mr. Smythe stepped forward. "Would you like help with that, Mr. Zhao?"

"No, thank you, Mr. Smythe. It is a joyous burden. Wen-shan and I will manage."

"I will show you out then." He held open the door and Wen-shan and her uncle exited.

Wen-shan turned back to look at Master Quan. He was slowly making his way to the window as the last rays of warm light flickered on the walls.

NOTES

Media and postal control: One of the first things Mao did upon taking power was to seize all media outlets. Print firms, newspapers, radio, television and film production studios, and theaters were all placed under government control. "We need the policy of 'keep people stupid'" was one of Mao's famous quotes concerning the dissemination of information to the masses. The same went for postal control.

Guilin: A city in the Guangxi province. It is an area known for its unique limestone peaks and has inspired artists and poets for thousands of years.

Chapter 4

ZHONG KUI DID NOT PROTECT her from bad dreams in the night. Even when she called for him to save her, the only answer was the sound of rain—rain that made the stones slick and the darkness terrifying. She could still feel the small hands on her back pushing her along—still feel the cold breath of the qweilo as it floated into the shadows and grabbed her around the waist.

Wen-shan opened her eyes and looked to the sunlit bathroom window, the frosted glass shimmery and white. She continued brushing her teeth. Variations of this dream had haunted her for many years, and as always, the day after such a night she was cranky and tired. She and her uncle had returned home from Mr. Smythe's well after dark because her uncle had wanted to walk home after they'd exited the ferry and also because he'd wanted to stop for snake soup. Wen-shan did not argue. She loved snake soup, but for the taste, not because she believed the notion that it heated and stimulated the digestive system or that it gave a person extra strength.

Uncle Zhao had eaten his soup without speaking or acknowledging her, and she knew better than to ask questions when he was in such a mood. Letters from her mother lay in the box sitting inches from her on the restaurant table, and Wen-shan's emotions had fought between curiosity and anger: curiosity about what the words would reveal about a stranger from a time and place she could not remember, and anger at that same stranger who abandoned her in the middle of the night.

Wen-shan rinsed her mouth of toothpaste and looked at her haggard face in the mirror. She had caught the looks of many of the people in the restaurant, who were eyeing the box with curiosity and envy, and she was glad when her uncle had finally hefted the box and they'd headed for home. There was no discussion about reading any of the letters that first night. They were both exhausted and bed had been a refuge. But the fitful night's sleep had brought her no relief, and she carried her scowl with justification.

Wen-shan went to the kitchen to find her uncle cooking rice gruel and fish balls. Her nose wrinkled in disgust. She went to the cupboard to retrieve her cornflakes. As they jingled into the bowl, her uncle grunted.

"There is nothing good there for you."

"I like them," Wen-shan replied, pouring more into the bowl.

"So Western," her uncle challenged.

She liked Western, and she was grateful to Mr. Pierpont, her uncle's boss at the furniture store, for supplying her with cornflakes, British biscuits, and marmalade. Her uncle thought all those things tasted bad and carried no strength.

"You should be glad you have good food to eat in Hong Kong. We have much. In Taiwan, they eat bananas; in China, they eat banana peels."

Her uncle could bother her about cornflakes all he wanted—it just made her like them more.

She sat at the table and put a big spoonful of flakes into her mouth. After a few crunches, she asked, "Why have you never spoken of Master Quan?"

"Don't talk when you have food in your mouth."

She swallowed. "Why have you never spoken of Master Quan?"

"That was a long time ago. Too long to remember."

"No, you remembered many things when you saw him."

"Do not be disrespectful. Now, you must hurry to school."

"I want to stay home today. I want to read some of the letters."

Her uncle put a fish ball into his mouth and chewed slowly. "Tonight, when I get home from work."

Wen-shan opened her mouth to protest and then shut it. She remembered she'd agreed to meet with Li-ying after school to study, so it was no good arguing. It was no good arguing anyway. She finished her cereal and went to get her schoolbag. She tried to convey disinterest as she went out the front door, but her worry over the letters and the images of the nightmare rain followed her to school and throughout the day.

● ● ●

"Where did you go with your uncle?" Li-ying questioned as soon as they were out of school.

Wen-shan looked around at her passing classmates. "Let's start walking." She headed for Li-ying's house at such a fast pace that her friend had to run.

"Slow down! I have long legs but I can't keep up."

Wen-shan slowed. Part of her wanted to tell the story of traveling to Mr. Smythe's big house in Kowloon, of meeting Master Quan, of being given the jade dragon box. But part of her felt stingy and secretive. Why should she tell Li-ying, who had lots of brothers and sisters and aunties and uncles? Would she really care about her one mother and one grandfather? Would she understand Wen-shan's anger at an uncle who never told her anything about her family?

"So?" Li-ying asked after they had broken free of the noise and jumble of the school yard.

Wen-shan sighed. It was no use keeping the news from her friend, and since she hadn't thought up a story to take its place, she pushed down her agitation and tried to speak as nonchalantly as possible.

"We went to Kowloon."

"Kowloon? What for?"

"Business."

"Business? Who with?"

"Mr. Smythe."

Li-ying pushed her glasses up. "Who is that? Someone your uncle knows from the furniture business?"

"No, not from the furniture business."

Li-ying stopped. "If you don't want to tell me, Wen-shan, no worries. Don't tell me." She pushed up her glasses again.

"No, it's not that. It's just difficult to explain." Li-ying stared at her until she continued. "A messenger came on a bicycle and gave my uncle a note."

"From Mr. Smythe?"

"Yes."

"Who *is* he?"

"The curator for the Hong Kong Museum of Art."

"Ah, that is an important position. What did he want with your uncle?"

"*Me* and my uncle."

"You? What did he want with you?"

Wen-shan began walking again. "If you will be quiet, Li Li, I will tell you."

"Sorry. Go on."

"Well, we had an appointment at Mr. Smythe's big house in Kowloon. The note said he had information that would be of interest to our feelings."

Li-ying opened her mouth to speak, but quickly closed it.

"Anyway, in his office he asked my uncle many questions, and when he was satisfied with the answers, he brought in a man—Master Quan—who was my great-uncle's art teacher in Guilin." She adjusted her schoolbag. "It seems Mr. and Mrs. Smythe work at sneaking people out of China."

This was too much for Li-ying's curiosity. "You mean like smuggling?"

"Yes. I think so—people and art pieces too."

"That is a great work," Li-ying stated. Wen-shan noted the fierceness in her friend's voice and knew she was thinking of her own family's escape from China when the Communists took over after the civil war.

"So, what about this teacher—Master Quan?" Wen-shan nodded. "Did he have news of your family?"

Wen-shan smiled; she was glad for the excitement in her friend's voice. "Yes, Li-ying. Master Quan brought news of my grandfather and my mother."

Li-ying's hands flew to her mouth. "Ah! That is a wonder, Wen-shan! You don't talk of them, but I know your thoughts must travel to the misty mountains in search of them."

Wen-shan swallowed her emotion.

"So what did he tell you?"

"It was not so much what he told us, but what he brought us."

"Something from your family?"

"Yes. A box filled with my grandfather's artwork and letters from my mother."

Li-ying stared at her. "Such a treasure, Wen-shan," she whispered. "Have you read the letters yet?"

"No, we will begin tonight."

Li-ying smiled, showing her crooked teeth without embarrassment. "And you will tell me a little about them?"

Wen-shan nodded. "Of course. We're friends."

They reached Li-ying's home, and Wen-shan could hear the sound of her friend's younger brothers and sisters playing under the banyan tree.

Li-ying opened the gate. "Come, we must tell my mother all about it. She will eat it up like grapes on a hot day."

● ● ●

Wen-shan had finished her homework, cleaned the kitchen floor, cut hydrangea flowers for the vase in the front room, and made her uncle's favorite noodles. Now she sat staring at the box on the coffee table and daring herself to open it without her uncle's permission. If he caught her, he would frown and then quote some wise saying from Confucius about patience. But Confucius wasn't sitting here looking at the box that contained words from his faraway mother.

Wen-shan traced her finger along the jade carving. The anger and confusion surfaced again as she tried to recall her mother's face. *"This one looks like her mother,"* Master Quan had said. Did she? She didn't remember much from when she was five—certainly not her mother's face.

Wen-shan jumped up. She'd heard her uncle's footsteps across the courtyard and didn't want to be caught staring at the box. She went to the kitchen and began rearranging food stuffs in the refrigerator.

Her uncle opened the door and stepped inside. He called out, "Hello?"

"Hello."

"What are you doing?"

"Cleaning the refrigerator."

He came to the kitchen. "Why are you doing that?"

"It was messy."

"Did you make noodles?"

"I did."

"I will wash, and then we can eat."

Wen-shan set the bowls on the table as well as the pickled daikon and the thin strips of pork and the fried vegetables in sesame sauce. She prayed her uncle was hungry and would eat quickly, but when the blessing on the food lasted the usual amount of time, and his arranging of meat and vegetables was done with the same slow precision, Wen-shan began biting her lips and trying to think of ways to calm her stomach. It was no good. As she raised the chopsticks to her mouth for the third time, the food stuck in her throat.

Her uncle pushed back his chair, thanked her for dinner, and stood. Wen-shan nodded, picked up dishes, and turned to the sink.

"Leave it until later. Let us look at the letters."

Wen-shan nearly dropped the dishes. She took a breath and set the bowls carefully in the sink.

Her uncle sat in his chair and she sat on the sofa. It was odd. She never sat with her uncle in the evening as he read his paper or his scriptures or worked on the bills. She normally went to her room after dinner to do homework or watch television. The small black-and-white floor model was her prized possession. Mr. Pierpont had given it to her uncle as a bonus for a very good year at the furniture store. Her uncle did not want to take it, but since it would have been shameful to refuse a gift, he accepted it, and then gave it to Wen-shan with a stern warning.

"No programs with rock and roll, and you can only watch a little *after* your homework is finished."

Her uncle sat with his hands folded in his lap, staring at the box, and Wen-shan wondered if he was nervous too. Probably not. He had been a soldier for Chiang Kai-shek.

"You may open it, Wen-shan."

"Thank you, Uncle." She knelt in front of the coffee table and undid the latches. Her uncle held the box as she removed the lid. Though it no longer contained her grandfather's calligraphy brushes, there was still a faint smell of ink. There was also the hint of something floral. Wen-shan had not been aware of that scent at Mr. Smythe's; perhaps it had been masked by the smell of books, leather, and furniture polish.

Wen-shan took a deep breath and set the lid on the soft cushion of the couch.

Her uncle nodded several times. "Mr. Smythe said the letters were numbered, so let's take them out and lay them in a row from first to last. Then we can place them in the drawer in the coffee table."

Wen-shan obeyed, not daring to break the affable mood her uncle was showing. "And the paintings?"

"Hand those to me."

Wen-shan took each parchment scroll, checked the tag, and began placing them in order. The silk scrolls she handed to her uncle. She worked silently until the box was empty. She peered inside and saw a small bud of incense. She picked it up and brought it to her nose, breathing in the soft scent of woodsy floral.

Twenty-two parchments lay in front of her. Twenty-two attachments to a world of floating mountains, a silver river, and family.

Her uncle laid his hands carefully on the silk parchments. "Confucius himself would call Master Quan a gentle man."

"Yes, Uncle. I agree. And a brave man, too."

"Yes. He risked much to bring us these things."

"Should we read a letter or look at one of grandfather's paintings?"

"Letter first."

Wen-shan's heart fluttered. "Yes, Uncle."

She reached for the parchment labeled as number one, untied the ribbon, and unrolled the scroll.

She fought the urge to cry as hundreds of delicate characters opened before her. She'd never be able to make such characters; her hands were too large.

Her uncle leaned forward. "Do you want me to read it?"
"No, no! I can. I will."
She took a breath and read.

*If you were near me, I would whisper in your ear
of China—of home. I would tell of the Guan Di Peak
and the Elephant Hill. We would walk together near
the Li River and over the Flower Bridge. I would buy
you dried plums, and I would braid your hair.*

*But I do not know where you are. When you were
a daughter of Guilin, your face was round, and in your
eyes there were many questions. Your baby feet would
kick the dust in the courtyard, and your laugh would fill
my heart.*

Wen-shan hesitated. She glanced at her uncle, but his head
was bowed. She began again.

*If you were near me, you would have lived through
sorrow. Or maybe you would not have lived at all. You
were too young to understand the need to send you to
Hong Kong. So I will write you letters. Perhaps they
will reach you in that faraway place. Perhaps they will
soften the sorrow. Perhaps in these letters I can tell you
why. For I will tell you of the turning of China, the
beautiful land weeping for its children. I will tell you
of the thousands of Gui that wail in the night. They
have gouged a scar in the heart of China that will
never heal. Here we hide everything: food, paper, ink,
paintings—feelings. Paper is a treasure, so I will use it
carefully to paint a picture of our life.*

Here in Guilin it is just father and me. Mother died many years ago, and Uncle Zhao Tai-lu, and his wife, Mei-lan, left for Hong Kong just as Chiang Kai-shek was retreating to Taiwan.

Her uncle's head came up at the mention of his wife's name, and Wen-shan stopped reading to see if he would say anything. He was silent, so she continued.

The Chinese people have suffered years of want and oppression—misery created by the corrupt emperors and tribal warlords, by invasion from Japan and bloody civil fighting. This has made the people hungry for the food of stability. The words of the Communist Party leaders sounded good in many ears as they promised us a government that would care for us equally—no emperor, no peasant. A government run by the common man. A government that would give us food. They promised us a peaceful China.

I was ten when Mao Tse-tung and the Communists fought their way into power, and I didn't care anything about it. I cared only that my Auntie Mei-lan was going away for reasons I could not understand. She was the woman who cared for me after my mother died. My Auntie Mei-lan, who loved me. My Auntie Mei-lan, who loved to listen to Benny Goodman and to dance the quickstep.

"Stop."
Wen-shan started at the sound of her uncle's voice.
"Is there more about my wife?"

Wen-shan looked at the next characters.

"No, the rest seems to be about Grandfather."

Wen-shan noted the anguished expression on her uncle's face before he hid it behind his stoic mask.

"Should I continue to the end?"

"Yes, if there is not much more."

"Not much."

She read.

One night when the wind blew and the bamboo swayed, I went to my father's workroom. He had just finished a calligraphy writing. It lay on the table, drying. My father did not hear me, as I came on quiet mouse feet. He sat looking out at the half-moon and his face was sad. I crept to the table, hoping to see my name, but in his graceful hand my father had written "Stone does not yield." I was young. I did not know the meaning of the words. Now I do.

Wen-shan slowly rolled the scroll. Even if her uncle had been willing, there were too many questions and feelings that needed sorting before she could talk about what she had just read. She laid the scroll on the table and stood.

"I . . . I think I'll go to my bedroom."

Her uncle looked at her and nodded.

"You don't mind?"

"No. I understand. There is much to think about."

"Yes. Good night, Uncle."

"Good night, Wen-shan."

"Oh, the kitchen cleanup!"

"I'll take care of it."

"You will?"

He nodded.

"Thank you, Uncle." She moved toward her bedroom.

"Wen-shan?"

"Yes?"

"You do look like your mother."

Her breath caught, but she kept walking.

NOTE

The "true gentle man": In Confucian philosophy, the gentle or superior man's goal was to set his feet upon the Way: "A gentle man has nine aims: to see clearly; to understand what he hears; to be warm in manner, dignified in bearing, faithful of speech, painstaking at work; to ask when in doubt; in anger to think of difficulties (consequences); in sight of gain to remember right."

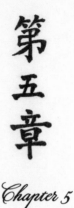

Chapter 5

T HE LINE FOR THE MOVIE was getting long. Wen-shan looked around. Where were her friends? She turned again and bumped into Wei Jun-jai.

"Ah! Jun-jai! I didn't see you."

"That's because you were looking the other direction."

"Very funny."

"Is Song Li-ying here?"

"Not yet. I've been saving places."

"You're a good friend."

Wen-shan's face colored, and she turned away as though looking for Li-ying.

"I hear this is a good movie."

"Me too." Wen-shan turned back. "*Benji*. It's a strange name for a dog, isn't it?" She began giggling.

"What is it?"

"Li-ying didn't want to come at first. She thought it was going to be a movie about a Chinese warlord."

Jun-jai laughed too. "Ah, Benji the Ruthless."

"When she found out it was about a cute little dog, she was happy."

"Yes. We should all be safe with this film. No ruthless warlords, or improper words, or rock and roll." He gave her a crooked smile.

Wen-shan growled. "My uncle is so old-fashioned! No rock and roll, Western food is terrible, and if it were up to him, he'd have me with two long braids down my back." She stopped her tirade abruptly as she thought about her mother's letter and how she would braid her hair.

Jun-jai noticed. "My parents are old-fashioned too, Wen-shan."

"Really? But you are always so up-to-date, Jun-jai."

"They are old-fashioned when it comes to behavior and family respect."

"Not clothing?"

Jun-jai smiled. "No, not clothing. In fact, my mother says the way I dress makes me look hip."

"She does not say that."

"She does."

"She says hip?"

"Just today she said it."

"I don't believe you, Jun-jai. I would have to hear her say it to believe you."

Jun-jai looked comically wounded. "You won't believe me? One who has set his feet upon the Way?"

Wen-shan giggled. "Oh, yes, I'm so sorry. I forgot. The great student of Confucius." She sobered. "But maybe someone can talk of the Way and not actually walk the path."

Jun-jai sobered too. "Do you think I would do that?"

"No! No, Jun-jai. I wasn't thinking of you. I was . . . I was just thinking of people in general."

The crooked smile was back. "I see."

"Really. I just mean that if someone was following the Way, then wouldn't their actions show it?"

"That is the point."

Wen-shan put her hands in her jacket pockets. "Of course. So, you would be sure to follow the Confucius saying about 'Don't do to others . . . something . . . something.'"

"'Don't do to others what you do not want done to yourself.'"

"Yes."

"A superior man would believe that and attempt to fulfill it."

Wen-shan felt tears pushing at the back of her throat. She turned away. "Where is that Song Li-ying? We may have to go in without her." Wen-shan could sense Jun-jai staring at her. She was afraid he would wonder why she was asking so many questions about Confucius. She didn't want to say anything directly about her uncle not following the Way, for Jun-jai admired her uncle and would think her a sour girl for disrespecting him. Luckily Li-ying appeared around the corner of the building at that moment, and Wen-shan stopped obsessing and waved.

"We're here, Li-ying!"

Her name being called out in public made Li-ying blush, but Wen-shan was glad for the distraction. Li-ying hurried quickly to them.

"Oh, I'm sorry I'm late. I had to walk my younger brother to his friend's house before coming," Li-ying said in a rush.

"No worries," Wen-shan said. "Benji the ruthless warlord is waiting for us."

"Don't tease me, Wen-shan. I didn't know."

The line began moving, and the three friends shuffled along.

"Good day, Wei Jun-jai," Li-ying said.

"Good day, Song Li-ying."

Two of Jun-jai's friends from school stopped to talk to him, and Li-ying took the opportunity to pull Wen-shan aside.

"Did you read any of the letters?"

"We did."

"And?"

"I'm . . . I'm not ready to talk about it yet, Li Li. I hope you understand."

"Of course, Wen-shan. I do, really. Does Jun-jai know anything about it?"

"No, and I don't want him to. Not yet anyway. You're the only one I've told."

"And I will keep your secret."

Wen-shan thought she caught a glimpse of satisfaction flicker on Li-ying's face but dismissed it. Li-ying was a true friend who was always honest.

● ● ●

Wen-shan arrived home from the movie to find two of her grandfather's paintings unrolled on the kitchen table. One was the painting of the Guilin Mountains she and her uncle had seen at Mr. Smythe's home, but the other was new. Wen-shan felt a coil of resentment snake into her mind as she wondered why her uncle hadn't waited until they could see it together. Had he read another of the letters too? Wen-shan took off her jacket and threw it over the back of the kitchen chair.

"That doesn't belong there."

She jumped at the sound of her uncle's voice. He'd come quietly from his bedroom, catching her unawares.

"You opened another of the silk scrolls?"

"As you can see, I did."

"Why didn't you wait for me?"

"How was your movie?"

"What?"

"Your movie—how was it?"

"I don't want to talk about the movie."

Her uncle calmly walked to the front room and picked up his paper. "So, it wasn't good?"

Wen-shan followed. "No. I mean yes, it was good, but that's not what I want to talk about."

"I know. You want to talk about the painting, but I will not talk with you about it until you are calm."

Wen-shan seethed. She wanted to yell and stamp her feet, but she didn't. She hadn't done that since she was little, and she knew instinctively that it would not produce the desired results. She took a breath and calmed the thoughts bumping around in her head.

"Was there a reason you opened the painting without me?"

"Yes."

Wen-shan waited.

"It was addressed to me."

"Oh." She was glad she hadn't yelled and stamped her feet. "My grandfather addressed it to you?"

Her uncle laid down his paper. "You must remember, Wen-shan, that he is your grandfather, but he is also my brother."

She felt small. "Oh, yes, of course."

"Come. I will show you why I think he meant this painting for me."

They went into the kitchen and Wen-shan looked carefully at the stunning picture spread across the chrome and Formica table. It was done only in black ink and showed a gnarled cypress tree clinging to an outcropping of rock. The detail in the twisted trunk and limbs gave the tree character and life.

"It is stunning, isn't it?"

"Yes." She looked at her uncle as he studied the picture.

"Do you know what the cypress tree and the rock signify?" he asked.

Wen-shan shook her head.

"Endurance." He touched the edge of the paper. "This is taken from a work done hundreds of years ago by Master Wen-Zhengming. Master Quan had us study it in school. There is poetry that goes with it. Would you like to hear?"

"Yes, I would." Wen-shan held her breath. Never in their ten years together had she heard such gentleness in her uncle's voice.

> *Weighed down by snow,*
> *Oppressed by frost, with the*
> *Passing of years and months*
> *Its branches become twisted*
> *And its crown bent down,*
> *Yet its strength remains majestic.*

The word *majestic* floated in the air for several moments.

"That was beautiful, Uncle."

He slowly drew his hand across the paper. "*This* is beautiful." He was silent for a long time, and when he finally spoke, his voice was full of acceptance. "I think this is one of the reasons I joined the military. I had some talent, but I knew I would never do this." He looked at her. "Come. Shall we read a letter?"

"Yes. I'd like to."

They settled into their accustomed seats and Wen-shan unrolled the second scroll.

I was four when my mother died, but I remember things about her. For many years my father would not listen. He told me it was impossible for me to remember anything. He said I was recounting some dream— some imagination. But when I finally told him of the great loom and my mother's gentle hands moving the blue thread so fast, he was silent. I told him how I remembered that she limped when she walked because her mother had broken her toes and bound her feet. I told him that many times my mother would place her gentle hands on my head and say, "Kai-ying, I will never bind your feet. You might not marry well because of it, but you will make your own way on your big, comical feet."

Then my father opened the linen chest and brought out my mother's tiny shoes. He gave them to me with a piece of soft blue cloth and an apology. I kept the cloth in the trunk with my clothes and toys. The shoes I threw in the trash heap. I did not like to think of my mother limping.

Wen-shan looked up to find her uncle staring at her.

"I remember the beautiful cloth your grandmother wove; blue was her special color."

"And her mother broke her toes?"

"Foot binding was a common practice."

"It was barbaric."

"Yes."

"Were your wife's feet bound?" Wen-shan could not believe those words had escaped her mouth. She was expecting a gruff reprimand, so she was surprised when her uncle smiled.

"No. She had big, comical feet."

"Really?"

"Actually they were just average-sized, but compared to feet that were four or five inches, they must have seemed large."

Wen-shan looked down at her own feet that were somewhat bigger than average. She'd never thought about them as beautiful or not beautiful. They got her from place to place just fine.

"And my great-aunt was a good dancer, right?"

Her uncle nodded. "A fantastic dancer."

"I wish I'd gotten to meet her."

"Hmm." He picked up his paper, and Wen-shan knew the conversation was over.

She held out the letter. "Can I take this with me to bed?"

Her uncle nodded and she headed off.

"Hang up your jacket."

She took it with her into the solitude of her room.

After her nightly routine, Wen-shan climbed between the cool sheets and unrolled the parchment. *I was four when my mother died, but I remember things about her.* She was five when she was sent from Guilin. Why couldn't she remember anything about her mother? She wanted to remember blue cloth, and her mother's voice. Wen-shan read and reread the characters until they began to slide off the page. She laid the scroll on her night table and turned off the light. Just before the cozy blue of sleep overtook her, she thought she heard the mellow sound of Benny Goodman's clarinet.

Notes

The Way: In Confucian philosophy, the practical teacher was concerned with the problem of man in society. The ideals which set a man's feet on the path of the Way were the ideal of the "true gentle man" and the ideal of proper conduct, which included the proper reverence for ancestors.

Mao Tse-tung's political and philosophical opinions were diametrically opposed to the teachings of Confucius. When asked about the Confucian sentiment "Do not do to others what you don't want done to your self," Mao replied, "My principle is exactly the opposite: do to others precisely what I don't want done to myself." Mao was also opposed to the idea of honoring ancestors. He believed the people should consider Mao their father and honor only him.

Foot binding: The practice originated in the Tang dynasty (928–936 AD), reportedly to imitate the small feet of an imperial dancer. When a girl was around the age of three, her toes were broken, curved under the ball of her foot, and then tightly bound in order to keep her feet from growing more than four inches. Small feet were considered beautiful, resembling a three-inch lotus.

So, WHAT DO YOU THINK, MADAM? The antique table for twenty-five pounds and the sofa for sixty?"

Wen-shan ran her hand imperiously over the fabric of the sofa. "I won't pay more than fifty pounds. That's my final offer."

The British salesclerk put his hand on his heart. He shook his head and his jowls wobbled. "Oh, dear. Oh, dear dear dear."

Wen-shan covered her mouth to stifle a laugh. "Besides, the fabric is second-rate."

Now a look of shock jumped into the man's expressive blue eyes. "Second-rate, madam? I'll have you know that Pierpont and Pierpont Limited sells *nothing* that is second-rate."

"Oh, really?" She held his gaze. "Well . . . in that case, I'll take four tables and two sofas."

A wide smile broke onto the clerk's face as he hastily brought out his account book and wrote up the order. "Very good, madam." He ripped off the slip and handed it to her with a flourish. "The goods will be delivered on Saturday!"

Zhao Tai-lu came to the side of the man. "Is she bothering you, Mr. Pierpont?"

"What? Oh, dear no, Mr. Zhao! Best customer of the day." He winked at Wen-shan. "She is always a delight to have in the store. In fact, if you don't mind, I think I'll put her to work. She can help me close up."

"Yes, of course. It will take me about thirty minutes to check in the rest of the new shipment."

Mr. Pierpont clapped his hands. "Ducky!"

Her uncle gave her a cautionary look as he turned back to the office.

"He's a fine man, that uncle of yours. I'm thinking of making him a partner."

Wen-shan stared. "Really?"

"Yes. But don't go blabbing about it, right?"

"Of course not."

"He's been with me since my brother died."

"The other Mr. Pierpont."

"Yes, indeed! The other Mr. Pierpont. Some eighteen years ago."

"That's a long time. That's before I came to live with him."

"Indeed. Before you came. Before his wife died. Before my wife died." Mr. Pierpont began walking around the sales floor, clicking off lamps and readjusting pillows. "Run and get the feather duster."

Wen-shan went to the front counter and rummaged in the cupboard until she found the duster. It was her favorite job. She followed closely behind Mr. Pierpont so they could talk.

"You knew my great-aunt."

"I did, yes." He paused as he reached for a light switch. "She was a remarkable woman, considering all she had to go through."

"What do you mean?"

"Oh, yes, well. Don't you know, what with being chased all over China by the Communists and having to live in that wretched refugee camp upon arriving in Hong Kong. And then . . ." He switched off a light and moved on.

Wen-shan quickly maneuvered around a chair. "And then, what?"

"Just many troubles, that's all." Mr. Pierpont turned to look at her. "What's this all about anyway? You have never had questions about your great-uncle's life."

Wen-shan dusted a statue of a girl carrying a basket. "I'm older now. I guess I'm more interested."

"As well you should be. But the story of a man's life should be told by the man himself."

Wen-shan plopped down on one of the couches. "He never says anything."

Mr. Pierpont studied her. "But that never mattered before."

Wen-shan looked up. "Well, it mattered, but I was too young to know what questions to ask."

"I see." Mr. Pierpont sat down next to her. "Surely he's told you something about his illustrious military career."

"Illustrious?" Wen-shan shrugged. "Not really. Just that he was some sort of officer in Chiang Kai-shek's army."

Disbelief sprang onto Mr. Pierpont's face. "I'll have you know he was a high-ranking officer in the Nationalist army. He was one of Chiang Kai-shek's general field commanders. Had the Communists not terrorized their way into power, your great-uncle would probably have held a position in the Nationalist government."

"Really?"

"Indeed."

"He's never mentioned anything about that."

"As you said, he's not one to talk about himself."

"But *you* know about it."

Mr. Pierpont stood. "Well, we've been friends for a long time. Over the years some information is bound to be shared." He went to push the chairs in on a dining room set.

Wen-shan ran the feather duster along the backs of the chairs. "Where did you meet?"

"When?"

"Well, where and when."

"I met him in 1958—the same year I hired him at the store. We met at church."

"Church?"

Mr. Pierpont chuckled. "Don't sound so shocked, Miss Chen. There are many sides to Mr. Terrence William Pierpont."

"No, I'm not shocked that you go to church, Mr. Pierpont, just that it's the Mormon Church my uncle goes to. Well, went to."

"Well, there you have it."

"He doesn't go all that much now."

Mr. Pierpont indicated a side table that needed dusting. "I think it's been difficult for him since his wife died."

"He used to take me with him."

Mr. Pierpont raised his eyebrows. "Oh, yes, I remember. You did not like it much."

"I did make a little fuss, didn't I?"

"A little fuss? Oh, my dear, everyone in the congregation went home with a headache."

"I was afraid of people."

"Of course you were. Poor little thing. Very understand-able."

"Probably another reason why he stopped going." Wen-shan finished dusting the table. "Why didn't I know that you went to the same church?"

"Like you said, you've just begun to ask questions."

Mr. Pierpont headed for the front of the store. "Your uncle is a good man. When he came into the Church, I had been baptized for only a year."

Wen-shan looked shocked. "Baptized? You were baptized as a grown-up?"

"Yes."

"And my uncle too?"

"Yes. In the swimming pool at the mission home."

"Excuse me?"

"Ah . . . yes . . . well, that's a story for another day."

"But isn't baptism for babies?"

Mr. Pierpont chuckled. "Indeed, it's for all of us who want to be born again."

Wen-shan didn't understand the joke. She found it difficult imagining two grown men being baptized.

"I wonder why he doesn't go to church more often," she said.

Mr. Pierpont patted her on the arm. "Perhaps that is a question you should ask him. Just know that he is a good man of faith." He smiled. "You should ask him to tell you the noodle story."

"The noodle story?"

"Yes. Like I said—a good man of faith."

"Well, he reads his Bible a lot."

Mr. Pierpont turned over the CLOSED sign on the front window, and Wen-shan looked around at the store's dim interior. She liked the lumpy shadows surrounding the pieces of furniture and the stillness caused by the cushions and pillows. She'd had a long day at school, and the idea of lying down on one of the soft sofas and covering herself with dozens of throw pillows seemed very appealing. Maybe she would magically disappear and wouldn't have to go home and fix dinner. Could she get away with tomato soup and cheese sandwiches? She doubted it. She put away the feather duster and latched the cupboard door.

Mr. Pierpont smiled at her. "So, there you have it. I'll lock the door and we'll go out through the back. Your uncle should be nearly finished with his task. Ah, and don't forget your box of biscuits."

"That was so nice of you, Mr. Pierpont. Thank you."

"You are entirely welcome, my dear. What's life without a nice sweet biscuit?"

Wen-shan figured her uncle would say life was better.

● ● ●

Walking home in the gathering darkness, Wen-shan's mind jumped from subject to subject: her grandmother's small shoes, math homework, dinner, her crying at church, the sunlit window at Mr. Smythe's home, and the jade dragon box. Her uncle was quiet beside her, and Wen-shan was sure his mind was focused calmly on one subject. A calm mind had never been one of her strengths. She tried to think of one of the sayings of Confucius her uncle had taught her.

There are three friends that do good, and three friends that do harm. The three friends that do good are a straight friend, a sincere friend, and a friend who has heard much.

The friends that do harm are a smooth friend, a fawning friend, and a friend with a glib tongue.

She wasn't really sure what *fawning* or *glib* meant, but she liked the saying overall.

"What are you thinking, Wen-shan?"

Her uncle's voice brought her to the present, and she was glad she had actually been thinking about something worthwhile.

"I was thinking of the Confucian saying on friends."

Her uncle seemed pleased. "An important saying. And your friends—what kind are they?"

"Oh, they're friends that do good."

"Yes, I think so. Wei Jun-jai is very bright."

Wen-shan knew he said that because Jun-jai was a student of Confucius, but she was glad for the compliment.

"Thank you, Uncle. I think Mr. Pierpont is a friend that does good, too."

"Oh? And why is that?"

"I think he tells the truth, and he's very kind."

"Yes, that's true."

"And he's known you a long time so he must know stories about you."

Her uncle was silent as an evening lark called out. Wen-shan stammered, "I . . . I mean, he didn't say anything, I just figured."

"And?"

"Well, we talked a little about your military career, and he said that you'd both been baptized and that I should ask you to tell me the noodle story."

"Hmm. That was quite a bit of talking from someone who didn't say anything."

"I'm sorry, it was me. I'm just full of questions lately."

They reached their gate and her uncle undid the latch. "No questions tonight."

"There is time for one letter, isn't there?"

"Yes. I think there's time for that."

1955

I have come home from working in the fields. I cross the ancient bridge over a tributary of the great Li River, and I feel the setting sun on the back of my neck. My hands ache from working in the rice fields, but I must not complain. This is the noble work that will make China a superpower. I am sixteen and my days at school are ended. Our great leader Chairman Mao says we do not need school. If we think something hard enough we can become it. That is the great power of Mao Tse-tung thought. Though I want to be a doctor, I must first learn the work of the peasant, and then the knowledge of the scholar will come to me.

I pass huts on my way home, and everyone wears the face of loneliness and hunger. I remember when the old men played mah-jongg, and the old women shared stories. Now everyone wears the blue uniform of communism, and the old have put on sullen faces. They do not understand the new ways that our leaders are teaching. They think only of how things were before. They think things were better, but they will learn. I

*walk on through the shadows of a bamboo forest. I
smile. I am proud to be a worker for the new order.*

*A crane flies overhead into the mist of the heavenly
mountains. Tonight I will eat noodles, and perhaps my
father will take his brush and write my name in his
beautiful hand. Tonight I will sleep quietly under a
Guilin moon.*

NOTES

Mao Tse-tung thought: These were the slogans and ideas of Chairman Mao that
were sent out to the Chinese people, which they were to follow without question.
Many of these thoughts were brought together to form the basis for the pocket-
sized edition of *Quotations from Chairman Mao Tse-tung.*

Party members: People who were members of the Chinese Communist Party, or
the CCP. By the late 1950s, an estimated seventeen million people were working
for the CCP.

第

七

章

Chapter 7

W EN-SHAN SAT ON HER FRONT porch with her
head in her hands. She hadn't slept peacefully under
a Guilin moon. No. Her sleep had been filled with dreams
of rice fields and hot sun, of squalid huts and old men playing mah-jongg. And worse, she kept asking everyone where she
could find her mother, but no one paid her any attention or even
looked at her.

"You have a headache?"

Wen-shan's head jerked up.

"Ouch!" She rubbed the back of her neck.

The neighbor girl laughed.

"Ya Ya! Leave me alone, you little brat."

"I'm not a brat. You are."

"Just get off my porch."

"I'm not on your porch. I'm in the garden."

Wen-shan looked down and forced her eyes to focus. Ya Ya made an ugly face and stuck out her tongue.

"Confucius says, 'Girl who makes terrible faces will have ugly babies.'"

Ya Ya's expression changed to a sneer. "He did not say that."

"That's what my uncle told me, and he's a great scholar of Confucius."

Ya Ya hesitated, and Wen-shan could see her brain trying to come up with a reply. The girl started to say something, when the door to her house opened, and Mrs. Tuan peered out.

"Ya Ya! What are you doing? Don't talk to her. Come in to breakfast."

After her mother had closed the door, Ya Ya made another face. "We're having rice pudding and cold watermelon. Bet you're not having that. Bet you're having stupid cornflakes."

"Go away, Ya Ya." It was muggy, and Wen-shan's shirt was sticking to her back. The heat only intensified her headache and her crankiness. *Cold watermelon does sound good.*

"You're just mad because I have a mother and you don't."

Wen-shan grabbed a sandal off the porch and chucked it at the scrawny girl. Ya Ya yelped and ran for the house.

"Mother! She threw a shoe at me!"

Too bad I missed. Wen-shan put her head in her hands again. Why didn't she have a mother, and a father, and brothers and sisters? She couldn't even remember images or smells from childhood—not her mother's face or her grandfather's house. She couldn't remember! She stood abruptly and saw movement at the gate. She looked over. Jun-jai stood there, raising his hand into the air. Wen-shan took a deep breath to still her emotions. *Stop being such a child.* She picked up the sandal, threw it back onto the porch, and went to the gate to greet her friend.

"Jun-jai, what are you doing here?"

"I didn't need to work at my uncle's store today, so I thought I'd take a trip up the Peak. Do you want to come?"

She brightened. "I'd love to! It will be cooler up there, for sure."

"That's what I thought."

"I'll go and get money for the tram." She ran back into the house, grabbed her coin purse, and left a note for her uncle. She knew she'd be home long before her uncle returned from work, but it was better to be safe.

● ● ●

The ride up the side of the mountain was soothing, even with the clatter of the metal tramcar on its steep ascent. The air cooled and a slight breeze moved the leaves of the thick vegetation and stirred up the smell of flowers.

Wen-shan sighed. This was just what her headache needed. Now if she could only find a nice cold slice of watermelon. She smiled.

"What are you thinking about?" Jun-jai asked.

"Watermelon."

He laughed. "That's what I like about you, Wen-shan. You're practical."

Wen-shan smiled, though she didn't know if she liked being thought of as practical. She shrugged. Well, maybe she was. *The chubby, short, practical girl.*

The tram reached the summit, and on disembarking, the two decided to hike a path that curved into the face of the peak. It would take them to a place where they'd have a view of Victoria Harbor, Central Hong Kong, and Kowloon. Jun-jai had long legs and Wen-shan had to hurry to keep up. When they reached the lookout, she was puffing.

"Oh, sorry, Wen-shan. I should have slowed down."

She was offended. "No, you shouldn't. I stayed right with you."

"You did." He reached into his pocket. "And as a reward, I think we should have a candy."

He held out a handful of sesame-seed candies wrapped in amber wrappers.

Wen-shan took half. "I don't see why *you* should get a reward, Jun-jai."

"What do you mean? It was hard to keep ahead of you."

Wen-shan laughed and sat down on a rock to look out at the vista. Jun-jai did the same.

"Ah, it's a clear day today," Jun-jai said. He pointed out over Victoria Harbor. "Look, you can see the mountains of the New Territories."

Wen-shan had just put a candy in her mouth, so she simply nodded.

"And beyond those mountains is mainland China."

Wen-shan's throat tightened.

"I wonder what will happen in Communist China without Mao Tse-tung to control things?"

"What do you think, Jun-jai?"

He was quiet for a long time, and then he shook his head. "I don't know. The Communist government only lets people hear what they want them to hear, and only lets people see what they want them to see. I don't know if that will change now that Mao is dead."

"Do you think life was really that bad? My teacher, Mrs. Yang, seemed sad the day Mao died."

"She wasn't sad for Mao's death; she was grieving for her parents. My family knows her family, Wen-shan. She and her brother escaped from Yan'an in 1947, but not before they watched their parents be tortured to death in front of the whole village."

Wen-shan could not swallow her candy and spat it out. "What?"

"Yes. They were tortured by the Communists. It was during the civil war, and they were caught hiding food from the Communist soldiers."

"Killed for hiding food?"

"Yes. And guess who ordered them dragged to the square, and who ordered their children and the whole village to watch?"

"Mao Tse-tung."

"Yes."

"But he wasn't the leader of the country."

"But during the civil war, he was the leader of his own little Communist country, and he made sure people were frightened of him."

"So things probably weren't good when the Communists took over."

"Probably not, but we don't know. Not much information gets out, and a lot of it is propaganda. People who escaped to Hong Kong have stories to tell, but most of them keep quiet."

"Like my uncle."

"Yes. They have learned fear to the center of their hearts."

They both said nothing for a long time.

Wen-shan thought of her mother being forced to give up her dream of being a doctor; of Mrs. Yang's face the day of the announcement of Mao's death; and of her uncle and aunt, running for their lives.

"Jun-jai?"

"Yes?"

"I have something to tell you."

He looked at her and waited.

She told him about the note, the trip to Mr. Smythe's home, meeting Master Quan, and being given the jade dragon box.

"And the letters tell you about your mother's and grandfather's life in Guilin?"

"Yes."

"And this is the first you've heard from them?"

"Yes. My uncle couldn't tell me anything because he and my great-aunt left China long before I was born." She looked out to the New Territories. "Besides, he doesn't tell me much anyway."

"This must be very hard for you."

Wen-shan put all her effort into not crying. "Yes."

Jun-jai didn't say anything else. He picked up some pebbles and began tossing them down the slope. Wen-shan was grateful for his silence. It gave her time to get control of her emotions.

"Jun-jai?"

"Yes?"

"In the letters, if my mother says things about life under the Communists, would you like to know?"

He looked at her with admiration. "That is very generous of you, Wen-shan, but you must decide."

"I think my mother's words will be the truth, Jun-jai, and people need to know the truth. Master Quan risked his life for the truth." One tear escaped and rolled down her cheek.

Jun-jai stood. "Come! Let's go see if we can find some jasmine flowers." He held out his hand and pulled her up. "And on the way, we'll eat more candy."

Wen-shan shook her hair back in the breeze. With Jun-jai

she would share her mother's thoughts about change and revolution, and with Li-ying she would share her mother's heart.

● ● ●

1956

I am rolling the last of my father's paintings for
there is no longer space to hang them on the walls. We
have been ordered by the new First Party Secretary of
Guilin to allow two other families to move in with us.
When he inspected our home with its two floors, indoor
toilet, and large courtyard, he shook his head and
scolded my father for his bourgeois excess.

Father nodded politely. "Yes, yes, Secretary Zhang,"
he said. "You are absolutely right. I have known this for
a long time, and have been waiting for a high official to
tell me how to remedy this offense."

First Party Secretary Zhang said my father and I
must be criticized publicly for our "Capitalist Roader"
ways, and then we must make way for two more families.

Wen-shan stopped reading.

"What is it?" her uncle asked.

"I am ashamed of myself."

"Why?"

"The day Mao Tse-tung died, I accidently bumped into a man on the street and he yelled at me."

"Why does that make you ashamed?"

Wen-shan shook her head. "Not because of what he said, but because of what I called him when I was angry."

"What was that?"

"I called him a Capitalist Roader."

"Ah, and now it has a different meaning."

"Yes. I'm sure Confucius must have said something about my terrible behavior."

Her uncle gave her a slight smile. "'When anger rises, think of the consequences.'"

"Perfect. I'll try to remember that the next time I lose my temper." Wen-shan looked down at her mother's writing. "Uncle?"

"Yes?"

"I don't know if I want to read what happened."

"That is up to you, but your mother wanted you to know— wanted us to know. These are the things she has chosen to share with you."

Wen-shan took a moment to slow her heart rate, and then continued.

There were two hundred people at the criticism meeting. My gentle father was made to stand in front of the crowd, and they put a heavy sign around his neck that said "Running Dog for the Capitalist!" I had a dunce cap put on my head while people yelled insults and called us names. My face burned with shame.

They called my father a selfish landowner, a gluttonous pig, and a thief of the people.

Many of these people were our neighbors and friends. I know that most were participating out of fear. They knew Secretary Zhang was watching and they wanted to make a good show. Some people we didn't even know came forward during the session and spoke strong words against us.

*After two hours, they took the sign roughly from my
father's neck and he stumbled and fell to his knees. The
crowd jeered at him and said the secretary had made
my father kowtow.*

*I helped my father to stand, and he looked straight
into the crowd and smiled at them. They became silent.
He said to them, "My thanks to the secretary and to all of
you for showing me my faults. It is a good thing for a man
to know his faults. I will now go my way and hopefully
be a better Communist." He bowed, and several people in
the crowd, without thinking, bowed back.*

*When we got to our little piece of home, I rubbed
a soothing camphor balm on his legs and had him
sit in his favorite chair. I sat by him, listening to the
sounds of the night and trying to rid myself of vengeful
thoughts. In my mental wanderings I discovered that
my father taught me a great lesson. He taught me that
he is not stone, but bamboo.*

*I put his paintings safely in a box under his bed. He
slept with a grin on his face.*

"The jade dragon box is the box under Grandfather's bed,
isn't it?"

"That is what I think."

Wen-shan tried to imagine the house in Guilin, her mother
placing the paintings in the box, and her grandfather sleeping
with a smile on his face. She needed to think of that, because
she did not want to think of him kneeling in front of the ugly,
smirking Secretary Zhang. She did not want to think of her
mother wearing a dunce cap. Wen-shan reached under the coffee table and laid her hand on the smooth wood of the box.

"Uncle?"

"Yes?"

"The people of China wanted peace."

"Yes. Like people everywhere, they wanted food and stability."

"Do you think they realized that they weren't going to get stability?"

He nodded. "All they had to do was look around them."

Wen-shan stood and went to the kitchen to get a drink of water for bed. "Well, I would have done something. I would have fought back," she said over her shoulder.

Her uncle joined her in the kitchen. "How were they to fight back, Wen-shan? They did not have weapons. If someone tried to start a riot, I am sure they were dealt with right away. That is why your grandfather taught the lesson of the bamboo—to be flexible in the storm."

"Well, I still don't understand."

"That is because you are a girl of Hong Kong."

She yawned. "I guess so."

"Go to bed now, before you fall down."

She nodded and headed for her bedroom, wondering what she would do if someone tried to put a dunce cap on her head.

Notes

Yan'an: A city in North Central China, Shaanxi province, Yan'an is located near the endpoint of the Long March. It also served as the capital of the Communist Party from 1936 to 1948.

The Long March: The Long March was the forced military retreat of the Red Army of the Communist Party to evade the pursuit of the Nationalist Army under the direction of Chiang Kai-shek. During the year-long, six thousand-mile trek from Jiangxi province to Shaanxi province, seventy to ninety thousand troops of the original 100,000 troops died. The march lasted from October 1934 to October 1935.

The war in China, which ended in 1949 with Mao Tse-tung's rise to power, is called the civil war by the Nationalists and the War of Liberation by the Communists.

Class struggle meetings: Meetings were held within a work unit or a neighborhood to publicly criticize someone. These meetings often included humiliation and physical assault.

Kowtow: This is an act of worship or submission where a person kneels and puts their forehead on the ground.

Chapter 8

T HE BELL RANG TO END CLASSES, and Wen-shan took her time gathering her belongings. Li-ying came to her side.

"You are slow today."

"Will you wait for me outside, Li-ying? I need to speak to Mrs. Yang."

"About your mathematics assignment?"

"No, about something else."

"How long will you be?"

"Just a few minutes. Then we can go to my house and watch my television."

Li-ying brightened. "In the middle of the afternoon? I thought you couldn't watch until after homework."

"I don't have much. Plenty of time to get it done." The last of the classmates were exiting. "Go on now. I'll be out in a minute."

Li-ying left, and Wen-shan timidly approached her teacher's desk. Mrs. Yang looked up.

"Yes, Wen-shan?"

"I am a friend to Wei Jun-jai."

Mrs. Yang nodded. "I know his family."

"Yes, I know. He told me." Wen-shan looked down at her shoes. "He . . . he said you lost your parents in China's civil war."

"No."

Wen-shan's head came up. "No?"

Mrs. Yang's gaze was steady. "I did not lose them, Wen-shan. They were murdered by Mao Tse-tung." She closed a book on her desk. "We call it the civil war, but the Communists call it the War of Liberation. Remember, Wen-shan, it is all in how one looks at something. Be diligent when you look."

"Yes, ma'am."

Mrs. Yang turned her head to look out the window. "I'm afraid the mythology surrounding Mao will last for a long time." She turned back and gave Wen-shan the same steady gaze. "But I was an eyewitness. I know differently."

"Yes, ma'am. I'm sorry for your pain."

"And I for yours."

Wen-shan's breathing accelerated. "Mine?"

"You came from mainland China at age five. You are being raised by a great-uncle. Surely there is some pain in your story."

"Yes, ma'am." Wen-shan thought of her mother at sixteen dragging in from the rice fields. "My mother and grandfather are in Guilin."

Mrs. Yang laid her hand on her chest. "The heavenly mountains."

"You know Guilin?"

"Everyone knows Guilin. When I was young, growing up in the stark landscape of Yan'an, I would dream of green mountains touching the sky, and swaying forests of bamboo. Especially after the Japanese bombed our village during World War II and there were no buildings standing. My family, like most others, lived in a yaodong—"

"A what?"

"Yaodong—an artificial cave cut out of the stone hills."

Wen-shan was fascinated, but she simply said, "Oh."

"I would stare at the lime-cast walls of my dugout and imagine seeing bamboo and tall mountains."

"I've never seen the great mountains either. Well, I mean, I've seen them, but I don't remember."

"Do you hear from your mother and grandfather?"

Wen-shan adjusted her satchel. "No. Just recently my uncle and I have received a box from them with letters, but they were written more than a year ago."

"And in Mao's China, a year is a very long time."

There was silence.

"May I ask a very personal question?" Wen-shan said.

"You may ask, but I may not answer."

Wen-shan nodded. The question came slowly. "Did you ever want revenge?"

Mrs. Yang looked down at the book on her desk as though images danced there. Finally she answered. "Yes. Both my brother and I wanted revenge. But my grandfather said to me, 'Before you start on a journey of revenge, dig two graves.'"

"Confucius."

"Yes. Our family had suffered many deaths, actual and spiritual, and my brother and I did not want to add any more grief."

"So you escaped."

"Yes, we put our energy into escaping."

Wen-shan was surprised that Mrs. Yang was sharing so much of her story. Perhaps with the death of Chairman Mao, people's hearts were letting out the poison of trapped sorrow.

"Thank you, Mrs. Yang."

Mrs. Yang smiled at her, and Wen-shan was warmed by the rare occurrence. "We must think of China as our beautiful land, Wen-shan. A land that is ancient and permanent." Absently, her fingers tapped the cover of the book. "'All the world's a stage, and all the men and women merely players.'"

"Yes, ma'am. I'll see you tomorrow." Wen-shan turned to leave the classroom.

"Work harder on your mathematics, Wen-shan."

Wen-shan left smiling. "Yes, ma'am."

• • •

As soon as the door to the bungalow opened, Wen-shan knew her friend was no longer interested in television. Li-ying gasped when she saw the paintings and calligraphy of Wen-shan's grandfather. She stood in front of the new scroll Wen-shan and her uncle had unrolled the night before. It showed a thousand vivid pink plum blossoms festooned on dark, curved branches. Some blossoms were cascading through the air and the accompanying strokes of calligraphy read "falling petals—fragrant rain."

Li-ying reached out to touch one of the petals. "I've never seen anything so beautiful, Wen-shan. I can sense your grandfather's feelings." She took a breath. "Thank you."

"For what?"

"For sharing this with me."

Wen-shan looked more carefully at her grandfather's painting. "You're welcome."

Li-ying moved next to the ink drawing of the cypress tree, and then to the mountains of Guilin.

"This is where you lived your young life," she whispered.

Wen-shan felt a momentary irritation. "For all I remember, I could have been born in the Gobi desert."

"Oh, of course, Wen-shan. How thoughtless of me."

Wen-shan nipped her sullen feelings. "It's all right, Li Li. It is a beautiful place. Maybe I breathed in some of its magic before I left."

"And you don't remember anything?"

"Rain."

"Rain?"

"But that may just be a bad dream I have every once in a while. A dream of rain, and darkness, and a ghost."

Before Li-ying could reply, Wen-shan turned to the kitchen, making a bold decision. "I say we eat something and read one of my mother's letters."

Li-ying followed. "You mean it, Wen-shan? Your uncle won't be upset?"

"He won't know." She opened the refrigerator door. "How about an orange?"

"That sounds good."

The girls went to the front porch to eat their orange wedges and watch people as they walked in front of the half-moon arch.

Wen-shan swallowed a piece of sweet orange. "Did you know that Mrs. Yang's mother and father were killed by the Communists?"

Li-ying looked stricken. "No. Is that what you talked about?"

"Yes. I'd found out from Jun-jai. His family knows the Yang family. Anyway, I wanted to tell her how sorry I was. Her parents were tortured and—"

Li-ying held up her hand. "Na, na, na, na! Don't say anything more, Wen-shan. I don't want to hear."

"But they—"

"No! Please, Wen-shan. Don't!" Tears filled Li-ying's eyes, and she took off her glasses to wipe them away.

"But the Communists treated your family badly."

"My father was a manager for a British oil company in Shanghai, Wen-shan. When the Communists took over all the industries, he was told he could work in a lower position under a party boss or leave the country. He and my mother chose to leave."

"Well, that had to be hard."

"My father lost his job and they lost their home, but that was all. We didn't suffer like—" She teared up again. "Like so many." She dabbed the tears away again with her napkin and put on her glasses. "Sometimes I forget how lucky we are to be here."

Wen-shan agreed, though not quite understanding the sentiment. Then she thought about her grandfather and mother being criticized and having more than half their house taken from them. She had her own bedroom and a television.

"I'm finished with my orange if you want the rest," Li-ying said, holding out the bowl of wedges.

"Are you sure?"

Li-ying nodded and Wen-shan took the bowl. She swallowed the last slice of orange as they moved to the kitchen to wash their hands.

Li-ying was quiet as they went to the front room and sat down on the sofa.

"Would you like to see the box first?"

"Yes, I would."

Wen-shan went down on her knees and lugged out the box from under the coffee table. She set it on top.

"Oh, Wen-shan, it's beautiful," Li-ying said. "Simple and beautiful." She ran her fingers over the jade carving. "A powerful dragon."

Wen-shan sat back on the sofa and opened the drawer of the coffee table. Her friend leaned over to see all the neatly arranged scrolls.

"There are so many."

Wen-shan actually thought the opposite—so few to represent a life. She reached for the next in the order, undid the ribbon, and opened the scroll. She saw a flicker of apprehension cross Li-ying's face and knew she was hoping there wouldn't be anything too sad to deal with. *The truth isn't always easy.*

"Ready?"

Li-ying nodded.

Wen-shan cleared her throat and read.

> *I have met a man. It is not customary, but nothing is customary in China anymore. His name is Chen Han-lie.*

Wen-shan choked and Li-ying gasped.

"Wen-shan, is that your father? Is your mother writing about your father?"

Wen-shan found it hard to speak. "I . . . I think so."

"Read, Wen-shan. Read!"

His name is Chen Han-lie, and he has been sent from Peking to teach the farmers how to double their crop production. He is tall—a head taller than the other men in the community. He wears the cap of a special worker and he is a fiery speaker.

He spoke at our monthly compulsory meeting.

"Our wise leader Chairman Mao says that you must grow more rice!"

Li-ying sat back. "Your father was a Communist."

Wen-shan's head pounded. *My father was a Communist.*

"Do you want to stop reading, Wen-shan?"

"No. I want to know. I want to hear my father's words."

"In the country, the peasants are lazy. You must be taught to work night and day for China. China must race towards Socialism, and you must run beside her or be trampled. Chairman Mao says 'Production first! Life takes second place!' All industry and commerce have been nationalized and now the farms must be brought together in one grand commune! The government has unified purchasing and marketing power over grain, cotton, edible oil, and meat. You will sell your goods to the government, and the government will take care of China's many people. Our great leader, Mao Tse-tung, will take care of the proper distribution of food and clothing so that everything is equal."

None of us believed that everything would be equal. We knew that the local party officials went to the back of the store to pick up their extra eggs and meat and milk. Most of us received meat once a week, and milk

*hadn't been available for years. But Chen Han-lie was
a good salesman and soon everyone was praising the
wisdom of Mao Tse-tung and the Great Leap Forward.
Our farm leaders began bragging that they could bring
in triple the crop production. Chen Han-lie taught us
a song and we all sang it together. We sang loudly to
make sure our neighbor heard us singing.*

> *Communism is heaven.*
> *The commune is the ladder.*
> *If we build that ladder*
> *We can climb the heights!*

*To show he was a good Communist, father did a
woodprint of happy people working together in the rice
field. Comrade Chen saw it pasted on the wall outside
our home. He liked it so much that he asked father
to make several more for the local party offices. Soon
everyone wanted a "happy worker" poster.*

*Comrade Chen then paid my father a small
amount and gave us two chickens. Of course we invited
him to dinner.*

Wen-shan let the scroll roll together on her lap. She was silent.

"Maybe it was good in the beginning. Maybe your father thought he was helping. The Great Leap Forward. That sounded good."

But everything Wen-shan had been learning said the Communist rule wasn't good. Mr. Pierpont had told her that the Communists had gotten rid of opium and gambling and had brought the people together under one government. Those were good things, but the cost was tyranny. The Communists, under Mao Tse-tung, had complete control over people's lives.

• • •

That night Wen-shan confessed to her uncle that she'd read the letter and left him to read it by himself. The thought of hearing her Communist father's words again made her stomach hurt.

She climbed into bed but couldn't get comfortable. The humid air was oppressive, and she found it hard to breathe. She knew some of the pressure would release with tears, but tears did not come.

When she finally did begin to drift into a gray nothingness, ghost voices whispered warnings in her mind of their power and told her to walk carefully because their icy fingers were always waiting and the black water was always lapping on the shore.

Wen-shan moaned and turned on her side. *Oh, go away,* she thought groggily. *I have a math test tomorrow and I need my sleep.*

Notes

Yaodong: A dwelling place carved into the side of a cliff. As a leader of the fledgling Communist Party in Yan'an, (1936–1948), Mao Tse-tung lived in a yaodong. It is kept now as a national shrine.

The Great Leap Forward: The Great Leap Forward (1958–1962) was a campaign begun by Mao Tse-tung to bring China into the forefront of economic development. Everyone in China was to be involved in steelmaking, and the rural communities were expected to triple their crop production so that China could become a superpower. Much of the food produced, however, was sent to Russia in exchange for machines and industrial goods. The experiment was a disaster, causing nationwide famine and the deaths of thirty-eight to forty million people.

Chapter 9

WEN-SHAN TAPPED ON THE store window just as Mr. Pierpont was flipping over the CLOSED sign. The man jumped, and then broke into a big smile. He motioned her to the front door.

"Mrs. Chen, so good to see you again! Are you here for more furniture?"

"Yes, Mr. Pierpont," Wen-shan said imperiously, stepping into the store. "I'm here to furnish my entire mansion."

Mr. Pierpont beamed. "Words of glory to a furniture man, Mrs. Chen!"

Wen-shan giggled at being called "Mrs. Chen," but then, remembering she had questions for Mr. Pierpont, she sobered. "Actually, I'm here for something else."

Mr. Pierpont grunted. "I knew I couldn't be lucky enough for an entire house. Oh, well. Come in! Come in, Wen-shan.

What can I do for you? Your uncle is not here. He and Mr. Ng are overseeing a delivery to . . ."

"A new office building. Yes, I know. He told me he'd be late getting home tonight."

"Ah, quite the knowledgeable one, aren't you?"

"It's you I wanted to see, Mr. Pierpont. I need to ask you some questions."

"Well then, come to my office. I have a few things to put away, and then we can talk." He started off and then stopped. "I have a better idea! What say I take you out for dinner? Have you eaten?"

"No. I was going to get wonton on my way home."

"Well, whatever you'd like. I just hate eating alone, and I thought if . . ."

"Actually I'd love dinner out, Mr. Pierpont. That's nice of you."

They stopped briefly in his office where he gave his secretary some final instructions, filed a few account papers, and picked up his raincoat and hat.

They walked several blocks, all the while debating whether mathematics was really useful. Wen-shan concluded no, Mr. Pierpont concluded yes, but only as far as adding up sales was concerned.

As the sun set, a light wind picked up, and Wen-shan hoped it meant a break in the muggy weather.

"Here we are!" Mr. Pierpont said, stepping up to the entrance of Xiao Nan Guo.

"Do you like to eat here?" Wen-shan questioned.

"Love it!"

"This place is very Chinese," Wen-shan said as he opened the door for her.

He hesitated. "You don't like it?" He closed the door. "We can surely go elsewhere. Someplace with meat and potatoes."

Wen-shan laughed. "No, this restaurant has wonderful food. I'm just surprised you like it."

Mr. Pierpont tipped his tweed hat. "Don't judge a book by its cover, Miss Chen."

They stepped inside the small space and were assaulted by Chinese voices, scraping chairs, calls for orders, and clattering dishes. Flavor-filled steam permeated the air, and Mr. Pierpont took a deep breath.

"Ah, heaven."

Mr. Pierpont hung his coat and hat on the coatrack, and he and Wen-shan squeezed their way to an empty table at the back of the restaurant. It was not an easy trip as space between tables was miniscule. Mr. Pierpont held Wen-shan's chair for her as she sat down.

"Thank you, Mr. Pierpont."

"My pleasure." He sat down across from her and gleefully rubbed his hands together.

An older woman came up, yelling a Cantonese litany to the kitchen. She plopped down two teacups and a pot of tea, and then glanced at the two new customers. "Ah, Mr. Pierpont, sorry." She grabbed up one of the teacups. "You not want tea. I get you glass of water." She scurried away.

Wen-shan chuckled. "You *must* love this place."

"Indeed I do. So, what would you like?"

"I like the prawns in garlic sauce."

"Yes, that's good. What else?"

"I usually only order one dish, Mr. Pierpont."

"Well, we'll have to remedy that. How about goose meat with noodles or shoyu chicken?"

"Both sound delicious."

The woman returned with a smile and a glass of water. "Here you go, Mr. Pierpont. You want your regular?"

"Yes, and an order of prawns with garlic sauce, goose meat with noodles, and shoyu chicken."

Wen-shan could tell the woman was delighted.

"Oh, all good choices. Good choices." She turned toward the kitchen, snapping off the order in rapid Cantonese.

Mr. Pierpont picked up the teapot and addressed Wen-shan. "Would you like some tea?"

"Yes, please." Wen-shan pushed forward her cup. "You're not having any?"

"No, I don't drink tea."

"You don't like it?"

Mr. Pierpont smiled. "Oh, I like it very much. When I was a young man, I think I had tea in my veins instead of blood."

"But?"

"The Church asks that I not drink tea or coffee or alcohol."

Wen-shan put down her cup. "Of course. Is that why my uncle doesn't drink tea?"

"I would imagine so. Have you never inquired?"

"I did once when I was about ten."

"And?"

"All he said was that there were more healthy things for the body. I didn't think much about it."

"And now?"

"I guess I'm more interested in what my uncle's life was like before I came along."

"The best way to find out, Wen-shan, is to ask him."

Wen-shan raised her eyebrows.

"You might be surprised."

Actually, over the past week, she had been surprised by her uncle's reaction to things. It seemed as though the paintings and letters were making little cracks in the wall that surrounded him.

Wen-shan realized that her thoughts had been drifting. "So how did you get mixed up with the Mormon Church, Mr. Pierpont?"

Mr. Pierpont grinned. "By the best of luck. I would love to share it with you, but it's a long story."

"I love long stories."

He tapped his fingertips together. "Hmm . . . where to begin? When we started the furniture business, my brother and I had two stores, one here in Central and one on Nathan Road in Kowloon."

"Impressive."

"And a furniture factory."

Wen-shan really was impressed.

"Now this is going back to 1955, so don't fall asleep."

"Not me," Wen-shan promised.

"So, one day I went to check on the Kowloon store, and my able employee Ng Kat-hing told me he had just made the biggest sale of his life: eight custom-made beds—extra long—and eight nightstands. Well, I thought it was too good to be true, especially when he said the young man who ordered it was a very tall American who spoke perfect Cantonese and who had a young wife and little baby boy with him."

"He was making it up to tease you."

"That's what I thought. But, no! It was true, every word of it. The tall American was Elder Grant Heaton. He and his wife, Luana, had just arrived in Hong Kong to set up a mission home for the Church. In fact, Elder Heaton was going to be the mission president for the Southern Far East Mission."

"What did that mean?"

"That meant missionaries from the Mormon Church were coming to Hong Kong, Taiwan, Guam, and the Philippines."

"How many missionaries?" she asked, picturing hundreds.

"Well, they started out with eight, right there in Kowloon, Hong Kong."

Wen-shan chuckled. "That's why they needed the eight, extra-long beds."

"Right you are."

"How old was Mr. Heaton? He couldn't have been too old to have a little baby like that."

Mr. Pierpont smiled. "Twenty-six."

Wen-shan frowned. "Now you're teasing me."

"I'm not. He was twenty-six."

"How could your Church send someone so young to do such a big job?"

"A very good question. I think it had something to do with revelation."

"Revelation?"

Just then the platters of food began arriving, and Mr. Pierpont's attention was diverted by vegetables, meats, and sauces. Wen-shan was hungry too, but answers seemed more important than prawns in garlic sauce. After they had both taken several bites, Wen-shan pursued the conversation.

"You were talking about revelation, Mr. Pierpont. Did you mean revelation from heaven?"

"Yes." He took a drink of water. "Revelation from heaven to a prophet."

"You mean like the Hebrew prophets?"

He gave her an admiring look. "How do you know about Hebrew prophets?"

"My teacher, Mrs. Yang, had us read some of the Bible. She says we have to learn about everything."

"A wise woman, indeed."

Wen-shan sat unmoving, her chopsticks poised over her food. "But, you're talking about a prophet in modern days."

"Yes."

"And my uncle believes this?"

"I imagine so."

"And you?"

"Yes."

"And that's why you were baptized."

"Me, and my wife, Minnie, and Ng Kat-hing."

"The one who sold Mr. Heaton the beds?"

Mr. Pierpont beamed. "Yes, indeed. We all took the plunge!"

"In the swimming pool?"

Mr. Pierpont laughed.

"You *were* teasing me about the swimming pool."

"Only a little." He put some shoyu chicken on each of their plates. "Actually the mission home where the Heatons lived had a swimming pool in the backyard. They'd fill it up about thigh-deep and use it for baptisms."

Wen-shan stared at her jovial dinner companion.

"Eat, eat, eat!" he ordered. "Don't let my babbling stop you from eating."

She picked up a bite with her chopsticks. "Mr. Ng is delivering furniture with my uncle. Is it the same Mr. Ng who joined the Church?"

"It is. While studying the doctrine, he helped the missionaries with their Cantonese."

"And he still attends church?"

"He's actually a leader of a small congregation—a branch president." Mr. Pierpont dished up the last of the goose meat. "Indeed Brother Ng is the one who brought me and Minnie along. So there you have it. What did you think of my swimming pool story?"

Wen-shan ate a bite of shoyu chicken and thought about all Mr. Pierpont had told her.

"I think there's a lot to think about."

"Exactly, Wen-shan. There is a lot to think about."

"And how did my uncle become interested in the Church?"

Mr. Pierpont gave her a gentle smile. "That is a story for your uncle to tell."

They ate in silence for a time and then finally, between bites, Mr. Pierpont spoke. "May I tell you something, Wen-shan?"

"Yes," she said warily.

"I like this new you. The question-asking girl."

Wen-shan blushed. "Better than the screaming little girl in church?"

He laughed loudly. "Yes, yes. I would have to say yes."

As she looked at Mr. Pierpont's happy expression, Wen-shan knew he truly was a good friend to her uncle.

● ● ●

1959

We have been killing sparrows. Chairman Mao Tse-tung says they are pests like rats because they eat the grain, and so we are killing them by the thousands. We should be harvesting the grain, but everyone is mad with sparrow killing. Comrade Chen says the government might pay us money for the dead birds. I wonder why people want money—there is nothing to buy. I must criticize myself for thinking against the wise commands of our great leader.

We spend much time killing sparrows and making steel. Our great leader, Mao Tse-tung wants China to make more steel than Britain and America. We are many millions of people, he says. If we all work together we can do anything. There are small neighborhood smelting furnaces to melt the metal that we find. Chairman Mao says that "to hand in one pickax is to wipe out Imperialism, and to hide one nail is to hide one counterrevolutionary." So everyone looks for metal. We have all thrown our woks and cooking utensils into the furnace. No one cooks anymore anyway. We all eat at the neighborhood canteen. The government takes care of feeding us, and we make steel and kill sparrows.

Wen-shan tore her eyes away from the parchment. The look on her face was a mixture of anger and disbelief. "They killed sparrows? Why would they follow such an order?"

Her uncle looked at her with an even expression. "What were they suppose to do, Wen-shan? You read what your mother wrote about the criticism meeting. Out of fear, people were turning on each other. There were party officials everywhere. What do you think would have happened to someone who spoke out?"

Wen-shan stood and began pacing. "I don't understand. I

don't understand. Why didn't someone in the government stand up to Mao? Why did they let him get away with such stupid things?"

Her uncle's voice was stern. "Fear. You don't know how much power lives in fear."

Wen-shan stopped pacing and stared at him. "You do. You know about fear."

He looked at her straight on. "Yes. I do."

Wen-shan followed his gaze to her grandfather's painting of the heavenly mountains.

"When your Auntie Mei-lan and I left Guilin, there had already been many killings of captured Nationalist soldiers. The death of an officer and his wife would have been made into a great public spectacle. There is no doubt that the entire family would have been killed."

Wen-shan felt again that icy water being poured on the top of her head. "My mother?"

"Yes. Your mother and your grandfather." He clasped his hands together. "Mei-lan and I hid in the small vault under our family's ancestor shrine. The entrance is not detectable unless you know about it. We were there five days. My brother—your grandfather—would bring us food. For others to see, he was bringing food for the ancestors, but Mei-lan and I ate it."

Wen-shan could tell these memories were causing him anguish as he gripped his hands tighter and tighter.

"In the dark morning hours of the sixth day, we escaped. It took us three months to make our way to Canton, and then we floated on a log to Hong Kong." His jaw muscles tightened. "Mei-lan was so brave. She was so brave. She did not know how to swim. We were in the water for ten hours." He stopped talking.

Wen-shan respected his silence. Finally she went to the

cabinet and retrieved one of her grandfather's paintings. She knelt down by her uncle's chair and unrolled the scroll onto the floor. A cocky copper, black-and-orange feathered rooster paraded on the silk paper. Surrounding him were several fat yellow chicks, scratching and pecking for food. The rooster looked offended to be in such company.

Wen-shan and her uncle laughed. They couldn't help it. The painting evoked such joy that any other emotion fled at first glance.

"How can a rooster have an expression?" Wen-shan laughed. "My grandfather is brilliant!"

Her uncle nodded. "Yes, he is." His voice became intense. "And I will tell you one thing, Wen-shan. Where others may not have survived this evil regime, my venerable brother will have found a way."

NOTE

The early days of the LDS Church in China: Elder David O. McKay dedicated the land of China for the preaching of the gospel on January 9, 1921, in a garden area located in the heart of the Forbidden City, Peking.

Elder Grant Heaton was called to be the first missionary to Hong Kong in 1949. He returned in 1955 with his wife, Luana, to serve as the mission president of the Southern Far East Mission. He was twenty-six years old at the time. He and Sister Heaton served faithfully in Hong Kong until 1959 when they returned to Utah to work, raise their family, and continue to serve the Lord.

Ng Kat-hing was baptized May 31, 1956, and became one of the first Chinese members of the Church in Hong Kong. He became interested in the Church when he sold furniture to Brother and Sister Heaton, who were looking to furnish the new mission home. Brother Ng served as a branch president, district president, mission president's counselor, stake president, and stake patriarch. When the Hong Kong Temple was dedicated in 1996, Brother Ng became the first temple president.

第十章

Chapter 10

C OOL MORNING AIR—THAT'S WHAT I NEED. Wen-shan got out of bed, dressed in an old shirt and pants, and went into the bathroom. She brushed her teeth, ran a comb through her hair, and washed her face. She avoided looking in the mirror. She knew her skin would be sallow and her eyes puffy.

Her dreams in the night were not of rain, but blood: of dead sparrows littering the ground, each lying in a little pool of blood, of red flags made from drops of blood, and of refugees pouring out of China like blood from many wounds.

She threw her mind to the picture of the rooster and smiled. *Cool morning air—that's what I need.*

She went to the kitchen and got a char siu bao out of the refrigerator. She was so hungry she didn't even think about trying to resteam it, but ate it cold.

She went quietly out of the house, secured the needed tools from the shed, and went to trim the Chinese Pepper Tree.

It was cool and quiet in the garden, and Wen-shan concentrated on the *snip snip snip* of the clippers. Whenever her thoughts began to turn toward her dreams, she would breathe in the fragrance of the morning, watch the dead twigs fall, and think about misty mountains, or baby chicks, or men being baptized in swimming pools. She was fascinated by the brave Mr. Heaton and his wife, who had traveled thousands of miles from their home, and with a baby too. Why would they do that? She wondered what her uncle thought of them and decided to ask him at the first appropriate opportunity. *Snip. Snip. Snip.*

She was suddenly aware of someone watching her and turned quickly to see Yan in his pajamas, about to throw a rock at her. Ya Ya stood beside him, grinning broadly.

"Yan! Don't!"

Both he and Ya Ya jumped at the sharp command, especially since it was accompanied by the threat of garden clippers. Yan dropped the rock and both children ran into their house, screeching.

"Little demons," a deep voice said.

Now it was Wen-shan's turn to jump.

Mr. Yee shut his door, picked up his shoes, and sat down on his porch chair to put them on. "Good-morning, Wen-shan."

"Good-morning, Mr. Yee."

"You're up early this morning."

She nodded. "I wanted some cool air."

"It is nice, isn't it?"

It was the longest conversation the two had ever shared— probably because Wen-shan was never out in the yard early in the morning when Mr. Yee went to work. Or more likely, it was because she'd never been interested in talking to him. Now, she just felt awkward.

"Do . . . do you like the morning coolness?" Wen-shan felt it was a stupid question, but Mr. Yee answered it without critique.

"I do. I like walking to work in it."

The Tuans' front door opened, and Mrs. Tuan looked out with an angry face. As soon as she saw Mr. Yee, she pulled her head inside and slammed the door.

Wen-shan cringed. "Uh-oh. I think I'm going to get a scolding sometime today."

Mr. Yee stood and picked up his briefcase. "Someone should put those two children in a box."

Astonishment covered Wen-shan's face. Mr. Yee was funny.

He came down the steps and headed for the front gate. "Have a good day."

She bowed. "You too, Mr. Yee."

The sun was now peeking into the garden, and Wen-shan decided she didn't want to hang around for a scolding. She put the tools back in the shed and escaped into the house. She was surprised to find her uncle sitting in his chair and reading his scriptures. That was normally a nighttime activity.

"Good morning, Uncle."

"Good morning."

She moved toward her bedroom.

"Before you get ready for school, I'd like to read another letter. Do you think you have time?"

"Of course. Let me wash my hands first."

He nodded.

Wen-shan went into the bathroom, washed her hands, and splashed water on her face. She looked into the mirror, and her tired eyes looked back. She really didn't want to read another letter. She felt heaviness descending with just the thought. She splashed more water onto her face.

When she returned to the front room, she saw that her uncle had already placed the parchment on the coffee table. She picked it up slowly and untied the ribbon. Her voice seemed unwilling and she had to clear her throat several times before she started reading.

Autumn 1959

> *The leaves on the Ginkgo trees have changed to brilliant yellow, and I have made a marriage contract with Chen Han-lie.*

Wen-shan stopped reading. "I can't."

Her uncle nodded. "Would you like to put it away?"

She held out the scroll to him. "No. I just can't read it. Would you?"

Her uncle took the parchment and unrolled it.

> *Chen tied a red scarf around my neck. He told me it represented the blood of our Liberation army. We stood in front of a large poster of Mao Tse-tung at the party offices and vowed our loyalty to the state. I wore my best pair of trousers, but there was still a patch on the knee. I am grateful to Chen Han-lie. He is a level twelve on the civil service ranking, and he made a marriage contract with me at great risk to his standing. I am the daughter of a onetime landowner and my uncle was a known Nationalist. I think he only took the chance*

*because when CCP leader Liu Shao-ch'i visited our
city, he picked up one of my father's "happy worker"
posters to take back to Peking. He is the top man next to
Chairman Mao, and it gave my father great status. For
weeks after, the neighbors all said that Chairman Mao
himself would probably look at my father's picture. Every
day people would come to our courtyard wall and run
their hand over the "happy worker" poster pasted there.*

Her uncle stopped reading and looked over at his brother's
picture of the cypress tree. He shook his head and turned again
to the letter.

*There were only six people at our ceremony: Chen
Han-lie, myself, the registrar, Chen's assistant (a level
thirteen), my father, and my friend Lin Kuan-yin. She
was very sweet. She brought me a handful of Ginkgo
leaves as a gift. They looked happy against my faded
blue uniform.*

*After the ceremony, Chen walked us to the
courtyard where a group of people were waiting. They
clapped politely when we came out, and my husband
gave a speech. I had him write it down:*

*"The Socialist man is responsible not only for
his life, but for other people's lives as well. His job
is to monitor the business and thoughts of the people
around him and to correct any improprieties or
counterrevolutionary thoughts or actions. The Socialist
man is required to put the state before himself or his
family. He is to be able to face others with self-criticism
and confess wrongdoings.*

"He is to be animated by five loves:
"Love of country.
"Love of people.
"Love of labor.
"Love of science.
"Love of common property!"
The people clapped loudly when he finished. He gave each person a bag of rice and they went away.

I know my husband's speech was for me and my father. He was reminding us of the chance he had taken in making a contract with me and that we needed to be mindful of our new status.

I will take the Ginkgo leaves and place them under my pillow. They will give me bright dreams.

Her uncle rolled the scroll.

"Do you think she loved him?"

"I don't know, Wen-shan. I think *he* must have loved her."

"Why?"

"He could have married someone safer."

Wen-shan was offended. "I don't understand that."

"Of course not. Your life is very different."

She stared at the picture of Guilin, trying to imagine her mother as a young woman walking the paths along the Li River and working in the rice fields. Did she have any feelings at all for the man she married?

"You'd better get ready for school."

Wen-shan stood. "Yes, Uncle."

He went back to reading his scriptures, and she went to turn on the shower.

• • •

After school she and Li-ying went to the Golden Door Bakery to get Chinese donuts and roasted melon seeds. Mrs. Wong was not giving away any free food today. After they paid, and she'd counted the coins carefully, the girls went to sit outside on a bench and watch the people and the traffic.

"I would like to drive one of those," Wen-shan said, pointing at a passing blue scooter.

"You would not!"

"Yes, I would. I could go everywhere on one of those."

"They're only for boys."

"Who said?"

"Your uncle would never let you ride a scooter."

"Well, he won't have much say when I'm off on my own."

Li-ying shrugged. "Well, that's true, but they're very dangerous."

"Life is dangerous, Li Li. A car could roll over and smash us flat while we're sitting on this bench."

"That's a terrible thing to say."

Wen-shan grinned at her. "Don't worry, it's not going to happen. Here—have some melon seeds."

They watched the traffic for a while in silence. Then Li-ying asked timidly, "You haven't said anything about your mother's letters. Have you read any more?"

Wen-shan crumpled her donut wrapper. "We read about my mother's wedding."

"Oh?" Li-ying sounded hopeful.

"No, it wasn't like that. It wasn't really a wedding. They just sort of signed a contract."

Li-ying was disappointed. "Really? There weren't gifts, and food, and a beautiful dress?"

Wen-shan felt sad and irritated. "No, Li-ying. There were Ginkgo leaves, bags of rice, and patched trousers."

Li-ying pushed up her glasses. "I'm sorry, Wen-shan. Of course. I should have known better."

Wen-shan threw the paper in the trash bin. "And my Communist father gave a speech about being a good communist."

Li-ying sighed and made a disappointed face. "Well, that wasn't very romantic."

Wen-shan burst out laughing and her friend joined her.

"Oh, Li Li, what would I do without you?"

The girls walked to Li-ying's house, chatting about many subjects. Wen-shan told her friend about her mother placing the Ginkgo leaves under her pillow to give her bright dreams. They both agreed *that*, at least, was romantic.

NOTES

Char siu bao: A steamed or baked bun filled with sweet, slow-roasted pork that has been diced and mixed with a savory sauce.

CCP: An acronym for the Chinese Communist Party.

CCCP: An acronym for the Central Committee of the Communist Party. This was the core of the ruling elite in China. Mao Tse-tung was the Chairman.

The Communists kept detailed files on every citizen and their family background. On every form a person filled out, they had to enter their family background, which was labeled either black or red. Black meant you were an enemy of the Communist Party and belonged to any one of the "Five Black Categories": landlords, rich peasants, counterrevolutionaries, criminals, or rightists. This information was kept by the Organization Department of the CCP.

Civil service ranking: All officials and government employees were divided into twenty-six grades. Grade twenty-six was the lowest. The system determined almost everything: from whether a person's coat was made of wool or cheap cotton to the size of a person's apartment and whether it had an indoor toilet or not. Grades fourteen and above had better subsidies and perks.

Chapter 11

FATHER HAS ALWAYS WORN THE LONG *dress of the scholar. I see the wide sleeves tied back as he dips his brush into the ink. My father's inkstone is as long as my arm. It is fashioned of hard black stone and is four hundred years old.*

My fingers follow the rises and depressions in the carved surface. I think of the artisan chipping away and forming the flying cranes. How graceful—the cranes' wings stirring the clouds.

Now my father wears the padded jacket and loose trousers of the masses, and his inkstone is buried in the garden.

Wen-shan read the characters again. She and her uncle had read the letter the night before but she loved the image of her grandfather in his scholar's dress writing bold strokes of calligraphy.

She sat alone on her front porch listening to the distant sound of traffic and enjoying her solitude. The Tuans were gone on a two-day trip to visit relatives in the New Territories, and her uncle and Mr. Yee would not be home from their jobs for hours.

She looked again at the letter. She could not picture her grandfather in the clothing of the Communists. How boring it would be if everyone wore the same thing.

The bell rang at the front gate and she looked up.

Wei Jun-jai. She rolled the scroll and carried it with her to open the gate for her friend. He toted a raffia bag, and Wen-shan could see that whatever was inside seemed heavy.

"Hello, Jun-jai. Why are you here?"

"I've brought you a gift, and I insist you open it now."

They moved to the porch.

"What is it?"

"You'll see." He set the bag on the porch and stepped back.

Wen-shan pushed back the bag's soft covering to reveal a watermelon. She was delighted. "Jun-jai, how wonderful! You remembered about my wanting watermelon from the other day."

"I did. And all I could give you then were sesame candies."

"I loved those!"

"You are a diplomat."

She picked up the melon. It *was* heavy. "Would you like a slice?"

"Well, that's not why I brought it."

Wen-shan giggled. "I know, but I want to share it with you."

"Then I would love some."

"Good. Why don't you sit here on the porch where there's a nice breeze."

Jun-jai opened the door for her then sat in one of the porch chairs.

Wen-shan navigated her way to the kitchen to cut slices, returning in a short time with wedges of succulent red watermelon on a platter. She also brought a stack of napkins and two of her mother's letters. She set the platter on the small porch table and handed Jun-jai several napkins.

"Please, help yourself."

"After you."

She picked up a small wedge and smiled when she took the first bite.

"Is it good?"

She swallowed. "It's delicious. Thank you, Jun-jai." *I bet Ya Ya isn't eating watermelon today,* she thought with smug satisfaction. She finished her piece, wiped her hands, and picked up her mother's letters.

"Here, Jun-jai, I would like to show you two of my mother's letters."

He set down the piece of fruit and cleaned his hands. "Are you sure?"

She nodded.

He took the first scroll and unrolled it. "What a delicate hand."

"I would like you to read them, Jun-jai. The first tells of a campaign against sparrows, and the second is a story about my parents' wedding contract. I want to know what you think." She had thought of sharing the letter about the criticism meeting, but that was too personal. The wedding story should have been personal, but all the emotion had been taken away. Besides, she figured Jun-jai would be interested in her father's speech about the duty of the Socialist man.

Jun-jai was very focused as he read. Wen-shan ate another

wedge of watermelon and watched for any reaction. A few times his head nodded, and his eyebrows went up once. She wondered what part he was reading at that moment.

He rolled the scrolls and handed them to her. "How would that be to have to spy on your neighbors and have them spying on you?"

"Well, one of my neighbors would love it, and I know several girls at school who would be turning people in all the time."

"But that's just the thing. They would try and secure their place by turning people in."

"They'd inform on people just to keep themselves safe?"

"Of course. The government had an automatic secret police."

"My uncle says the people did it because of fear—fear about just staying alive."

"I agree. And that kind of fear brings out the worst in people."

"Did any of your family come from mainland China, Junjai?" She felt foolish that this was the first time she'd ever asked him. Of course, he'd never asked much about her family either.

"Two of my uncles and their families from my mother's side escaped to Taiwan. My father's father was a doctor in Peking, but he was studying in Britain when the Communists took over. He thought about going back to Peking, but since all his family was with him, he decided to settle in Hong Kong."

"So, Auntie Ting is your father's sister?"

"Yes. My father has seven brothers and sisters."

Wen-shan could not imagine so many relatives. Her family was small by comparison.

"Should we open one of my grandfather's paintings?"

"Really? Oh, I'd like that, Wen-shan—if it's all right."

"Yes, of course." She was telling a bit of a lie, but she figured there wasn't any harm in sharing a picture with her friend. "Stay here and I'll go get one."

She went to the cupboard, lingering for a moment over her decision. She finally chose one with a blue ribbon and returned to the porch.

Jun-jai looked anxiously at the silk scroll. "This is a great honor, Wen-shan."

She was delighted by his enthusiasm. She undid the ribbon and opened the scroll. As she did, another rolled-up paper fell out. Jun-jai caught it. He traded the scroll for the paper.

"Oh! That's odd! What is this?" Wen-shan unrolled and unfolded the paper. It was a poster. It was not an artist drawing, but a photograph. It showed a huge field of wheat with the wheat so densely packed together that three children were standing on top of it.

Wen-shan gasped. "How is that possible?"

"It's not," Jun-jai said, derision coloring his voice. "The picture has been manipulated. This is part of the propaganda for the Great Leap Forward—lies about how much food was being grown."

"Like my mother talked about."

"Yes."

"And killing the sparrows was part of the Great Leap?"

"Killing the sparrows was insanity. What do you think happened after they did that?"

Wen-shan shook her head. "I don't know."

"The next year they had a swarm of insects."

"That destroyed the crops."

"Exactly."

"Did they kill sparrows all over the country?"

"When one of Mao's campaigns went out, Wen-shan, it went to everyone."

Wen-shan felt sick. She ran her hand over the poster. "This happened right before I was born."

Jun-jai was silent. He worried the edge of the silk scroll. Unrolling it a bit more, he revealed the dark ink stroke of a character. He opened the scroll quickly to unveil stunning calligraphy characters. The strokes were fierce and determined. A rumble of sound escaped Jun-jai's chest as he stood. "Ah, Wen-shan. Look! Look at the stroke of a Master!"

Wen-shan stood slowly, her eyes never leaving the scroll.

"Truth."

NOTES

Calligraphy: In China, calligraphy is considered as a treasured artistic form of Chinese culture. The strength, balance, and flow of the strokes made with a highly pliable, hair brush are believed to convey the calligrapher's moral and psychological makeup as well as his momentary emotions. The ink stick, inkstone, writing brush, and paper are the four essential implements of the artist.

Refugees and their escape from mainland China: When the Communists took control of the country in August 1949, hundreds of thousands of people sympathetic to the Nationalist government fled the country. Some people went abroad, but most went to either Taiwan or Hong Kong. It is said that at one time Hong Kong harbored some sixty thousand refugees.

Propaganda: Mao Tse-tung controlled the dissemination of information and manipulated reality. Without opposing voices, the people were systematically brainwashed.

Chapter 12

H ER GRANDFATHER'S CALLIGRAPHY was put in a place of honor on the wall near the small shrine for their ancestors. The shrine was only a table in the corner of the room that held a statue of Confucius, a tray for food offerings, and an incense burner. Wen-shan liked the idea that the curling smoke from the incense was a way to communicate between the world of the living and the world of the dead. Of course, she kept the picture of Zhong Kui in her bedroom to ward off ghosts and demons. Ghosts and demons were very different from the spirits of departed ancestors.

She'd worried when she'd presented her uncle with the opened scroll, but he had been so overcome with emotion when he saw his brother's writing that he made no mention of her opening it without him.

Truth. Why had her grandfather written that word, and why

had her mother sent it? Wen-shan knew that there had to be dozens of her grandfather's paintings, and while she realized the box only had so much room, she wondered how they had decided to send the pieces they did. How, too, had her mother decided which letters to send? In her imagination, Wen-shan could see hundreds of letters. She imagined her mother sitting someplace secret, in the late hours, writing out her grief and fear.

Wen-shan sighed and continued dusting the furniture. She watched the clouds through the front room window. The afternoon weather had turned gray and heavy and Wen-shan wished for rain—not just a light sprinkle, but a drenching rain that pounded the streets and clattered the rooftops.

She wished for a rain that would wash away her melancholy.

Wen-shan picked up the statue of Confucius for dusting and noticed a folded piece of paper underneath. She opened it and saw her uncle's writing.

What is Truth?

She looked at the bold characters her grandfather had painted. *Truth.* She replaced the paper and set Confucius on top.

"And what do you think of truth, Master?" she asked the statue. "Did you ponder truth, or was the Way for you more practical? Simple things like, 'Do not do to others what you would not like done to yourself,' or 'To see what is right and not do it is want of principle,' or 'Study the past if you would define the future'?"

Wen-shan stopped babbling.

She was learning the truth of the past and it was smothering her. Before the letters came, Wen-shan had wondered about her mother, had fashioned stories in her mind of their life together in Guilin, and had suffered discontent at her uncle's reluctance to share the truth of that life with her. *Truth.* Was it sunlight or a dragon with claws? Now each time she read a letter with her uncle, Wen-shan's stomach ached and her heart closed in. She had longed for words from her mother, but she wanted those words to be hopeful.

Wen-shan thought of her grandfather laughing as he painted the feathers of the comical rooster. She thought of her grandfather in his scholar's dress, dipping ink from his ancient inkstone, and of her grandfather's hand gracefully making the characters of her mother's name. She thought of her mother watching the shimmering clouds as they gathered around the tops of the heavenly peaks, and sleeping peacefully under the Guilin moon. That truth was sunlight, but the truth of her mother working in the rice fields, and having to wear a dunce cap, and never having enough to eat—that truth was the dragon with claws.

Would her uncle agree not to read any more of the letters? Could they shut them back into the box and forget about the note from Mr. Smythe, or meeting Master Quan? Perhaps they could make up their own letters? Wen-shan considered that if they did stop reading, the new openness between her and her great-uncle might drain back into the pond of silence and neglect. She was torn; there were reasons to keep reading and reasons to stop.

Melancholy surrounded her and she turned and looked at the cypress tree painting. She did not have that kind of strength; she was just a little sapling being blown about in the wind.

Just then a bang of thunder rumbled across the sky and Wen-shan jumped.

"Ah!" She looked out the window and saw the clouds—a

turmoil of dark and light gray. Another clap of thunder sounded and she cheered. "Yes!"

It was going to be a big storm with the kind of rain that would wash the streets clean. She hoped her uncle had remembered his umbrella.

● ● ●

She'd made goulash for dinner, and it was not successful. Her uncle hadn't complained, but he ate more of the rice and sliced fruit than the main dish. Wen-shan knew her uncle liked Cantonese dishes, but she liked to experiment with new things. She remembered a German recipe she'd tried once with dumplings and veal. That had ended up in the garbage can.

"You don't have to eat it, Uncle."

"It's not bad. Just a little spicy—more like Sichuan cooking."

"Well, like I said, you don't have to eat it." She picked up the pot of thick goulash and took it to the sink. "Besides, you need to save room for dessert."

"You made dessert?"

"I did. Steamed milk with ginger syrup."

A look of delight appeared on her uncle's face. "Ah, my dear niece, you have just redeemed yourself."

Wen-shan's hand hesitated as she went to pick up her uncle's plate. *My dear niece?* He had never said that to her. She felt a momentary press of tears and pushed them back with a cough. She quickly picked up his plate and took it to the sink.

They ate the delicate dessert and talked about their day. Wen-shan told him about a good grade she'd received on a mathematics paper, and her uncle talked about another delivery he supervised at the new office building. She asked him if Mr. Ng had also supervised, and when her uncle said yes, she'd plunged ahead.

"Uncle?"

"Yes?"

"Isn't Mr. Ng a member of that church you belong to?"

Her uncle hesitated. "He is."

"Don't you like the church anymore?"

"Why would you think that?"

"Well, you don't go very often. I mean, you read your scriptures and everything, but you don't go to church."

"Why is this important to you?"

She licked the last of her dessert off her spoon and thought about it. Why *was* it important to her? "I just think it's interesting that you would join a Christian church, that's all. Especially since you're a scholar of Confucius."

Her uncle studied her face, looking deep into her eyes until she became uncomfortable.

She looked away. "I just wondered."

He leaned back in his chair. "It is a very practical answer, Wen-shan. It just does not show me in the best light."

She waited for him to continue.

"I am a coward."

She did not expect those words. "You? Impossible."

"Not impossible. True. After my Mei-lan died, I felt that I had lost my strongest connection to the Church. From the beginning, she was the one who believed everything the missionaries said. I listened more from a sense of duty. It was difficult to go to church without her. Then when you came to live with me—"

Wen-shan interrupted. "It was impossible to go because of my temper tantrums."

"Do you remember?"

"Oh, yes, and Mr. Pierpont reminded me."

Her uncle nodded. "As the months went by, it became easier and easier not to go. And then, I was too embarrassed to walk into church; I felt that people would judge me."

"But they wouldn't. Think of Mr. Pierpont. He wouldn't judge you."

"Not all the members are like Mr. Pierpont."

"Well, too bad for them."

Her uncle smiled.

"Oh, by the way, Mr. Pierpont said I should ask you about the noodle story."

"Oh, he did?"

"Yes. And this seems like a good time. Will you tell me the story? I'll give you more dessert."

"Are you bribing me?"

"Yes."

He shook his head. "All right, but you're probably going to find it very boring." She widened her eyes and waited. "When Mei-lan and I came to Hong Kong, we had almost nothing—a little money and a few pieces of clothing. We lived in the refugee camp with thousands of other displaced Chinese. While we were in this terrible condition, we found the Mormon Church and joined."

Wen-shan interrupted. "How did you find the Church?"

"That is a story for another day. Just know that we joined, and we began learning the different doctrines of the Church."

"Like not drinking tea."

"Yes, the Word of Wisdom. And other things like faith in Jesus Christ, priesthood authority, honesty, tithing, and service."

"What's tithing?"

"It's the money contribution we make to the Church."

"Oh."

"And this is where my noodle story begins."

Wen-shan was intrigued. She was also surprised that her uncle was sharing a story with her, and a long story at that. Mentally she crossed her fingers that the miracle would continue.

"I was always concerned about money. There were so few jobs and so little money. Mei-lan and I prayed and prayed about what to do. One morning, I sat straight up in bed and said, 'Noodles!'"

"Noodles? What did that mean?"

"I had this clear idea about getting a noodle-making machine and making noodles for all the people in the refugee camp. The noodles would be fresh, I'd sell them at a good price, and people would trust me because I was a refugee myself. There was only one problem."

"What?"

"I didn't have money to buy a noodle-making machine. So, I wrote out a plan and I went to see the mission president."

"President Heaton? Really? Mr. Pierpont told me all about him."

"Did he?"

"And you knew him too?"

"All the early members knew Brother and Sister Heaton. We were amazed that they would come so far to bring us the gospel of Christ."

"And they had a little baby boy."

"Yes, they were a very young couple." His thoughts drifted. "Very young, but very capable."

"So, go on with the noodle story."

Her uncle smiled. "You're not bored?"

"No!"

"I met with President Heaton for advice. I just wanted him to look over my plan and tell me if he thought I could be successful. I wasn't asking for money, just advice. He read over everything carefully and asked me a few questions. At the end of the interview, he loaned me $75 for a noodle machine."

"Oh, my," Wen-shan whispered.

"Yes. Oh, my." Her uncle cleared his throat. "He told me I could pay back the money when I could, and that I should give him updates every couple of months."

"What happened?"

"After about three months, I sent a message to the mission home for President Heaton to come see Mei-lan and me in our little, ramshackle house. President Heaton told me later that he was nervous because he was afraid we were going to ask for more money."

"But you didn't."

"Now, don't get ahead of me."

Wen-shan grinned.

"We brought the president into our little noodle-making production facility and showed him all the packaged noodles. On each package we put the price and the purpose for the noodles. We had clothing noodles, food noodles, savings noodles, and tithing noodles. The tithing noodle packages were the biggest because we received more money for those. President Heaton loved our tithing noodles and bought three packages." Her uncle grinned at the memory. "That day I was able to pay him $25 on the loan. President Heaton patted me on the back and told us he was glad for our success and touched by our faith."

"He was a good man."

"Yes." Her uncle's head nodded several times. "Yes, a superior man." He looked at her and smiled. "So, that is my noodle story. Did you like it?"

"Very much." In truth she loved it, and for more than just the story. She stood and picked up the dessert dishes. "Uncle?"

"Yes?"

"I'd go with you if you wanted to go back to church."

Her uncle's look turned soft. "That's very kind of you, Wen-shan."

"And I promise I wouldn't scream or kick or cry."

He chuckled. "In that case, I'll have to think about it."

Wen-shan took the dishes to the sink, thinking about the amazing thing that had just happened. "Thank you, Uncle, for the noodle story. It's my favorite."

Her uncle stood up from the table. "I think we should read another letter before it gets too late." He moved toward the front room, and then turned back. "Oh, and thank you for dinner."

She gave him a wry look. "Well, the dessert anyway."

● ● ●

Wen-shan sat staring at the scroll in her hand.

"What is it, Wen-shan?" her uncle asked, noting the hesitation.

She took her time in answering. "Are you getting tired of reading the letters?"

"Tired?"

"Well, not really tired, but . . ."

"Tired of feeling helpless?"

"Yes, that's it exactly. There's nothing I can do about what happened to them, or what is happening to them. Does that make any sense?"

"Yes."

She looked at him. "But you want to keep reading?"

"Yes. I want to know as much about them as I can. And you?"

Wen-shan played with the ribbon on the scroll. "I want to keep reading."

She untied the ribbon.

1960

We come in from the field with burned faces and flat hearts. There is no water and the insects rage like monsters on the land, and still we are told to grow rice. Many people die, and many more want to die. Many take their own lives in protest or desperation. People with arms and legs like sticks lie down by the side of the road and die there like mongrel dogs. When people die, we are told to show no emotion. Mao Tse-tung tells us that we are not to cry for the dead because death is good—the bodies can be fertilizer. And so we are told to plant crops over the graves.

Wen-shan looked at her uncle, the color draining from her face. She waited for him to speak because her words caught in her heart and made it hard to breathe. Her uncle's jaw was clenched, but finally bitter words escaped. "That is a great disrespect to the ancestors. There must have been so much anguish in the hearts of the people." He shook his head. "So much anguish."

Numbly Wen-shan looked back to the paper.

We no longer put on the faces of the "happy worker" poster. We show no gentle emotion. One night someone broke the curfew and scraped my father's poster off our courtyard wall. I was glad. When I walked by the poster, my anger would make me grind my teeth. One of our neighbors accused my father of removing it and so he was put up for another criticism meeting. He had to kneel for several hours on broken pottery. When he collapsed, one of the policemen beat him until he crawled back onto his knees. Finally Secretary Zhang let me and my husband carry my father home.

I had bitter words for my husband that night. I asked him why he didn't stop the torture of his father-in-law. Why he didn't go to the demon Zhang and speak for my father. He told me that that would be showing favoritism, and the party might take away his standing. That would mean less food for us. I yelled at him. I said I didn't care about the extra food. As I cleaned my father's wounds and put him to bed, he told me that Han-lie was right. He was our only protection, and that I needed the extra food or I would lose the child growing inside me.

Wen-shan's voice faltered.

I laid my head on the side of the bed and cried. I cried for my father, for my aching body, for the child

who might never live. I cried because my hunger forced
me to ask for my husband's forgiveness.

When my father could stand, Secretary Zhang
came to our house and told him he must now paint
only revolutionary paintings, and that he was to
expect no payment. If he did a good painting—a
painting that the party liked—he would receive more
supplies. This was supposed to be a great honor for
my father. Secretary Zhang told him that he must
kowtow whenever he saw a party official and show his
gratitude. He was warned that he was close to being
labeled a counterrevolutionary and that he must work
hard to dispel people's suspicions. Zhang gave my father
a list of the things he must paint and things he must
not paint. First on the list of things he must paint were
happy faces. If he painted people working in the fields
or attending meetings, they must always be smiling.
My father would have to invent those images because
no one smiles anymore. First on the list of things he
must not paint were pictures of Chairman Mao. The
reason for this was that no artist could adequately
represent the great leader's image. Father must take one
of the approved photographs of Chairman Mao and
incorporate it into a painting.

I stood supporting my father as he listened patiently
to all of Secretary Zhang's words. My father bowed
several times and thanked him for the instruction. I
could not look at the secretary. His face was scarred
with smallpox and a welt ran across his jawline where,
rumor had it, a Nationalist soldier tried unsuccessfully

*to slash his throat. I was angry that the soldier had not
been successful.*

*My father limped to open the door for the demon.
I watched until the evil man was out of the courtyard
and down the street, then I took what little water we
had and scrubbed the floor where he'd stood.*

The food in Wen-shan's stomach had soured and she felt
sick. The look on her uncle's face told a similar story. She rolled
the scroll, tied the ribbon, and placed it back in the drawer.

"Are we sure we want to know all about them?"

Slowly her uncle nodded.

Wen-shan went off to bed, forcing her mind to remember
the noodle story.

Notes

Chinese painting: Chinese painting falls into two large divisions—painting on
walls and painting on the portable media of paper and silk. The greatest glory
of the Chinese art of painting is landscape painting. According to Su Dongpo
(1037–1101), the purpose of painting was not to depict the appearance of things
but to express the painter's own feelings, making it much more like poetry.

Chinese art during the time of Mao Tse-tung: Mao believed that art was a tool
for leading the masses. In a quote he said, "There is in fact no such thing as art for
art's sake, art that stands above classes, or art that is detached from or independent
of politics."

Chapter 13

RAIN. WEN-SHAN KNEW THE RAIN was not real. She knew the shadows were only dark places in her nightmare and the small hands pushing on her back were phantoms, but her body accepted the terrifying suggestions without question, and so her heart pounded and sweat covered her skin. The qweilo came floating out of the darkness, reaching its cold, icy fingers for her, and catching her around the waist. The ghost whispered in her ear to be still and not to scream, but her mother's face was fading and the rain became a curtain.

A bell rang, and Wen-shan sat up, slapping off her alarm clock. She blinked open her eyes to a dim morning. She lay back down and listened to her uncle opening a drawer, shutting a drawer, walking across the floor, and moving into the hallway. The familiar sounds were comforting. She heard the shower and jumped out of bed. She snuck into her uncle's room and fished his transistor radio out of his dresser drawer. She hurried back, jumping into her bed, and pulling the comforter over her head. She quickly found the rock-and-roll station and prayed there would be a song and not a commercial or some dumb contest. The Beatles' voices sang out, "She's got a ticket to ride, and she don't care." Wen-shan quickly adjusted the volume so only she could hear. Blissfully she listened to two more songs then crept back into her uncle's room before the shower was turned off.

The nightmare had faded with the upbeat music and secretive foray into her uncle's room, so that by the time she went to the kitchen for her breakfast of cornflakes, she was almost cheerful. Her uncle came into the kitchen a few minutes later and fixed himself orange juice and an English muffin. It was the only exception he made to Western breakfast food. Of course, he never ate the muffin with butter and marmalade, but covered the little rounds with sardines out of a tin.

"Wei Jun-jai telephoned last night."

Wen-shan nearly dropped her bowl. "He did?" She'd heard the telephone ring after she'd gone to her bedroom, but was sure it had nothing to do with her. "What did he want?"

"He's going to Kowloon after school to pick up a suit for his father."

"Oh?" Wen-shan was confused. What did she have to do with Jun-jai's father's suit?

"He asked if you could go with him."

"To Kowloon?"

"Yes."

"What did you say?"

"I told him it would be fine, but that it depended on your homework."

Wen-shan tempered her excitement. "I'll make sure I finish my work at school."

"That is acceptable."

Wen-shan's face clouded. "How will I let him know?"

"He said he would stop by the house to see if you could go, or couldn't go."

"Cool."

Her uncle frowned. "Excuse me?"

"I mean good . . . good. That will give me the chance to come home from school and change my clothes."

"Do you have money for the ferry ticket?"

Wen-shan shook her head. "I don't think I have enough."

"The yard needs raking. If you do that after school, I will leave money for the ferry."

"Thank you, Uncle." She finished her cereal and rinsed her bowl in the sink.

As she dressed for school, Wen-shan's mind kept ranging through the different emotions she'd experienced since the letters in the jade dragon box had come into her life, and also the different feeling now shared between herself and her uncle. Her mother didn't know what the letters meant to them. As she worked in the fields or looked to the misty mountains, did she think about the letters and wonder if they were being read by her daughter in Hong Kong? Wen-shan ran a brush through her hair and checked her image in the mirror. And what of her mother's life? Was she still alive? Wen-shan did not let her mind stay long on that thought, but forced her heart to take over. Her heart always told her that her mother was alive. Of course she was. Master Quan had said both her mother and her grandfather were alive when he left Guilin, and that was only a year ago.

Wen-shan came out of her bedroom and found her uncle standing in the front room with a silk scroll in his hand.

"Oh! I'd love to see a painting before I leave for school."

Her uncle nodded and untied the ribbon. "You looked a little tired this morning. I thought maybe this would chase away a nightmare."

"Yes." She put down her schoolbag and tried to look more awake. She moved to her uncle's side as he unrolled the scroll.

In tones of gray, white, black, and cream, two sparrows sat snuggled together on a dark, leafless branch. Snow was falling and the bird's feathers were puffed out to keep them warm.

Wen-shan let out an audible sigh. "How sweet! Aren't they sweet?"

"They are beautifully painted."

"Yes, they are." Wen-shan sighed again. "And they are so sweet." She touched one of the birds' round tummies expecting to feel soft fluff. "Please, read the characters, Uncle."

"'Wearing winter's coat.'"

"Ah, look, that's exactly what they're doing." Wen-shan touched a snowflake that was just about to land on one of the sparrows' heads. "Thank you, Uncle."

He nodded. "Now off to school."

Wen-shan picked up her bag and impulsively left a kiss on her uncle's cheek before going out the door.

Because she did not turn back, she missed his look of astonishment.

• • •

Wei Jun-jai came to the gate while she was still raking. Wen-shan had hoped to have the job done before he arrived and hurriedly wiped the sweat from her face.

When she approached the gate, she thought Jun-jai looked a little embarrassed.

"Did your uncle forget to tell you I'd called?"

"Oh, no. No. I was just doing a little work for . . . ah . . . before we left. I was just finishing." She opened the gate and Jun-jai stepped in.

"I'll put the leaves in the bin for you, if you'd like," he said.

"That would be nice, Jun-jai. Thank you. The bin is there by the side of the shed." She headed for the house. "I'll just go wash my face." *And change my shirt,* she thought. *Why does Jun-jai always look so . . . so . . . well, not like me?*

Wen-shan quickly washed her face, changed into a pale yellow button-up shirt, and grabbed her cloth purse with the long straps. She went to the coffee table, got out her mother's letter about the famine, and placed it in the bag. When she turned around, she saw Jun-jai standing at the open door, staring at the painting of the plum blossoms. He snapped his gaze away when he realized she was looking at him.

"Oh! Wen-shan, sorry. I was just . . ."

"It's all right, Jun-jai. Please, come in and see my grandfather's paintings."

"May I?"

"Yes, of course."

He walked to the painting of the rooster and started chuckling. "It's wonderful."

Wen-shan smiled. "It is, isn't it?"

Jun-jai looked carefully at each painting, finishing with the baby sparrows.

"We just opened this one today."

Jun-jai shook his head. "They are so full of life." He scanned all the pictures, his eyes resting on the heavenly mountains of

Guilin. "Your grandfather has such a gift." He stared again at the sparrows, and then back to the plum blossoms.

"Jun-jai?"

"Yes?"

"Should we be going to Kowloon?"

His body became animated and he checked his watch. "Yes, we should!" He put his hand on her back and moved her out the door, shutting it behind them. "Oh! Sorry! It's your house."

Wen-shan laughed. "That's all right, Jun-jai." Though she was glad that Mrs. Tuan wasn't home to see a young man escorting her out of her house.

The two walked to the Star Ferry talking about rock and roll, television shows, movies, cars, and school. Jun-jai was very smart. He went to a private school and was going to be an international businessman. His father was a successful businessman and that's what he wanted for his son.

Jun-jai looked over at her. "What do you want to be, Wen-shan?"

She swallowed. She had no idea. She'd never even had a job. She didn't think he'd be impressed if she said she'd be happy dusting the furniture at Pierpont and Pierpont Limited. "I'd love to travel to other countries. Maybe I'll be a stewardess."

He looked at her. "Well, you have the personality for it. You may have to grow a few inches."

She gave him a haughty look. "I still have several years to grow before I apply, Jun-jai."

He laughed. "I know, I'm just teasing. We both have plenty of time. These are our crazy, carefree years, as Auntie Ting says."

"I like her."

"Me too." They reached the ferry station. "Wait here and I'll go buy the tickets." He started off.

"But, I have money!"

He waved. "My treat!"

She smiled. *Now what will I do with all my extra money?*

• • •

The heat of the afternoon had given way to a refreshing breeze, the ferry crossing was smooth, and the man who had tailored Jun-jai's father's suit was a toothless comedian. They left the shop with their sides aching from laughter.

On their way back to the ferry, they stopped at a small eatery to buy braised spare ribs in black vinegar sauce. Jun-jai again insisted on paying, so Wen-shan insisted on buying them both a soda. They sat outside at a table overlooking the harbor. Wen-shan felt happy. It had turned out to be an excellent day. She looked at Jun-jai and thought again of the Confucius teaching on good friends. She knew Jun-jai was a good friend to her.

They boarded the ferry as the sun was setting and found seats on the upper deck. After the noise of the initial launch subsided and people settled into their own areas, Wen-shan brought out her mother's letter.

"I brought another letter, Jun-jai. Would you like to read it?"

"Yes. Yes, of course." He carefully took the scroll.

It was the letter about the famine and the cruelty to her grandfather. Wen-shan stood. "I'm going out to the deck."

Jun-jai nodded, already caught up in the first words of the letter.

On deck, Wen-shan watched the passing boats. She loved the large wooden Chinese boats with their red sails. One of the boats sailed close to the ferry and Wen-shan saw a bridal party, the happy celebrators dancing and drinking champagne. A lobster boat slid behind the party boat, and Wen-shan watched the captain with his tattered clothing and weathered face as he maneuvered the boat with ease.

She looked over to see Jun-jai standing beside her. "Oh, Jun-jai, I didn't hear you." He gave her the letter without speaking. He put his hands on the rail and looked out over the water.

Wen-shan busied herself with putting away the letter, and then she quietly joined him at the rail.

Finally Jun-jai spoke. His voice was husky with emotion. "I am so angry about the grief men cause because they want power. They want to rule things and people when they cannot even rule themselves." His voice broke. "I'm sorry, Wen-shan. Sorry for what your family has had to suffer."

She looked away from him. His anger and sadness were so intense, and she had no words but agreement.

Jun-jai looked back toward Kowloon, the New Territories, and mainland China. "The Master says, 'He who exercises government by means of his virtue may be compared to the North Polar Star, which keeps its place and all the stars turn toward it.'"

Wen-shan looked straight at his face. "Most men don't rule with virtue, do they?"

Jun-jai put his hand tenderly on her hand. "No."

● ● ●

Her uncle had come home early from the store and fixed congee with pork for dinner. Wen-shan thanked him sincerely but was only able to eat a little, partly because she had eaten late in Kowloon, and partly because her stomach was unsettled by all the conflicting emotions she was feeling.

"It's not good?"

"It's delicious, Uncle, really. It's just . . ."

"Is your stomach upset? The porridge will settle your stomach."

She didn't want him to worry about her. "No, Uncle. It's just that Jun-jai and I ate something in Kowloon."

"Oh, I see." He put another slice of pork into his porridge. "Did he pay?"

"Yes."

"Good. I knew I liked him."

"He paid for the ferry tickets too."

"Oh? Hmm. Maybe he likes you."

Wen-shan felt heat on her face. "We're friends."

She didn't see the slight smile that played at the corner of her uncle's mouth. "Oh, I see. Friends. . . . Well, that's good. Maybe just being friends is better because he seems very Western to me."

Wen-shan was immediately defensive. "Well, he is Western in some things, but he's very traditional in others. *You* know him; he's a student of Confucianism."

Her uncle kept his detached demeanor. "Yes, that is one plus in his favor."

"He's very smart too. He's going into business like his father."

"Well, he will make some woman a fine husband someday." He stood and took his dishes to the sink, leaving Wen-shan to close her open fish mouth.

Is he teasing me? She turned to watch her uncle at the sink. *I'm not going to play his game.* She decided to change the subject.

135

There was a question that had been bothering her for weeks and she wanted to know her uncle's thoughts.

"Uncle?"

"Yes?"

"Do you think they're still alive?"

The clattering of dishes stopped. He was quiet for so long Wen-shan wondered if he'd heard the question correctly.

"Do you think—"

"I heard you." Another pause. He turned to look at her. "I don't know. I think they are both very wise and will figure out a way to survive, but I think it is hard to survive against evil."

Wen-shan stood. It was not the response she wanted. "Well, I think they're alive. Master Quan said they were alive when he left Guilin." She moved to help him with the dishes. "I think they're alive."

"Good. We will have faith."

"Yes. And I will have faith that I'll see them again."

He looked at her for a long moment and then nodded. "Good. Now, you go and get another letter ready, and I'll be there in a minute."

"Yes, Uncle."

He came to his chair a few minutes later, and Wen-shan began reading.

1960

The yellow leaves have fallen from the Ginkgo tree
and the barefoot doctor has placed a daughter in my
arms. This baby has a round moon face and a spirit
like the mountains surrounding the Li River. She cries
loudly and defies death and starvation. Chen Han-lie is

concerned for her fierce nature. He will not hold her for
fear she will conquer some of his strength.

Wen-shan looked up. "That was me."

Her uncle gave her an encouraging smile. "Yes. I've heard
that cry."

Wen-shan did not react to that, but went back to reading
her mother's words.

> *I walked from the field to the hospital, and as soon*
> *as I stepped in the door, the water poured from my*
> *body.*
> *There were two know-nothing student doctors in*
> *the room with me but neither one had ever delivered*
> *a baby. Dr. Han, the regular doctor, had been sent*
> *to the detention center for refusing to place a picture*
> *of Chairman Mao in the operating room. One of the*
> *doctors fainted when she saw blood, and the other ran*
> *out of the room when I started screaming from the*
> *pain. Twenty minutes later, Dr. Han's nurse came*
> *in and helped me. My little daughter was born ten*
> *minutes later. I will name her "bright kindness" for*
> *that is what she is to me.*
> *To protect my daughter's strength, I will be grateful*
> *for my husband's place. There is so little food that*
> *people are eating the corn husks and wild grasses.*
> *Coming home from the field several days ago, I saw a*
> *man and two children crouching around a pile of rags.*
> *As I passed by, I looked closer. It was not a pile of rags,*
> *but a dead woman. It was probably the man's wife*
> *and the mother of the children. They were guarding*

the body until the wagon could come to take it to the grave. We have heard of unspeakable things. People are hungry.

Rain falls on the mountain. Heaven is weeping.

Given his position, Han-lie secures what grain he can for the people, but there is so little. He says most is sent to Moscow in exchange for machinery. Machinery? Do the party leaders think we can eat a tractor?

No one feels attached to the land anymore. We do not feel that we grow our own food or raise our own cattle—that is done by the commune, and the commune has no heart. The peasants sing, "In the past when a cow died, we cried because it was our own, but now when a cow dies, we are very happy because we have meat to eat."

Han-lie is worn out with trying to get starving people to work. Secretary Zhang says he must beat them, but Han-lie says that will only send another worker to the grave and that will make the problem worse.

Han-lie worries that if he cannot bring in the quota, he will be demoted. Or worse, he will be labeled a counterrevolutionary and sent to detention.

But I cannot worry or look beyond the world of my small home. I see only my daughter's moon face and my father's thin arms as he paints the happy people of Communism.

Neither Wen-shan nor her uncle moved or spoke. Wen-shan felt a weight pressing down on her chest and she found it hard to breathe. Without permission her mind went back to the images conjured by her mother's words: her mother walking the path to the hospital, the man and his children crouching around the pile of rags, and her father's tired face. But she did not know what her father looked like. When she imagined her grandfather, she printed her uncle's features on the face. Her mother became Auntie Ting. Perhaps her father could look like Jun-jai.

Wen-shan turned her head as her uncle stood.

"I'm going to bed," he said.

She nodded.

He hesitated as he passed her, laying his hand on her shoulder. "Don't stay up too long."

"I won't. Good night, Uncle."

"Good night, Wen-shan."

She noticed a slower pace as he shuffled to his bedroom. She looked at the painting of the cypress tree. *Endurance.*

Notes

Congee: Congee is a type of rice porridge popular in many Asian countries. It can be served with savory items or with crullers (fried bread) for breakfast.

Barefoot doctor or student doctors: Many urban youth were given minimal medical training and sent to the countryside to provide basic healthcare and promote hygiene.

第十四章

Chapter 14

E VERY MORNING WE GO TO A *neighborhood meeting where one of the party officers reads us* the newspaper. There is always a large photograph of Chairman Mao on the front of the paper. We are tired. It is hard to listen. If you fall asleep, someone kicks you to wake you up. After the reading we stand and sing—

> The East is Red
> The sun rises
> China has produced a Mao Tse-tung
> He seeks happiness for the people
> He is the people's savior.

Then we go to the fields to work and to die.

The other day Zhang read to the women a new slogan from Chairman Mao. The secretary's face was *stern and his tone uncompromising as he recited the words, "Capable women can make a meal without food." We thought he had read it wrong for we all remembered our mothers and grandmothers saying, 'No matter how capable, a woman cannot make a meal without food." We all shuffled away thinking, Ah, well, if our great leader Chairman Mao said it then it must be true.*

● ● ●

Wen-shan was awoken in the middle of the night by the sound of rustling paper. What time was it? She lay in the warm bed, drifting in and out of sleep, her mind catching snatches of the letter she and her uncle had read the night before. Sleep was about to overtake her when she heard the sound again. She slid out of bed and crept to her door, rubbing sleep from her eyes. She looked down the hallway. There was a light coming from the kitchen. She put on her robe and went out to investigate. As she came from the hallway, she saw her uncle kneeling on the kitchen floor. Spread out in front of him were large pieces of paper covered with characters. Her uncle dipped his brush into the ink pot and created another character. *Tears.* He was so intent on his work that he was unaware of her watching him.

It was such odd behavior it frightened her. Wen-shan quietly backed into the hallway, returned to her room, and slipped into bed. Had nightmares disturbed her uncle's sleep? And what was he writing on the big posters? She yawned. Tomorrow she would ask him. Her mind began to drift. *It might just be a dream.* She rolled onto her side and yawned again. Warmth surrounded her. *Odd behavior. Such odd behavior.*

• • •

Wen-shan woke in the morning thinking that seeing her uncle kneeling on the kitchen floor had been a dream. She convinced herself that she really hadn't gotten out of bed and walked down the hallway. It was just a dream. Quickly she slipped on her robe and went to the kitchen. It hadn't been a dream. There on the floor in front of her were big posters covered in her uncle's writing. She moved closer and some of the characters leapt off the page: *famine, scattered, moon.* Her uncle had written a poem.

"Good morning, Wen-shan."

She jumped. "Good morning, Uncle." She walked into the kitchen until her bare toes touched the paper. "What are these big posters?"

"I couldn't sleep last night. I hope I didn't disturb you."

"No," she lied. "No. I'm sorry you had a bad night."

Her uncle walked past her and went to the refrigerator.

"What are you having for breakfast?" she asked.

"Leftover congee."

"May I have some too?"

Her uncle gave her a look. "Really?"

"Yes, and don't look so surprised."

"I think I will make some crullers to go along with breakfast."

"That would be good."

Wen-shan walked to a drawer, rummaged around, and pulled out cellophane tape. "May I hang the writing on the kitchen wall?"

Her uncle nodded.

She picked up the first big piece of paper. It crackled as she carried it to the wall. She secured it in place and picked up the second. The posters dominated the wall behind the kitchen table, and Wen-shan found them beautiful.

"I didn't know you wrote poetry."

"They are not my words. I only copied. Those are the thousand-year-old words from Master Bai Juyi of the mid-Tang dynasty."

"Will you read it to me?"

Her uncle stopped the breakfast preparations and read.

> *The times are hard: a year of famine has emptied the*
> *   fields,*
> *My brothers live abroad—scattered west and east.*
> *Now fields and gardens are scarcely seen after the fighting*
> *Family members wander, scattered on the road.*
> *Attached to shadows, like geese ten thousand li apart,*
> *Or roots uplifted into September's autumn air.*
> *We look together at the bright moon, and then the tears*
> *   should fall.*
> *This night, our wish for home can make five places one.*

"That was written a thousand years ago?"

Her uncle went back to his cooking. "A little more than a thousand years."

Wen-shan silently read the final lines again. "How did he know our hearts?"

"Do you think hearts have changed so much?"

She hadn't thought about it like that.

"Uncle?"

"Yes?"

"Did you have nightmares last night?"

"No, not really. I just felt . . . unsettled."

Wen-shan sat at the kitchen table and put her chin in her hand. "I still have those nightmares about the rain and the white ghost. Did you ever read me a ghost story about that?"

"I never read you stories."

That was true. "Maybe my mother told me the story when I was little."

"Maybe." He kept working away on the breakfast, making finger-sized ropes of dough for the deep fryer. "You don't remember anything about Guilin?"

"No." She yawned. "I wish I did." She watched her uncle cooking. "Tell me about it."

She hoped the empty space of time that followed meant that he was gathering his thoughts and not ignoring her.

"When we were boys, your grandfather and I loved to run along the banks of the Li River. To us it was a pale blue dragon curving its way through the green mountain peaks. It was a place of wonder."

Wen-shan folded her arms on the table and laid down her head.

"We would make these flat, narrow boats out of bamboo sticks and twine. We tried to make them look like the fishermen's boats."

"Fishermen?"

"Oh, yes. Many fishermen. They each had their own bamboo sampan, only about this wide." He held out his hands to indicate a space of about three feet.

Wen-shan's head lifted. "That's narrow."

"Very narrow. They would stand on the boat and move it along with a pole. Tai-lang and I wondered how they kept their balance." He went back to cooking. "There was a basket on the boat and a diving bird."

"What's a diving bird?"

Her uncle looked over at her. "Ah, yes. You don't know about the magical diving bird. He is the real fisherman. It is natural for this clever bird to dive into the river and catch fish; what is not natural is that the man trains him to bring the fish out and drop it in the basket."

"You're teasing me."

"I am not. I have seen it many, many times."

"A fishing bird?" Wen-shan yawned. "I would like to see that." She thought how different her life was in Hong Kong with the noise and the traffic and the tall buildings. There were hills surrounding Hong Kong, and Victoria Peak was lovely, but somehow she knew they wouldn't compare with the heavenly mountains and the blue dragon river. "Do you have pictures?"

Her uncle hesitated. "I . . . I don't. I could probably find travel photos of the area."

Wen-shan yawned again. "That would be nice."

"Of course, we have the best picture hanging on our wall."

"We do," Wen-shan said as she laid her head on her arms again. "Tell me something else."

"You'd better get ready for school before you fall asleep at the table."

"All right," she said reluctantly. "Thank you for talking about Guilin." Wen-shan pushed herself to her feet. "And I like the poem, even though it makes me sad. Thank you for writing it out." She yawned again.

Her uncle waved a big spoon at her. "Yes, now hurry! Go get ready! Breakfast in ten minutes!"

● ● ●

"No, that picture is crooked. Miss Song, please put your side down a little."

"Yes, Mrs. Yang. Like this?"

"That's much better." Mrs. Yang narrowed her eyes at Wen-shan. "Miss Chen, make sure you secure the pin tightly."

"Yes, Mrs. Yang." Wen-shan looked over at Li-ying and they shared a grin.

"How is that, Mrs. Yang?" Li-ying asked when they were finished pinning.

"Oh, very good. Come down and see."

The girls stepped off their chairs and went to stand beside Mrs. Yang, who was admiring the bulletin board.

Wen-shan liked it too. At the top of the board was the title GREAT THINKERS. The rest of the board was filled with pictures of famous men and women with their names above and one of their great thoughts underneath. There were pictures of Aristotle, Mahatma Gandhi, Helen Keller, Confucius, Thomas Jefferson, and others she didn't recognize.

Li-ying pointed at one of the pictures. "Mrs. Yang, Albert Einstein was an American scientist."

"Yes."

"Did he think about things other than science?"

"Oh, yes. He loved science—the theory of relativity and all of that—but he was also a great thinker. Read. Read his words out loud."

Li-ying read. "'The significant problems we face cannot be solved at the same level of thinking we were at when we created them.'"

Mrs. Yang beamed. "That is smart thinking, isn't it?"

"Yes, ma'am."

"Now you, Wen-shan. You read one. How about Thomas Jefferson?"

Wen-shan swallowed. "'It is always better to have no ideas than false ones; to believe nothing, than to believe what is wrong.'"

Mrs. Yang tapped the side of her head. "Smart thinking, yes?"

"Yes." Wen-shan smiled. "Now you, Mrs. Yang. Read your favorite."

Mrs. Yang took a small step forward and adjusted her glasses. "My favorite is by Mahatma Gandhi. 'When I despair, I remember that all through history the ways of truth and love have always won. There have been tyrants and murderers, and for a time they can seem invincible, but in the end they always fall. Think of it—always.'"

Tears sprang into Wen-shan's eyes. It wasn't just the powerful meaning of the words, but the passion in Mrs. Yang's voice that gripped her emotions. At that moment she knew why Mrs. Yang had done the bulletin board. She could see her teacher looking up quotes from people she admired, reading words that gave her courage and comfort—words that helped her navigate the sorrow of her life. And, Wen-shan realized, the words gave her courage and comfort too.

The three stood for quite awhile, looking at the pictures and silently reading quotes. Mrs. Yang slipped her arms around the girls' waists. "Thank you for helping me with the bulletin board. I could not have reached some of those high places."

"It really is wonderful," Wen-shan said.

Li-ying nodded. "Maybe we can keep it up all year and just put up different pictures and quotes."

Mrs. Yang walked over to gather the scissors, extra pins, and unused bits of paper. "Now that is great thinking, Li-ying."

Wen-shan laughed. "Li-ying's picture should be on the board."

Mrs. Yang turned. "Hmm. That is great thinking too."

Li-ying protested. "Don't be silly, Wen-shan."

"Well, perhaps I will not display your photographs," Mrs. Yang said. "But at some point I will have the class members come up with great thoughts and we will put those on the board."

The girls were excited about the idea, although Wen-shan secretly worried about being able to come up with any great thoughts.

They said their good-byes to Mrs. Yang, gathered their books and bags, and left the school. Once outside, they stopped to take in the beautiful afternoon. Billowy white clouds floated in the blue sky, the humidity was low, and a light breeze tousled their hair.

"Shall we go up to the pagoda?" Wen-shan asked.

Li-ying frowned. "I can't. I have to go shopping with my mother. I wish I could."

"That's all right. Another time."

"See you tomorrow."

Wen-shan waved and called after her departing friend. "Keep thinking those great thoughts!"

Li-ying pushed her glasses higher on her nose and smiled.

Wen-shan turned in the opposite direction of her normal trek home and began walking up the road that would eventually wind its way to the old white pagoda. She was actually glad she was alone. She liked visiting the pagoda by herself, sitting on the dilapidated balcony and sorting through her thoughts.

As she climbed higher on the shoulder of Victoria Peak, Wen-shan passed the bungalows of the uppity British land-owners. It was a section of the peak where only British folks could own property. Wen-shan shrugged. *Oh, well. They can have their cold isolation.*

She passed a park-like area and caught sight of the pagoda through a stand of trees. As she drew closer, she saw the mounds of sand and piles of boards and bricks that indicated a construction site. She knew she didn't have to worry about anyone interrupting her solitude because the building materials had been sitting in the same place, untouched, for at least five years. Moss was growing on the boards, and the grass and bushes had overwhelmed the bricks.

One of the double wooden doors leading into the pagoda sagged on its hinges, and Wen-shan scrambled through the gap it created. She gingerly climbed the creaky wooden stairs to the third level and went out onto the balcony. This level was just the right distance from the ground—not too high to be scary, but high enough to have a good view. She could even see a bit of Kowloon and the New Territories to the west. She threw off her schoolbag and went down on her knees. She laid her arms on the balustrade, and peered out toward mainland China.

"What are you doing today, Mother? Are you still working in the rice field? It's harvesttime, isn't it? Are there big white clouds hanging over the heavenly mountains? Have you eaten today?" Wen-shan knew no one could hear her, so she continued the one-sided conversation with her mother in Guilin, until the sun hid itself behind the trees and vegetation, leaving an orange and gray smudge on the horizon.

Finally, Wen-shan stood. "Maybe if I look hard enough I

can see the path by the Li River, or the Flower Bridge. Maybe I can see your face."

But what she saw were only the trees and buildings of Hong Kong Island.

NOTES

Famine: When asked about the starving peasants during the years of the "Great Leap," Mao replied, "People were not without food all the year round—only six . . . or four months."

Tang dynasty: The Tang dynasty lasted from 581 to 907 A.D. North and South China were reunited at the end of the sixth century, and under the Tang dynasty, China became an expansive, dynamic, cosmopolitan empire. The Tang capital, Chang'an, grew to be the largest city in the world, housing perhaps a million people and attracting traders, students, artists, and pilgrims from all over Asia.

Li: A *li* is an ancient Chinese unit of distance.

Cormorant birds: The Li River fishermen train these birds to catch fish.

Chapter 15

I T WAS NEARLY DARK WHEN Wen-shan arrived home.
She hurried to change out of her school uniform and get
to the kitchen to fix dinner. Luckily her uncle had brought
home snake soup the night before and they had enough left for
another meal.

Her uncle came home from work late, and Wen-shan figured they wouldn't be reading a letter that night, but after dinner and a short rest, her uncle called her to the front room. "Are
you too tired to read a letter tonight?"

"No. Are you?"

"I am a little tired, but I want to hear your mother's words."

Wen-shan nodded and went to the coffee table drawer to retrieve another letter. There were very few letters left to read, and
Wen-shan tried not to think about the last ribbon being untied.

She pushed the parchment open and read.

1962

*I whisper to my daughter that Mao Tse-tung has been
made to change his mind. She rubs her ear and giggles
because my warm breath tickles. I can tell her these things
because she is only two and will not report me to Secretary
Zhang. I say the name of President Liu Shao-ch'i, and she
smiles. Yes! We all smile! He helped us. He listened to our
cries. At great risk, he stood up to Chairman Mao. The
quota was much lower this year, and while some grain
was sent away, more filled the people's stomachs. There
is cooking oil, eggs, and flour. And we have been given
permission to plant our own gardens. Father and I bring
in beans, peppers, corn, and eggplant. Wen-shan stumbles
around the garden, looking at plants, and poking her fingers
in the dirt. Han-lie watches her from a distance. He smiles.
I think in his heart he would like to stand up like President
Liu, but he is more comfortable being told what to do.*

*My father paints again—a secret painting of tiny
sparrows bravely wearing winter's coat.*

Both Wen-shan and her uncle turned to stare at the painting. It was odd to have her mother speak about something that
was hanging on their front room wall. It caused an ache in her
heart, and with difficulty, Wen-shan went back to the letter.

*He does not do a revolutionary painting. He paints
the sparrows and smiles. It is his way of being on the
other side of sorrow. We will hide it with the others.*

*Secretary Zhang was sent to Peking for a month of
training, and we were all joyful. The assistant who took*

*his place was lazy and did not care if we chanted Mao's
name or read the newspaper. We still had to work, but
we felt lighter not having to carry around heavy words in
our mouths. When Secretary Zhang returned, he brought
a wife with him. Wu Ming-mei. She was a former
actress in the opera like Mao Tse-tung's wife, Jiang
Qing. But Wu Ming-mei is pretty. We do not know her
heart because she does not come to the reading of the
newspapers or to the meetings. In the fields the women
talk, and we wonder why a lotus flower would marry a
scorpion. I think maybe she did not have a choice.*

*Father did an exquisite writing, and then he
burned it for fear Secretary Zhang would call him a
counterrevolutionary.*

Wen-shan's uncle moaned. "The world is mad, Wen-shan.
For such beauty to be burned? It's madness."

"I agree, Uncle. Maybe that's why Mr. and Mrs. Smythe
work so hard to get treasures out of China."

Her uncle nodded. "'A gentle man holds three things in awe.
He is in awe of Heaven's dome; he is in awe of great men; he is
awed by the speech of the holy. The vulgar are blind to the power
of Heaven and hold it not in awe. They are saucy towards the great,
and of the speech of the holy they make their game.'" He stared
at the picture of the cypress and rubbed his hands across his face.
"Perhaps I'm more tired than I thought. I think I will go to bed."

"Wait, Uncle. There's one more line."

*As the flames ate the writing, I saw what my father
had written: We do not ask for much—only to work
and to live.*

Her uncle nodded, picked up his scriptures, and moved toward his bedroom.

• • •

"He told me the noodle story, Mr. Pierpont."

"Did he now? Wonderful!" Mr. Pierpont quickly grabbed onto the delivery truck's armrest as the driver maneuvered a sharp turn around a corner. "Patrick! Slow down!" Wen-shan squealed with delight. "Oh, you like that, do you? Well, his driving is going to give me apoplexy." Mr. Pierpont leaned forward and looked around Wen-shan to the brawny British driver. "Truly, Patrick, slow down."

"Right ya are, Mr. Pierpont."

"There's precious cargo in the back."

"Yes, sir."

"And even more precious cargo sitting next to you."

The driver gave Wen-shan a wink. She was shocked, but found it funny too.

"Go left on Queen's Road West."

"Yes, sir."

"Ah, see there? He knows who pays his salary." Mr. Pierpont focused his attention on Wen-shan. "Now, tell me how you liked the story."

"It was wonderful. I didn't know you could make good money selling noodles."

"Well, your uncle is a hard worker."

Mr. Pierpont stopped talking to point dramatically down the street which the driver should be turning. The truck swung precariously around the corner and the passengers bumped against one another.

"Sorry, Mr. Pierpont."

"Patrick, I think this girl or I could drive better than you."

"Well, the girl anyway."

Wen-shan giggled as Mr. Pierpont gave Patrick a warning look. "That's enough of that. Just watch the road signs and slow down." He puffed out a big breath of air. "Now, where were we?"

"Making money selling noodles."

"Ah, yes. As I said, your uncle is a hard worker, and so was your aunt. Besides which, they paid their tithing." He turned to look at her. "Did he tell you about the tithing noodles?"

"Yes, sir." She looked puzzled. "But why would that make a difference?"

"Well, it's all part of the glorious gospel package, isn't it?"

"What does that mean?"

Mr. Pierpont paused. "Hmm. Well, it's rather difficult to explain if you're not in the thick of things."

"I beg your pardon?"

"Let's just say the Lord promises us certain things if we're obedient. If we follow the Word of Wisdom, we have better health. If we serve others, we have a better outlook on life. If we pay our ten percent tithing, our lives are more stable. Does that make sense?"

"I guess so. If you pay your tithing, your noodle business will be successful."

Mr. Pierpont laughed. "Something like that. You still have to put in your effort and work hard, but since you've been obedient, the Lord will bless you."

"It doesn't mean you'll be rich or anything, right?"

"Well, sometimes amazing things do happen. Don't you think your uncle's done very well, considering where he came from?"

Wen-shan thought of the refugee camp, her uncle's

bungalows on the slopes of Victoria Peak, and his job with Pierpont and Pierpont Limited. "He has done well." She held onto Mr. Pierpont's arm as they made another turn. "And you met my great-aunt and great-uncle at church?"

Mr. Pierpont beamed. "And liked them from the very beginning."

"But how did they get interested in the Church?"

Mr. Pierpont gave her a knowing look. "Ah, you're trying to wriggle information out of me, aren't you?"

She couldn't help but smile. "He's been talking to me much more lately about Guilin, and his escape to Hong Kong, and the noodle story, but he still won't tell me much about the war, or the refugee camp, or why he joined the Mormon Church."

"Some stories are more difficult to tell, dear girl. Give him time."

Patrick grunted. "I think I missed the street, Mr. Pierpont."

Mr. Pierpont shook his head and rolled his eyes. "Well, repent, man, and go back!"

By the time they reached the delivery point, poor Patrick had gotten a proper British taking down, and Wen-shan hadn't laughed so much in ages.

● ● ●

As Mr. Pierpont supervised the delivery and spoke with Mrs. Scott, Patrick took in the large items, and Wen-shan took in the more delicate pieces. She entered the elegant house with care and took her time removing the protective wrapping from the gilt mirror, the small table, and the Ming vase. She knew it wasn't an actual Ming vase because that would have cost thousands and thousands of pounds, but this was a very good copy and probably very expensive.

She breathed a sigh of relief when Mrs. Scott had inspected everything and signed the account form. It turned out that Patrick was a better moving man than a driver.

Mr. Pierpont shook Patrick's hand and patted Wen-shan's shoulder. "Well done. Well done, you two." He turned to Wen-shan. "Thank you very much, Miss Chen, for coming along and keeping us on our toes. I'm glad your uncle could spare you."

She mimicked his British accent. "You're very welcome, Mr. Pierpont."

"So, a ride back to the store?"

Wen-shan gave Patrick a terrified look. "I don't think so, Mr. Pierpont. I actually live near here. I think I'll walk."

Mr. Pierpont laughed. "Very wise choice. And if you don't mind, I think I'll walk with you."

"Hey now," Patrick protested. "I don't drive that badly. Besides, Mr. Pierpont, you don't live anywhere near here."

"That speaks to your driving skills then, doesn't it? Easy does it back to the store and tell Mr. Zhao that his great-niece is being well looked after."

"Yes, sir. But how will you get home?"

"There are these wonderful things called taxis, Patrick."

Wen-shan waved to Patrick as he pulled away. She let out a chirp of surprise when he didn't stop at the end of the driveway before pulling out into traffic. There was a car horn, but no crash. Sheepishly she looked over at Mr. Pierpont and found him shaking his head.

"If I wasn't so fond of the man . . ." He looked at Wen-shan. "Well, should we be on our way? A brisk walk sounds wonderful."

"And safe."

Mr. Pierpont nodded in agreement, and they started off. After a block or two of comfortable silence, a question came to Wen-shan's mind.

"Mr. Pierpont?"

"Yes?"

"Has my uncle told you about the jade dragon box?"

"Yes, my dear. He has mentioned it. What a significant treasure."

"And about the paintings and letters?"

"Well, those are the most significant treasures of all, aren't they?"

"Has he told you what any of the letters said?"

"Oh, no. I'm very sure those sentiments are much too precious for the two of you to share them with everyone."

Wen-shan nodded. "But I'm sure he would like you to see his brother's paintings."

"Really?"

Wen-shan could tell by the tone in Mr. Pierpont's voice that he was excited by the idea. "And I just thought, since you're walking me home, that you'd like to see them when we get there."

"How thoughtful, Wen-shan. I would love to see them."

The two walked on, chatting about Chinese painting in general, Guilin, and Master Quan. Mr. Pierpont was fascinated by Master Quan's escape from China, and Wen-shan wished she had more information to share. She figured it might be time to have Master Quan to dinner. Wen-shan did share bits and pieces from her mother's letters, and Mr. Pierpont was appropriately sad, angry, and in awe.

They reached the house and Wen-shan opened the front door. Mr. Pierpont removed his shoes and stepped reverently into the house. The room was dim, and Wen-shan went to the front window and drew back the drapes. Her grandfather's pictures were revealed in the golden glow of the late afternoon sun.

"Ah!" Mr. Pierpont turned slowly from side to side trying to take in all the paintings and calligraphy at once.

"I'm thirsty after our walk, Mr. Pierpont. Would you like a drink of water?"

"Yes . . . yes, Wen-shan, that would be nice." His eyes never left the paintings as he walked slowly toward the silk scroll of the brilliant plum blossoms.

When she returned with the water, he was still staring at the same painting. She handed him the glass of water and he took a drink. "Would you like me to read to you what it says?"

He shook his head. "'Falling petals—fragrant rain,'" he said in Cantonese.

Wen-shan nearly dropped her glass. "You read Chinese?"
He grinned. "And speak it?"

"I have lived here all my life, Wen-shan. What kind of a businessman would I be if I did not speak the major language of my home? Besides, you heard me ordering dinner at the restaurant."

"That's different. That was ordering food."

"I see."

"But you never speak to me in Cantonese."

He grinned again. "You need to practice your English."

He went back to admiring the picture, leaving Wen-shan speechless. He moved to the picture of the rooster, and Wen-shan knew what his reaction would be. Sure enough, he let go a hearty laugh.

"How delightful!" He handed Wen-shan his now-empty glass, and they shared a look of delight. "Your grandfather's paintings are so full of life, Wen-shan. How in the world did he get that expression on the face of a rooster?" He laughed again. "I wish I could meet him."

"I wish you could too."

Mr. Pierpont turned to her. "Yes, indeed." He looked back to the painting. "Well, we shall pray for a grand meeting someday."

Wen-shan took the glasses to the kitchen. If Mr. Pierpont thought praying to his Christian God would really help bring her grandfather and mother to Hong Kong, then she would ask him to teach her how to do it, and she would pray too. When she returned to the front room, she found Mr. Pierpont studying her grandfather's calligraphy.

"Truth," he said in Cantonese. Then in English he said, "What is truth?"

"That's what my uncle said. What does it mean, Mr. Pierpont?"

"What is truth? It's a question humankind has been asking for thousands and thousands of years." He moved to look at the painting of the heavenly mountains. "Here is an example, Wen-shan. Through the ages, prophets and philosophers have been searching for truth, and many have given us beautiful words and thoughts, but I look at your grandfather's painting and I see truth in every brushstroke."

She didn't understand, but nodded in agreement anyway.

Mr. Pierpont considered each painting carefully, and Wen-shan wondered what truths he was learning. After a time, he turned to her and asked to borrow the telephone. As he dialed the number for the taxi company, Wen-shan studied the painting of Guilin. She wanted to see the truth in her grandfather's painting. She saw his great ability, and the beauty of the heavenly mountains, but what truth did that teach her about life?

Mr. Pierpont came back to her side and together they chatted about the unique strengths in each painting. The taxi horn sounded, and with a sigh, Mr. Pierpont gathered his raincoat and hat.

"Thank you, Wen-shan, for inviting me to view your grandfather's work."

She moved with him to the outside. "You're welcome, Mr. Pierpont." She went to tell the taxi driver that his customer would be there in a minute as Mr. Pierpont sat on the porch and put on his shoes.

He joined her at the gate and tipped his hat. "You are welcome to join me on a delivery anytime, Miss Chen."

Wen-shan opened the gate for him and he stepped out. "As long as Patrick isn't driving," she answered.

Mr. Pierpont chuckled and got into the taxi. He waved to her as the vehicle pulled away.

Wen-shan stood at the gate for a long time, watching the shadows of evening creep across the sidewalks. A warm breeze tousled her hair, and she tried to imagine that it was her mother whispering in her ear.

NOTES

The end of the Great Leap Forward: Mao's miscalculations for the Great Leap Forward caused the deaths of 38 to 40 million people, engendered economic catastrophe, and precipitated agricultural devastation. Years after Mao's death, Chinese people, still cautious about voicing any criticism of the Chairman, would say, "Mao was a great revolutionary, but not a very good leader."

Liu Shao-ch'i: As president of the government, President Liu saw the devastation caused by the flawed programs of the Great Leap. He led the top echelon of the CCCP to force Mao to abandon his plans.

Chapter 16

1964

I T IS WINTER AND VERY COLD. *Ice forms on the windows. This morning at the neighborhood meeting we stood and chanted "Mother and Father are dear, but Mao Tse-tung is dearer." My husband, Chen Han-lie, led the chant as Secretary Zhang looked on. We chanted until our legs ached from standing and our throats were rough from shouting. Chen Han-lie chanted loudest of all though tears ran down his face. He is being sent away to the North Country. There was a charge that he cared more for his family than he did for our great leader, Chairman Mao. At the struggle meeting, people accused him of taking extra eggs from the people's store and of standing up for his wife, who was the daughter of a dirty landowner.*

Secretary Zhang made him stand barefoot on the frozen ground.

Wen-shan dropped the letter on the couch and went to look out the window. A light morning rain was falling and she watched as it gently tapped the leaves of the Chinese Pepper Tree. *What is truth?* Her father was a Communist, but he didn't love Chairman Mao more than he loved her mother . . . or more than he loved her. That was a truth she was sure of. She tried to picture her father in his green uniform. Did he ever hold her, or feed her, or tell her stories? Maybe her father was the one who told her the ghost story that gave her nightmares. Did he hate the words the Communists made him chant? Was he a coward because he did not stand up when people were starving to death, or was he saving his family?

"Wen-shan?"

Her uncle's voice was gentle. She turned away from the window. "Yes?"

"Do you want to read any more this morning?"

"Yes." She came back to the couch and picked up the letter. "Uncle, why do you think my father became a Communist?"

"I don't know, but like many, he may have been caught up in the words."

"What does that mean?"

"The people of China have lived with chaos and hunger for a long time, Wen-shan. Chiang Kai-shek was trying to change things, but it wasn't fast enough for most people. The words of the Communists sounded good: everyone is the same; no rich or poor; the government will take care of you."

Wen-shan interrupted. "But everyone *isn't* the same. I'll never be as smart as Jun-jai, or as good as Li-ying. And how does the government take care of people? The people still have to work to support the government."

"True."

"And what if those people who take charge aren't good men?"

"It usually works out that way, doesn't it?"

"Look at Secretary Zhang. Look what he did. And whoever put him in charge had to be just as bad."

"Probably."

She shook her head. "I don't know why my father would believe any of it."

"I cannot answer that."

"And now look at what the Communists did to him. He tried to do his best for the party and they sent him away from his family." There were tears in her voice, and neither of them spoke for some time.

Finally Wen-shan picked up the letter. "Stupid government."

She read.

> As we were chanting, Wu Ming-mei came to my side and took my hand. She told me to have courage. She told me that all things change. She told me to be careful. She said Zhang had it out for our family because he was jealous of my father. She said she wanted to help me because I reminded her of her sister in Peking. I looked at her with her cropped hair and her Mao cap, and I wondered if she was trying to trick me. She was so pretty. I wanted to believe I had an influential friend, but maybe she was just trying to get information for her husband, the demon Zhang. I

*took my hand away and shoved it into the air so my
husband could see.*

Wen-shan rolled the letter.

"She doesn't say anything about where your father was sent,
or when he left?"

"No. That was everything." She put away the letter and
stood.

Her uncle stood with her. "I'll be home late from work this
evening. Mr. Pierpont wants to see me after we close the store."

Wen-shan smiled. She had a good idea what Mr. Pierpont
was going to talk to her uncle about. "Should I wait dinner?"

"No, I'll get some wonton or something on the way home."

"Oh, well, your loss. I was going to make goulash again."

Her uncle raised his eyebrows, but said nothing.

Wen-shan headed for her bedroom to finish getting ready
for school. She wore a secret smile.

● ● ●

Mrs. Tuan was on her porch, sweeping. Wen-shan watched
her out of the corner of her eye as she knelt by the ornamen-
tal strawberries, pulling weeds. She had the suspicion that Mrs.
Tuan wanted to ask her a question or scold her about something,
and Wen-shan wondered what was holding her back. Wen-shan
really didn't want to have a conversation with the toad woman.
She was enjoying the late afternoon autumn sun. The leaves on
the Chinese Pepper Tree had turned a bright red, and that, com-
bined with the smell of moist soil and the warmth on her back,
filled her senses.

"Hello, girl!" Mrs. Tuan called.

Wen-shan grumbled quietly and looked over. She smiled and waved her trowel, which Mrs. Tuan took immediately as a sign to join her.

"Hello, Mrs. Tuan. And where are Yan and Ya Ya today?"

"Oh, those two? They are staying at their auntie's house this weekend. She picked them up from school."

Wen-shan thought she caught the sound of relief in Mrs. Tuan's voice. "Well, that will be fun for them," she said diplomatically.

Mrs. Tuan cleared her throat, and Wen-shan knew she was impatient to get to her questions. "So, you have new paintings?"

"New paintings?"

"Yes, in your house."

"How did you . . ."

"I was getting Yan's kite out of the tree. Your drapes were open. I just happened to look over."

"And you saw my grandfather's paintings?"

Mrs. Tuan was stunned silent for a moment. "Your *grandfather's* paintings?"

Wen-shan shaded her eyes and looked up at her. "Yes. Some of my grandfather's paintings were smuggled out of Guilin." She knew the word *smuggled* would send Mrs. Tuan into a fit of curiosity.

"Smuggled? Who smuggled them?"

"An old pirate that my uncle knows."

Mrs. Tuan narrowed her eyes. "It is disrespectful to tell me a lie."

Wen-shan stood. "Sorry. I'm sorry, Mrs. Tuan. I was just having a little fun."

Mrs. Tuan blew out a puff of air. "Young people these days. No respect."

"Really, I am sorry. Actually it was one of my uncle's old teachers from the university. Some people smuggled him out of Guilin, and he brought the paintings with him."

"Who smuggled him out?"

"I can't tell you that."

She gave Wen-shan a very conspiratorial look. "Ah, very secret, huh?"

"Yes. Very secret."

Mrs. Tuan tapped her finger on her lips. "That is what the message was about. The one brought by the boy on red bicycle."

Wen-shan was shocked at her recollection. "That's right."

Mrs. Tuan looked over at the bungalow. "Nice to have a grandfather who sends you such a treasure."

"Yes," Wen-shan said. She looked at Mrs. Tuan's eager expression and made a decision. "Mrs. Tuan, would you like to see the paintings?"

"Me?"

"Yes, I'd be glad to show them to you."

"Well, I would, but I'm dirty from doing housework all day."

"You're fine."

Mrs. Tuan seemed agitated and excited. "Let . . . let me go wash my hands."

Wen-shan hid a grin. "Of course. Whatever makes you feel comfortable."

Mrs. Tuan scurried into her house and emerged a few minutes later. She was still wearing her work dress, but she'd added a flowered pillbox hat to the ensemble.

Wen-shan opened the door for her. "That's a nice hat, Mrs. Tuan."

She touched it a bit self-consciously. "Thank you."

"If you don't mind, I'll just let you go in by yourself."

"It will be all right?"

"Of course. I need to finish out here in the garden."

"I promise I won't touch anything."

"I'm not worried."

"You leave the door open so you can be sure. You can watch me."

"Okay." Wen-shan grinned to herself again.

Mrs. Tuan entered the house slowly, and Wen-shan wondered how this could possibly be the same woman who yelled at her children and snooped on all the neighbors.

Wen-shan went back to her gardening, glancing up every now and then to the house. Once she saw Mrs. Tuan chuckle, and once she saw her timidly reach out toward one of the paintings. *Probably the sparrow painting,* Wen-shan thought.

She had just finished her weeding when Mrs. Tuan came out onto the porch. She gave Wen-shan a little bow and headed immediately for her house. Wen-shan waved at Mrs. Tuan's back as she and her flowered pillbox hat disappeared through the doorway.

Wen-shan wasn't sure, but she thought her neighbor was crying.

● ● ●

Wen-shan was watching *Charlie's Angels* when she heard the front door open. She jumped out of bed and went to see what news her uncle had to share. He was hanging up his raincoat when she came out.

"Good evening, Uncle. How was your day?"

"Good." He moved to his chair.

"Can I get you anything?"

"No, thank you." He sat down and picked up his scriptures. "How was your day?"

"Good." She sat cross-legged on the couch.

Her uncle frowned at her. "So American."

"No, it's not. I'm following Buddha's example."

He raised his eyebrows. "I see."

She wished he'd stop getting her off track. "So, how was your meeting with Mr. Pierpont?"

"Good." He opened his book.

Wen-shan was getting frustrated. "What did he want to talk to you about?"

"Just some business."

She tried to remember the Confucius saying about patience. She took a breath. "Oh, just business? I thought he might want to talk to you about something else."

Her uncle slowly turned a few pages of his Bible as though searching for a specific passage. "You mean like being his partner at Pierpont and Pierpont Limited?"

Wen-shan shot up from her seat. "Yes!" She caught herself. "Oh, I mean, really? Really? That's fantastic!"

Her uncle chuckled and closed the book. "He also told me that you knew all about it."

Wen-shan looked sheepish. "Oh."

"I must say you did a very good job keeping it quiet."

Wen-shan beamed at him. "I did, didn't I?" She sat down again. "Oh, Uncle, I'm so glad for you. You are a hard worker and you deserve it."

He was quiet for several moments. "I've been given many blessings." He reached over and took her hand. "And you are one of them."

Tears sprang from her eyes and ran down her cheeks. "Wen-shan?"

"Yes?" She hiccupped through her tears.

"Would you please get me a glass of water?"

"Yes, Uncle." Wen-shan stood quickly and went to the kitchen, letting the tears flow as she filled the glass ten times. Finally she took a deep breath, splashed some water on her face, and dried it on the tea towel. She took the glass of water to her uncle. She drew in a deep breath. "I'm very proud of you."

"Thank you, Wen-shan."

"I think I'll go to bed. It's been a long day."

Her uncle nodded, and she turned to go. "Wen-shan?"

"Yes?"

"I may be going to church on Sunday. Would you like to come with me?"

"Yes. I would."

"There's only one thing I ask."

"Yes?"

"When we get there, no kicking or screaming."

The tears started again. "Yes, Uncle." She moved quickly to the solitude of her bedroom.

NOTE

Mao Cap: Men and women wore a standardized uniform of loose trousers and a jacket designed to obscure the differences in rank or sex. As part of that uniform, men and women could choose to wear a blue or green cap. The cap had a soft pillbox that covered the head and a stiff brim. Often a red star was worn on the front of the cap.

Chapter 17

W HAT DID CONFUCIUS TEACH about peace in the world?"

Wen-shan pointed to her ears and shook her head. "I can't hear you, Jun-jai. The tram car is too noisy."

Li-ying hid her smile behind her hand as the corner of Jun-jai's mouth curved up. "It's not too noisy," he said. "You just don't know the answer."

Wen-shan pointed to her ears again and turned to look out the window. The glossy leaves on the banana and camphor trees spoke of the night's rain, but the morning had arrived with blue sky and a gentle breeze, and Wen-shan was glad that she and her friends didn't have to postpone their picnic outing on Victoria Peak. She glanced sideways and found Jun-jai looking out the opposite window.

"'If there be rightness in the heart, there will be beauty in the character,'" she began.

Jun-jai turned to her and nodded like a teacher prompting his student. "And?"

"'If there is beauty in the character there will be balance—'"

"Harmony."

"'There will be harmony in the home. If there is harmony in the home, there will be order in the nation.'"

"Yes? And?"

"'If there is order in the nation, there will be peace in the world.'"

Jun-jai nodded, but didn't say anything.

"So? I told you I knew it."

He stayed silent.

Wen-shan batted him on the arm. "Jun-jai, how about some praise?"

He pointed to his ears. "What? Sorry, I can't hear you. The tram car is too noisy."

Their bantering stopped as the tramcar arrived at the top of Victoria Peak and people rose to disembark. Jun-jai picked up the satchel with the food, Wen-shan gathered the blanket, and Li-ying brought the thermos. They hiked the trail to their favorite spot, and as they went, Li-ying surprisingly did most of the talking. She was upset with her mother, who had almost not let her come on the outing.

"She'd forgotten that I'd asked her weeks ago about it, and she scheduled an appointment with the dentist on the same day. She just expects that I'm always going to be around to watch the children. I do have a life other than being the big sister."

They arrived at the grassy overlook, and Li-ying abruptly stopped talking. She looked embarrassed. "Oh, sorry, Jun-jai. I'm not showing much rightness of heart, am I?"

Wen-shan laughed as she spread out the blanket. "You're just being normal for once."

"But it's very disrespectful to talk in anger about your parents. What does Confucius have to say about my disrespectful behavior, Jun-jai?"

Jun-jai grinned at her. "'When you have faults, do not fear to abandon them.'"

A mortified look appeared on Li-ying's face.

Wen-shan growled at him. "Ah, Jun-jai! That is a terrible thing to say. Li Li, don't listen to him."

"I was just teasing, Li-ying. Really. I can't see that you have any faults, and you are the most respectful girl I know."

Wen-shan gave him a look. "Compared to me, who is known for her faults and bad manners."

"Actually, Wen-shan, you've been doing much better lately."

Li-ying giggled, and Wen-shan glared at Jun-jai. "And what does Confucius say about boys who are mean?"

"Confucius says that mean boys should eat a good lunch and talk about the weather."

The girls laughed as they sat down on the blanket.

Jun-jai sat down with them and handed Wen-shan the satchel. "It was nice of you to make lunch, Wen-shan."

"I fixed everything American-style!"

Li-ying pushed up her glasses. "What does that mean?"

Wen-shan reached into the bag and began dragging out food. "Bologna and cheese sandwiches, potato chips, apples, and biscuits! The biscuits are from Mr. Pierpont."

"So those aren't really American," Jun-jai teased. "If they were American, we'd be eating cookies."

"Well, I like biscuits better."

Li-ying looked skeptical. "I don't think I've ever eaten bologna."

"You'll like it, I think," Wen-shan said as she handed each of them a sandwich wrapped in waxed paper. She watched as they both took a bite.

Jun-jai looked pleased. "I've had something like this before—Italian lunch meat. It's pretty good."

Li-ying looked like she was having trouble swallowing.

"How is it?" Wen-shan asked.

"Not bad." Li-ying answered, trying to smile as she chewed.

Wen-shan giggled. "You don't have to eat it, Li Li." She reached in the satchel again. "I brought some cold shoyu chicken, just in case."

Li-ying brightened as Wen-shan pulled out the container filled with tender chunks of meat coated in the savory sauce.

"Is there enough for all of us?" Jun-jai asked hopefully.

Wen-shan threw her own partially eaten sandwich into the heap and gave them both a half grin. "I guess I should have known better."

They divided the chicken, chips, and apples, and spent the afternoon sharing stories and experiences. Her friends were delighted when Wen-shan told them about her uncle's promotion to partner at the furniture store. When lunch was over, Wen-shan threw away the trash, reached into the satchel, and brought out Mr. Pierpont's tin of biscuits. She also brought out one of the parchments.

Jun-jai sat straighter.

"I thought you might like to hear another of my mother's letters."

"I would," Jun-jai answered quickly.

"Oh, yes," Li-ying added. "As long as it's not too sad."

"You'll have to decide for yourself," Wen-shan said as she unrolled the scroll. "My uncle and I read it last night, and I want to know what you think about it."

Li-ying sat with her back against a tree, and Jun-jai sat with his arms folded around his bent legs.

Wen-shan took a drink of water and began reading.

1965

I stand with a clump of grass in my hand. I throw it into the smoldering fire pit, and then use my wooden hoe to dig up another patch. Next I will destroy the peony bush and the yew tree. My daughter sits in her little Mao jacket pulling up starflowers. She is a good revolutionary. Our great leader Chairman Mao says that grass and flowers are habits of the Western rich and must be purged from our lives. So we are turning our courtyard into a wasteland. I ache as I cut branches from the peony bush. The delicate pink petals fall to the ground. For a moment they will bring splendor to the dark earth. I must hate myself for feeling miserable. I must work against any feeling that goes against the instructions of Chairman Mao.

"Wen-shan?"

Wen-shan stopped reading and looked at Li-ying. The expression on her friend's face was one of bewilderment.

"They were told to dig up flowers?"

Wen-shan nodded.

"That's impossible," Li-ying said.

"That's insanity," Jun-jai said flatly.

175

"But why destroy flowers? There's no reason for it."

Jun-jai shook his head. "It's not about reason, Li-ying. It's about power. If you can get an entire nation of people to do something as insane as pulling up their flower gardens, then you know you have control over their minds. You've created people who have no thoughts of their own."

"That's not possible."

"You heard Wen-shan's mother," Jun-jai pressed. "She said she had to hate herself for feeling miserable."

"But didn't Mao Tse-tung care about his people, Jun-jai?"

"No."

Tears came into Li-ying's eyes, and she took off her glasses to wipe them away. "Do you remember pulling up flowers, Wen-shan?"

Wen-shan shook her head. "No." She tucked her hair behind her ear. "I was only four and a half." She didn't want to remember pulling up flowers, but she would have liked to have remembered the peony petals scattered on the dark earth.

"Is there more? Do you feel like going on?" Jun-jai asked.

Wen-shan nodded and read her mother's words.

I told Father he did not need to come to the courtyard while we worked. I knew it would be hard for him, but he did not listen to me. After an hour of watching, he stood by the fire pit and took each plant and flower from us. He held each one tenderly before throwing it onto the fire. A butterfly came to the garden looking for its evening nectar. Wen-shan called it "light"—"light" because the sun reflected off its shiny blue wings. She cried when it would not stay. Why would it? There was no place for it to rest.

Secretary Zhang came to our courtyard with his wife, Ming-mei. He stood by the fire pit, kicking the last of the yew tree into the ashes and looking around at our barren yard. "This is better," he said. "Much more practical." Ming-mei's face showed no expression as she looked around at the torn earth. Even when her glance fell on Wen-shan who was twirling in circles and kicking around in the dirt, Ming-mei showed no signs of actually seeing her.

My father addressed Secretary Zhang very politely and asked him for an official pocket-sized photograph of Chairman Mao. He said he wanted to paint a special picture to honor our illustrious leader and his grand ideas, and he wanted to include the photograph. Secretary Zhang looked like he'd swallowed ink, but said he would get him a photograph. As they left, Ming-mei stooped down and picked up one of the fallen flower petals. She put it in the band of her Mao cap. It made my father smile.

Wen-shan rolled up the parchment.

"I think I like the secretary's wife," Jun-jai said.

"Why?"

"I think she's a very clever person."

Wen-shan frowned. "Really? I don't like her at all."

"Just because she married Zhang, doesn't mean she's like him."

"That's not the reason."

"Why, then?"

Wen-shan frowned. "I . . . I don't know."

Li-ying broke into the conversation. "I don't see why your grandfather would do a painting to honor Mao Tse-tung."

Before Wen-shan could speak, Jun-jai answered. "You two are missing the point. Sometimes things are not what they seem."

"What does that mean?"

"You said that Ming-mei was an actress, right?" Wen-shan nodded. "Maybe in front of her stupid, cruel husband she's always acting."

Wen-shan thought about it. "Maybe."

"And maybe your grandfather is doing everything he can to keep his family safe."

"From Secretary Zhang?" Wen-shan's face was resolute. "No matter what he does, it won't make a difference. Zhang is an evil person."

Jun-jai nodded. "Perhaps you're right."

"I mean, I don't think her grandfather should stand up to Zhang or anything," Li-ying said timidly. "I just don't think he should waste one of his beautiful paintings on Mao Tse-tung."

Wen-shan smiled. "You are a treasure, Li Li."

"I agree with that," Jun-jai said.

Li-ying blushed. "You're making fun of me."

"No, I'm not," Wen-shan said as she began gathering the picnic items. "You know how you feel when you look at my grandfather's painting of the rooster?"

The sides of Li-ying's mouth curved up. "Yes."

"Well, that's how you make me feel."

Li-ying blinked. "Oh. That's a nice thing to say. Thank you, Wen-shan."

"I mean it."

The three friends stood and Jun-jai folded the blanket. As

they walked back to the tram, Wen-shan thought about how lucky she was to have her friends. She wanted to believe what Jun-jai said about Secretary Zhang's wife being a good person. It would be nice for her mother to have an influential friend.

● ● ●

Wen-shan had made noodles with deep-fried yellow fish for dinner, and her uncle had taken three helpings. It had put him in such a good mood that he helped her with the dishes before they went into the front room together.

"Let's not read a letter tonight," he said as he sat down in his chair. "What do you say we just look at a painting?"

"Yes, I'd like that." She was glad to not read a letter. Thoughts from her afternoon conversation with her friends were still bumping around in her head. She went to the cupboard. Only four paintings left to open. She chose one and brought it to her uncle. "Only three more after this one."

He nodded and glanced around at the paintings on the walls. "Look how they've filled up our home." He stood and un-tied the ribbon. A stand of bamboo graced the unfolding page. Brilliant green poles of bamboo with branches reaching skyward were sporting hundreds of slender leaves in myriad shades of green. Wen-shan imagined a playful wind making the leaves dance. There were a few luscious golden leaves peeking from behind the green and the contrast of colors made the stand of bamboo appear all the more real.

Wen-shan was delighted, and she stepped closer to touch the bamboo. Then she paused. "What's that?"

"What?"

"There's something under your fingers at the top."

"It's nothing important, Wen-shan."

"Uncle, what is it?"

"I didn't want you to see." He slowly moved his fingers and exposed a small photograph.

Wen-shan stepped back. "That's Mao Tse-tung."

He nodded.

She stared at the photograph. "Uncle, this is the painting. The painting we just read about."

"Yes."

It was getting hard to breathe. "Please take that thing off."

"Wen-shan . . ."

"Please take it off, Uncle. Will it come off?" She stepped forward. "Take it off! Take it off!"

"You take it off," he said in a soft voice.

She snagged a corner of the image and pulled. The photograph ripped in half. She dug at the other corner and pulled the remaining paper from her grandfather's painting. She tore the pieces into bits and dropped them onto the floor.

Her uncle held out the scroll to her. "Here, you hold the painting while I get the hammer and nail."

Wen-shan took the scroll without speaking. When her uncle returned, she was standing in the same position. He hammered the nail in its place and hung the painting between the rooster and the sparrows. "Now they will have some shade."

"I don't understand, Uncle. Why would Grandfather paint such a beautiful painting for Mao Tse-tung?"

Her uncle looked at her, and then back to the healthy green bamboo. "I am sure it was not done for Mao Tse-tung. You see, bamboo is a symbol of survival in a storm. It is flexible. When the winds come, it bends without breaking." He ran his fingers over the delicate leaves of the painting. "I think he painted it for your mother."

Notes

"Peace in the world": The teachings of Confucius are connected to the practicality of life and how a person can use his life to make life better.

Tiananmen Square: The public square in Peking's central government compound was designed by Mao and is an excellent example of his dislike of gardens. It is a huge flat square without grass, trees, or bushes. Mao is quoted as saying, "Get rid of most gardeners."

Self-criticism: Mao taught that self-criticism was a necessary activity each citizen must practice. They were to criticize even the smallest fault in themselves which might have them questioning the government, its policies, and most importantly their leader, Chairman Mao.

Deception for survival: All the people of China became very good at double speak.

Chapter 18

1966

OUR LITTLE FAMILY GOES *to the canteen to get our piece of bread and bowl of fish broth. While we are waiting, a party official goes down the line, handing each of us a red book and a picture of Mao Tse-tung. We are told we must hang the picture in our house. Wen-shan reaches out to give the picture back because we always tell her not to take anything from anyone. My father catches her hand as the party official gives her an angry look.*

"She only wants a bigger picture," my father says. "This one is so small, and she loves Chairman Mao."

The party official scowls at her. "This is the only size. Don't be greedy." He calls out loudly to everyone and says, "This is the only size! Don't be greedy." He holds up the red book. "This is the red book of Mao Tse-tung thought!

*You will carry it with you. You will read it every morning
and every night at your neighborhood meeting."*

*I watch as many people rub their hands across
the cover, while others flip through the pages, perhaps
wondering what the characters mean. Some of the older
uncles and aunties place the small red book prominently
on the table in front of them. They do not want trouble.*

*My friend Kuan-yin comes to sit by us as we eat. In
her eyes there is news, but she waits for the right moment to
speak. She asks what we think of the book and the picture.
Father says we have all had pictures of Chairman Mao in
our houses for a long time. She swallows that, but presses on
about the book. She says Mao must think he's as important
as Confucius or Jesus to need his thoughts written down for
everyone to read. Father warns her to be careful of what she
says, or even thinks, but it is hard for her. Kuan-yin was
one of the top students at school, and all the teachers said
she would be the best at university studies. Now she cleans
the party offices and brings us news.*

Wen-shan's uncle stood and took his dishes to the sink.

"I would hate it if my picture was plastered everywhere,"
Wen-shan stated. "Why did Mao want to do that?"

"Because Mao was Mao."

"In school we read about the little red book, and afterwards
Mrs. Yang told us that great thinkers question everything."

"She is a good teacher."

"She is." Wen-shan looked at the letter. "Should I go on?"

"Do you have time before school?"

"I think so. There's not much more, and I don't have to
wash my hair." She found the place where she'd stopped.

*Kuan-yin tells us she had seen Secretary Zhang's
wife at the party offices the other evening and that
she had a big purple bruise on the side of her face. We
think Zhang beats her because she won't go to most of
the struggle meetings. She is not a very good wife for
him because she is not as red as she should be.*

*Wen-shan is scolded by the party official because
he caught her sitting on the photograph of Chairman
Mao. I tell him it is because she didn't want the picture
to blow away in the wind. He leaves, grumbling, and
Kuan-yin and I try very hard to keep smiles off our
faces. It would have felt good to smile.*

"I sat on the picture of Mao Tse-tung?" Wen-shan asked, beginning to giggle. "I wish I could remember that."

Her uncle chuckled too. "Knowing your personality, I don't think you did it to keep it from flying away."

"I was probably angry at the party official."

"That would be my guess. Is there more?"

Wen-shan turned the parchment over, looking for characters on the other side. "No, that's the end."

"Time to get ready for school then."

"Yes, Uncle." She rolled the parchment and took her dishes to the sink.

"Do not forget your promise to Mr. Pierpont that you would help with inventory after school."

Wen-shan brightened. "That's right! That's today."

"Don't be late."

"I'll hurry as fast as I can to the store when school ends."

She went to get ready for school, already anticipating a very good day.

● ● ●

"Ten blue pillows, ten beige, six white, eight brown—"

"Six brown, two bronze," Mr. Pierpont corrected.

"Oh. Sorry." Wen-shan corrected the error. "Six brown, two bronze."

"Good. Shall we take a little hiatus before we move on to lamps?"

"I'm fine to keep working, Mr. Pierpont."

"How glorious to be young again. Let's take pity on an old Brit, shall we? Give me fifteen minutes rest, and we'll be off and going again."

"Of course, Mr. Pierpont."

"Good. What say we grab a grape soda and go out front and watch the world go by?"

"That sounds good."

A few minutes later they were settling onto the bench. Each carried an opened bottle, and Mr. Pierpont brought along a tin of biscuits.

He sat with great drama. "Ah, this is more like it! And here's a treat for all our hard work."

Wen-shan was about to say that she didn't find the work all that hard, but she wanted to play along with his histrionics, so she talked instead about the biscuits. "I love shortbread biscuits!"

"Of course you do. That's how I got you to warm up to me when you first arrived."

"Really?"

"Oh, yes. I'd hide a biscuit somewhere in the store, and you'd have to find it."

"I remember that! Of course."

"But I don't think you ever really sufficiently covered your eyes."

"Of course not! I was five. Do five-year-olds play by the rules?"

"Quite right." He offered her the tin. "Have some biscuits."

Wen-shan took two. "Thank you, Mr. Pierpont."

"You're welcome."

"Mr. Pierpont?"

"Yes?"

"Thank you for making my uncle your partner."

Mr. Pierpont smiled broadly. "Oh, I'm thrilled. He practically runs this store anyway. I just made it official. He's a good man."

Wen-shan nodded.

"And I must say, I was glad to see you two out to church the other day."

"And I didn't even throw a fit."

"Yes, I noticed. So, how did you like it, this time around?"

"Church?"

"Yes."

"It was fine. A little different."

"A good honest answer. Not to worry. It takes time to get used to a new adventure."

She smiled and munched on her biscuit. "I was surprised how many people knew about Mr. and Mrs. Heaton when I mentioned their names."

"Indeed, they were well-liked among the early members."

"How long were they here?"

"Hmm. Let's see . . . Four or five years, I think." His brow furrowed as he thought. "Yes, about that. They came with the one little tyke, and when they left to go back to America, they had three children. Of course, they almost lost their first boy, Grant Jr., to polio while they were here."

"Really? What happened?"

"Just one day he was very ill, and then word went around to all the members that Grant Jr. was in the hospital. He was about three, if I remember correctly. Such an active little boy. Anyway, the pediatric specialist, Dr. Hsu, said it was polio. Grant Jr. was given a blessing, and we fasted and prayed, but the disease only progressed."

"That had to be terrible for them."

"It was. Oh, indeed, yes, it was. And the poor little boy just kept getting weaker. So much so that the doctor said if they couldn't find an iron lung within a few days they would probably lose him."

"What did they do?"

"Well, President Heaton searched for an iron lung, but the only one available in the mission was in Guam. It would never get here in time." Mr. Pierpont shook his head at the memory. "It got to a point that all the boy could move were his eyes."

"Poor little thing."

"A group of Chinese saints got together for a special fast. At the end of it, they sent two of their members to the hospital to check on the boy. When the Chinese members arrived at the hospital, they found Sister Heaton there alone. President Heaton had been at the hospital all night, but when his wife arrived, he left for a short time to interview a couple of newly arriving missionaries. Sister Heaton told Minnie and me later that the two Chinese members didn't speak any English, but she thought she understood that they wanted to pray for Grant Jr. She told them they could, and the two knelt by his bed and prayed. She said they stood up from the prayer, watched Grant Jr. for a few minutes, and then bowed and left. Sister Heaton said that Grant Jr.'s eyes were open and moving, so she went out to the small refrigerator in the hallway to get some Jell-O. She said she just wanted to get something to slide down his throat and give him nourishment. As she was turning from the refrigerator, the swinging door of his room opened and Grant Jr. came running out to her."

Wen-shan felt tears press at the back of her eyes. "How is that possible?"

"Plain and simple, it was a miracle."

"But there's no such thing."

"Really? Tell that to Grant Jr. He'd be what, eighteen now?"

"But . . ."

"Wen-shan, I saw the boy with my own eyes afterwards. He did not suffer one ill effect from the disease."

"It could have just been that the disease was going away on its own."

"Well, Dr. Hsu said he could not comprehend what had happened. Medically, Grant Jr. should have died."

Wen-shan was silent for several moments. "I . . . I just find it hard to believe."

"Of course, Wen-shan. It takes time to learn to navigate new waters."

A scooter went by and Wen-shan followed its journey with a longing gaze.

"I can see that you would probably like to navigate your way around on a scooter."

She was glad for the change of topic. "Yes. I would."

Mr. Pierpont finished his grape soda. "You wouldn't find it frightening?"

"After riding in the truck with Patrick?"

Mr. Pierpont chuckled. "I see your point." They watched the scooter disappear around the corner. "I'm afraid I'm made for the more quiet life. Give me cricket, the ballet, or a stroll in an art gallery." He selected a shortbread biscuit. "Speaking of which, any new painting to report?"

Wen-shan nodded. "Yes, actually."

Mr. Pierpont turned to her expectantly.

"My grandfather painted this beautiful stand of bamboo. It looked like you could walk right into it."

"Lovely."

"Except there was something about it that wasn't lovely."

"Really? What was that?"

"There was a picture of Mao Tse-tung glued to the top."

"That had to be a shock."

"I pulled it off."

"Very forthright of you, I must say."

"I didn't want his photograph on my grandfather's beautiful picture." She finished her soda. "Did you know that Mao Tse-tung ordered the torture and murder of my teacher's parents?"

"How do you know that?"

"My teacher saw it happen."

Mr. Pierpont lowered his head. "Oh, my."

"I don't understand, Mr. Pierpont. If God is so powerful and can make the Heaton's boy better, why couldn't he save Mrs. Yang's parents? Why can't He just make evil people get sick and die?"

"Well, Mao Tse-tung is dead, isn't he?"

Wen-shan hesitated. "Yes, but he caused a lot of suffering before he died. My mother wrote about people starving and people being sent away from their families and artists tortured."

"I don't have an answer for you, Wen-shan, other than to acknowledge that there is good and evil in the world, and that perhaps, at times, it seems evil is winning." He patted her hand. "But I know in the end, good will prevail."

"That's what Mahatma Gandhi said—that in the end, tyrants will fall."

"I think we can trust that."

She nodded. "It doesn't help much for right now though, does it?"

"No, I suppose not."

Wen-shan looked out at the passing traffic. But she wanted things to be better now. She shook her head. She couldn't understand it. It was all too complicated. She stood. "We should be getting back to work, Mr. Pierpont."

He smiled at her. "Absolutely! Right you are. Those lamps are not going to count themselves."

They moved back into the store, and Wen-shan was glad for the counting and sorting. She was only fifteen and didn't want to think about anything more serious than outings with her friends and possible adventures on a scooter bike.

Notes

Communal canteens: During the Great Leap Forward, individual cooking was eliminated and all eating was done in a communal canteen.

The cult of Mao: During the Cultural Revolution, the propaganda to enhance the cult of Mao was expanded. Pictures of Mao were everywhere, and badges bearing the Chairman's picture were worn by most citizens. It's estimated that some 4.8 billion badges with Chairman Mao's image were manufactured.

The Little Red Book: Compiled in 1964, this book entitled *Quotations from Chairman Mao* eventually grew to contain 33 topics and 427 quotations, with a total printing of 1,055,498,000 copies (from 1964 to 1976). During the latter half of Mao's rule, it was an unofficial requirement for every Chinese citizen to own, read, and carry the book at all times. This was especially true during the Cultural Revolution. The Ministry of Culture, under the direction of the CCCP, stated that their goal was for "ninety-nine percent" (of the population of China) to read Chairman Mao's book.

Healing of Grant Heaton Jr.: The healing of Grant Heaton Jr. is a true occurrence and is documented by both his mother and his father.

第十九章

Chapter 19

1966

TODAY IN THE SQUARE I WATCHED *as Red
Guards punished the brother of Ming-mei for
being too foreign in his dress. He was sent down from
Peking to be taught the ways of the farmer, and he was
being harassed by the Red Guards because he was not
wearing the wide pants and the round-toed cloth shoe
of the peasant. Secretary Zhang and Ming-mei stood to
the side as three male guards shoved him around and the
broad-faced female guard yelled insults.*

*"What? What are you doing in those pointed shoes
and pants that are not wide enough? Are you a running
dog for the capitalists? Take out your scissors, comrades,
and cut those pants! Rip them to the knee! We will do
our job! We are in charge of killing the four olds! Cut*

up his expensive shoes too! We do not want anything of the foreign evil! We need only the words of our great leader, Chairman Mao!"

Those of us standing around felt sorry for the young man's shame as the guards laid him on his back, stripped off his shoes, and carried out their orders. Ming-mei stood silently beside her husband seeming not to care, but when the female guard slapped her brother, I saw her hands turn into fists. The brother ran away, and the female guard called out more insults. "Look, look! He is a running dog for the capitalists!"

I recognized her—Han Yen-sui. It was odd because when we were in school together she never spoke a word. Learning was difficult for her. She always stared at the teachers with blank eyes when they asked her a question. She went about with her head lowered, and the boys made fun of her. They called her mouse and pulled her long thick braids. Now her hair is short and her voice is loud.

Mrs. Yang stared directly at Wen-shan when she looked up from the parchment. "Thank you for reading that, Wen-shan. Your mother paints a vivid picture of cruelty."

"Yes, ma'am." She rolled the scroll. "Mrs. Yang, I don't understand what the Red Guards were trying to do."

"They thought they were doing the work of the revolution. They were going to move the socialist ideals forward. They were young people caught up with Mao Tse-tung thought."

"But how did they get started?"

"I have met with teachers who fled China after Mao Tse-tung died. They said it began with a select group of young people in Peking—children of party officials in the Central Committee. Mao told them they did not have to respect their teachers, that they should seek out counterrevolutionaries even in their own families, and that they should destroy anything that was capitalistic or that distinguished someone as upper-class."

"Like a pair of pants?"

"Or books, or art, or higher education."

Wen-shan felt light-headed, and she put her head in her hands.

"Are you all right?"

She nodded and looked up. "It just sounds very frightening."

"It became frightening very quickly. Can you imagine high school and college students stirred up to do Mao's bidding? He loved chaos, and chaos is what the Red Guards gave him. They smashed up their schools and beat their teachers."

"No, they didn't."

"Yes, Wen-shan, they did. Many young people were thrilled to exercise their power over adults. One of the teachers I met from Shanghai said she quoted a passage from Shakespeare one day and her students beat her with their red books and ran her out of the classroom. One boy threw a rock at her and said she was showing honor to someone other than Chairman Mao."

The color drained from Wen-shan's face. "But we have always been taught to respect our elders."

"Which is what Mao Tse-tung wanted to destroy. He wanted the young people to follow only him, to love only him. One of the slogans for the Red Guards was 'We can soar to heaven, and pierce the earth, because our Great Leader Chairman Mao is our supreme commander!' Mao used them like pawns." She turned to look at the bulletin board of great thinkers. "Do you know what Lenin called young people?"

"I don't."

"Useful idiots." She looked back to Wen-shan. "Not such a great thought."

Wen-shan shook her head. She was trying to imagine young people beating their teacher. She looked at Mrs. Yang's gentle brown eyes and felt sick to her stomach at the thought of one of her classmates raising a hand to harm her. "How many Red Guards were there?"

"No one knows for sure. I understand that thousands of people, perhaps a million, joined in Peking and from there it spread to the entire country. Mao even encouraged the Red Guards to travel around the country to meet with other Red Guards. They were to be given free passage on any train. He wanted them to share methods for routing out the 'four olds.'"

"What does that mean?"

"Mao wanted to destroy old ideas, old culture, old customs, old habits. His lawless Red Guards broke into people's houses and tore up books and destroyed pieces of art."

Wen-shan thought of her grandfather's exquisite paintings. "Did Mao think that was going to make people's lives better?"

Mrs. Yang walked over, sat down on the other side of Wen-shan's desk, and took her hands. "Wen-shan, do you think Mao Tse-tung was concerned with making people's lives better?"

Wen-shan felt nauseous as she thought about the murder of Mrs. Yang's parents in Yan'an. She shook her head. "No, ma'am."

"So why do you think he did it?"

"Power."

Mrs. Yang took her hands away. "That's exactly what I

think. He lost power because of his failed policies. Don't you think the failure of the Great Leap caused many in the party to question his leadership?"

"Yes."

"That's exactly what it did. For a time, Mao was held back, but like a mad dog in a muzzle, I think he spent every waking minute trying to get back into full power and punish those who made him step down. Mao was out to get rid of anyone who would stand up to him, and he used another purge to do just that."

"How?"

"By calling it the Great Proletariat Cultural Revolution, he made it seem like the people were the ones rooting out the evil counterrevolutionaries, that the Red Guards were the heroes, destroying the old culture and establishing a new socialist order."

"But they weren't."

"No. It was chaos Mao wanted, and the chaos hid the fact that he was having perceived party enemies, intellectuals, and artists thrown into detention centers, beaten, tortured, and executed. He even got his wife, Jiang Qing, involved. She became the leader of the Red Guard activities, and she was ruthless."

"How do you know all this?"

"Facts are beginning to come out as refugees talk about their experiences. I am only fitting little pieces together."

Wen-shan nodded. It would be just like Mrs. Yang to fit little pieces together.

Mrs. Yang gently picked up the letter. "Your mother is one of those voices, Wen-shan. She is writing down the truth." She handed Wen-shan the scroll. "Thank you for sharing this with me." She stood. "Do you have any more questions?"

"I always have questions, but I can keep some until later."

"Very well then. Have a good weekend."

"Thank you, Mrs. Yang . . . for everything." Wen-shan picked up her schoolbag and headed for the door.

"And, Wen-shan?"

"Yes?"

"Remember what Mahatma Gandhi said about tyrants."

"In the end they always fall."

"Always."

Notes

Great Proletariat Cultural Revolution: The Cultural Revolution was Mao's major campaign from 1966 to 1976 to get rid of all dissidents and revisionists in the CCCP under the guise of the people breaking apart the shackles of an old culture.

Red Guards: The Red Guards were a loosely structured organization of high school and college students from "red" family backgrounds. They were ardent followers of Mao and became his machine for chaos during the Cultural Revolution. Millions of young adults joined Red Guard groups during the years of the Cultural Revolution.

Four olds: During the Cultural Revolution, Mao decreed that these "four olds" must be abolished: old ideas, old culture, old customs, old habits.

"Running dog for the Capitalists": Anyone sympathetic with or in agreement with any tenet of capitalism was labeled with this derogatory title.

Juang Qing: Mao's fourth wife. Mao put her in charge of the Small Group—the office that dealt with the Great Purge. She joined Mao in his personal vendettas and helped him discredit and destroy his enemies. During the Cultural Revolution, she was associated with Zhang Chungiao, Wang Hongwen, and Yao Wen-yuan. They were known as the "Gang of Four," a tight-knit political faction that used extreme and cruel measures to accomplish their goals. She was arrested shortly after Mao's death for crimes committed by the "Gang of Four." In the courtroom she said, "I was Mao's dog. Whoever Chairman Mao asked me to bite, I bit."

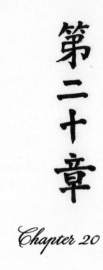

Chapter 20

W EN-SHAN TOOK HER TIME choosing the chopsticks she would place on the table. The serving bowls
sat ready to receive the food, and the house was cleaned to sparkling. Now she checked the food for the tenth time and went to
look out the window. There was a spot of dirt on the glass, and
she ran to get a paper napkin to clean it. She was breathing on
the window as she saw the taxi pull up in front of the half-moon
arch. She quickly rubbed the spot as her uncle got out of the
taxi and went around to open the opposite door. Master Quan
emerged and Wen-shan's stomach did a little flip. She ran to the
cupboard and tossed the napkin in the trash can. She took one
last look around the room as she heard the footsteps on the front
porch. The door opened and Master Quan shuffled in. He was
dressed in his scholar's robes and walked with a simple black
cane. Her uncle came behind, looking much like a mother bird
protecting its chick.

Wen-shan stepped forward and bowed. "Welcome to our home, Master Quan."

He grinned broadly, which made his eyes crinkle. He bowed too. "Thank you for inviting me. I smell many good smells."

"I hope so."

"This way, Master," her uncle said, guiding his teacher toward the kitchen. "Our home is small, so we eat in the kitchen."

"It is better," Master Quan said as he slowly made his way forward. "That means you are closer to the food."

Wen-shan giggled. "That is wise thinking."

As they passed the painting of the cypress tree, Master Quan stopped and focused on the picture. After several minutes, his gaze moved to the other hangings. He studied each without speaking. Finally he made a small turn to the right and saw the calligraphy. He pushed himself a little taller with his cane. A sound rumbled from low in his chest, and Wen-shan watched as tears washed his face. "Ah, I was a fortunate teacher."

"And I a fortunate brother."

"Yes."

Master Quan slumped a little, and her uncle held his arms. "Are you ready to sit and have a nice dinner?" her uncle asked.

Master Quan used his sleeve to dry his face. "Yes. After seeing that powerful writing I could eat a dragon!"

Her uncle took him to the kitchen and held the chair as Master Quan sat down. Wen-shan went to dish up the food. She had patterned the dinner after the one she'd eaten at Auntie Ting's, although she couldn't quite manage the pork knuckles. As she set the vegetables in sesame sauce, spring rolls, fried fish, cashew chicken, and rice on the lazy Susan in the middle of the table, Master Quan clapped his hands like a child and made excited comments.

"Look at the color of sauce. So beautiful. Like a Guilin sunset. The fish look like they are just caught. Very fresh. I have not seen vegetables like that since my mother cooked them for me."

Wen-shan was overwhelmed with all the praise and sat down a little out of breath.

"We say a prayer before we eat," her uncle said. "If that is all right with you, Master Quan?"

Master Quan beamed. "I like prayers!"

· Her uncle's blessing on the food that night added in words of gratitude for Master Quan and his bravery in bringing the jade dragon box to them.

When Wen-shan said her amen to the prayer, she really meant it.

They dished themselves the foods they wanted and, as dinner progressed, it seemed to Wen-shan that the lazy Susan went around and around many times.

Master Quan ate and talked with great enjoyment. "So, have you learned much from your mother's letters, Wen-shan?"

"We have, Master Quan, though much of it is very sad."

He nodded as he picked up a few more leeks with his chopsticks. "There was not much good news in China."

"No."

"But perhaps things will get better now."

"We can pray," her uncle said. He put more fish on top of his rice and gave Master Quan a searching look. "I cannot imagine how you escaped, Master Quan. It was difficult for me and Mei-lan. I cannot think what it was like for . . ."

"For someone as old as me?" Master Quan chuckled.

"You have hidden strength, that is all I can say."

"I would love to hear the story," Wen-shan encouraged.

"Of course. Of course," the old scholar said happily. "For

this dinner I would tell many stories! But Mr. and Mrs. Smythe have the main story to tell; they have much strength and intelligence. Like two clever monkeys."

"How did you meet them?" Wen-shan asked.

"They came to Guilin in 1930s to look for art."

"For the museum?"

"Oh, no. This long time before museum. They were young couple with much money. They own fancy Asian import business in London." Master Quan became reflective. "When things got very bad in Guilin, they snuck word that they were going to get me out."

Wen-shan's stomach clenched at the words, "very bad in Guilin."

"They must have some powerful contacts," her uncle stated.

Master Quan's head bobbed several times, and he gave them a meaningful grin. "Yes, but still they take big chance." He leaned forward. "One day an important official came from the Central Committee. He had much power and we were all afraid. He came to our university and ordered we hand over art pieces we were hiding from Red Guards. He was going to torture one of the teachers because no one would talk. I make decision. I order the art treasures brought out. One of the treasures is your jade dragon box."

Wen-shan was stunned. *How did our box ever get out of the grasp of the government official?* she wondered, but before she could ask, Master Quan went on with the story.

"The official was very angry. He put art pieces into truck. Then he beat me and put me into truck too."

"Oh, no! Oh, Master Quan!"

Master Quan patted her hand. "Not to worry. He beat me only a little bit to make it look good."

"What do you mean?"

Master Quan grinned. "This official was paid lots of money by smart monkey couple to get me out of China."

Wen-shan sat back in her chair. "The Smythes arranged it?"

Master Quan nodded. "After we drive for many hours, the truck stops, and governmental official dumps me out."

"In the middle of nowhere?"

Master Quan chuckled. "No. In the middle of airfield. Monkey couple is sending small plane to fly me out." His expression turns sober. "There was only one bit of trouble."

"What?"

"The official did not want me to take jade dragon box. He said he was told he could keep all the treasures."

"Oh, no."

"I tell him that monkey couple will never do business with him again if he does not let me take box."

Her uncle shook his head. "You were very brave, Master Quan."

"Ah, but I know the government official very greedy. He wants to do business."

Wen-shan leaned forward. "So he gave you the box?"

"Yes."

"And the plane came and flew you to Hong Kong."

"To secret airfield in New Territories. Mrs. Smythe pick me up in jeep."

"I wish I could meet her," Wen-shan said.

"Yes. She is amazing woman."

"And your story is remarkable, Master," her uncle said.

Master Quan's grin widened so that his eyes crinkled. "It is good story, yes?"

"Yes."

"But what I don't understand is how you had the box when the official came to the university," Wen-shan questioned.

"I went to hidden room under your family shrine and took the box. That is what your grandfather tell me to do if things were very bad for the family."

"What do you mean, very bad?"

Master Quan studied her face. "Have you finished reading letters yet?"

"No, not yet."

The Master's expression softened, but he shook his head. "Then I must not tell you. That is story for your mother to tell. Just know that I hide box away with other art pieces."

Wen-shan resigned herself to the fact that no other information about her family would be coming from Master Quan.

"And now, if you're finished with dinner, Master, we would like you to join us as we open another of my brother's paintings," her uncle said.

Master Quan's head bobbed. "Oh, I would be so honored. So honored." He went to stand and Wen-shan's uncle helped him. He asked to use the washroom, and as her uncle showed him the way, Wen-shan cleared the dishes from the table and put away the extra food.

Wen-shan smiled as she overheard a comment from Master Quan as he was coming back from the washroom. "So different from Chinese toilets. But better different, I think." She turned off the lights in the kitchen and joined the two men in the front room. Master Quan was sitting in her uncle's chair while her uncle sat on the sofa.

"Wen-shan, would you please bring a painting?"

"Yes, Uncle." She went to the cupboard and picked up one

of the last three paintings. She handed it to her uncle. "Only two left." He nodded.

As her uncle unrolled the scroll, Master Quan leaned forward. It was another magical scene of Guilin. The horizontal painting showed the Li River meandering through the stunning green peaks. The blue water curved around a crescent shoal of flat land that pushed up against the feet of the soaring cliffs.

"I know that place," Master Quan whispered. He cleared his throat. "First time I see Yellow Cloth Shoal, I am eight. I take boat ride with my family." He pointed to the mountains. "See these seven peaks?" Wen-shan nodded. "They are the seven fairies. Would you like me to tell their story?"

"Yes. I would love to hear a story."

Master Quan gazed at the beautiful painting as though magic was pouring out of it. "Seven fairies went to the king of the fairy court. They had decided they wanted to see what earth was like. The fairy king told them they would not like the earth. It was barren and filled with brutish beasts called humans. He told them they should stay in the fairy kingdom. The fairies were sure that they must go to earth and see for themselves. Finally the king gave his permission, and the seven friends dropped out of the sky and landed on the Yellow Cloth Shoal. They looked at the peaceful blue river, they walked along the beautiful yellow shoal of land, and they danced with the mist as it played among the heavenly mountains. They even dabbled their feet in the river and watched a kindly old fisherman paddling his boat. The fairies were so infatuated by the scene that they did not listen when the fairy king told them to return. They said they wanted to stay longer. The fairy king was angry that they liked earth better than his kingdom, so he granted their wish to stay longer by turning them into seven beautiful stone hills."

Master Quan pointed to each of the hills again, and Wen-shan smiled. "That is a good story, Master Quan. I can see why the fairies wanted to stay."

"Ah, yes. And I could stay gazing at this picture all night, but I am old, and sleep is calling."

Her uncle stood. "I will call the taxi."

• • •

Master Quan was helped to the taxi by both Wen-shan and her uncle. He thanked Wen-shan many times for the dinner, and both of them for sharing the paintings with him. Her uncle told her not to wait up because it would be late by the time he took Master Quan all the way to the Smythes' home in Kowloon and then returned.

Wen-shan went back into the house smiling with the satisfaction of a good evening. She had been nervous about the dinner, but all went well. She drew her fingers across the seven hills of the Yellow Cloth Shoal and thought about the look of wonder on Master Quan's face. It was a miracle that he had been able to get the jade dragon box to them. Her grandfather's paintings were hanging here because of Master Quan's bravery. She frowned as she thought about his daring escape. What had happened to all the other irreplaceable art pieces taken away by that greedy government official? How much of China's art had been lost or destroyed through the years?

She pulled her eyes away from her grandfather's painting and went to the kitchen to finish the cleanup. It was nice to have company. For ten years she could remember only one or two other people being inside their home, but now, with the arrival of the jade dragon box, there seemed to be a constant stream of visitors.

NOTES

Protecting art: Many people hid art during the Cultural Revolution to save it from destruction by the Red Guards. As one example of the level of destruction, in 1958 there were 6,843 monuments still standing in Peking. In the summer of 1966, 4,922 were obliterated.

Chinese versus American toilets: A Western toilet has a base upon which to sit. A Chinese toilet is simply a hole in the ground.

第二十一章

Chapter 21

S HE STOOD ON THE HUNDRED Flower Bridge with
Nui Gui. The ghost was silent and beautiful; her long silver
hair blew in the wind, and in her pearly white hand she carried
a red fan. Wen-shan looked away from her and down into the
dark water. The shimmering face of Shui Gui peered up and
beckoned her to come to the water's edge. His voice was cold
and pitiless, but his cunning words made the water tempting.
Her body swayed forward and small hands pressed at her back.
She felt her body fall, and she grabbed for the rough stones of
the bridge. She did not want to sink into the cold dark water
with Emperor Chan Lee! She did not want to feel the clammy
hands of Shui Gui pulling her down to drink the dark water!

Her body jerked awake, and Wen-shan found herself on her
bedroom floor with a very sore side and elbow. She groaned.

Suddenly the hall light was turned on and her uncle was at her door.

"Wen-shan, what happened?" He came to her side. "Are you all right?"

"I fell out of bed." She got onto her knees and he helped her to stand. "I . . . I think I'm all right."

"What happened? Did you have your nightmare again?"

"It was a nightmare, but not my normal one. Anyway, I'm sorry I woke you up."

"Don't worry. It was almost time to get up anyway."

Wen-shan rubbed her elbow. "Ouch."

"Come. Let's put an ice pack on that, and I'll make you a cup of chamomile tea." He helped her on with her bathrobe and the two trudged out to the kitchen. "Do you want cornflakes?"

She smiled. "No. Too early. The tea sounds good though."

"It will calm you."

"What I really need is shark soup to help me be strong against those stupid ghosts."

Her uncle put on the kettle. "Another ghost dream?"

She sat at the kitchen table. "Yes, but in this one Shui Gui was after me."

"Oh, he is a bad ghost."

"Yes, and I'm afraid of the water."

"See, I told you you should have taken swimming lessons."

"It's not too late. Maybe I'll sign up." Wen-shan yawned and looked at the pale sky outside the kitchen window. "I wish I could figure out what all these ghost dreams mean, especially the one with the rain. I hate that one."

Her uncle handed her an ice pack. "Maybe we can say a prayer and give the house a blessing."

"What? A blessing for a house?"

"Yes, we can ask for a better spirit to come in."

"Like the Buddhist teaching of sweeping the house with brooms to sweep out all the evil spirits?"

Her uncle smiled. "Not exactly like that." He put the tea leaves in the container. "I will ask Mr. Pierpont how to do it."

Wen-shan gingerly changed the position of the ice pack. "Uncle?"

"Yes?"

"The other day when I was helping with inventory, Mr. Pierpont told me the story of the Heaton's little boy. The time he had polio."

"Oh, yes. I remember that."

"Do you think it was a miracle?"

"How else can you explain it, Wen-shan? One minute he can't move, and the next he's running to his mother."

"But things like that don't happen."

"We all saw the boy when he was well."

"Maybe his body just got better."

"Well, that would have been amazing enough, right?"

"Yes, but it wouldn't be because somebody prayed and then God made him better."

"Is that what's bothering you? You're not sure there is such a thing as God?"

The teakettle started whistling, and her uncle lifted it off the stove. He poured the water into the teapot and replaced the lid. He turned to look at her.

"I'm not sure."

"It's good not to be sure. To know you do not know a thing is the beginning of true wisdom."

Wen-shan smiled. "I think it's funny how you can believe in God and Confucius at the same time."

Her uncle smiled back. "Confucius has perfect philosophies. God has perfect answers."

"You really believe there is a God?"

"Yes."

"Who lives in heaven?"

"Yes."

"But where is heaven?"

Her uncle brought the cups to the table and poured the tea. "Now you sound like Yan and Ya Ya."

Wen-shan laughed at herself. "I do, don't I?"

"It is good to ask questions, Wen-shan, but some questions are more important than others. Does it really matter where God lives?"

Wen-shan sipped her hot tea. "I guess not."

"What would be an important question?"

She tried to think of an important question. After a while she shrugged her shoulders. "I don't know."

"Does God watch over us or not?"

Wen-shan thought about the suffering of her family in Guilin, of Mrs. Yang's suffering, of all the people killed in China. "No."

"No?"

"If there is a God, He doesn't watch over us very well. There are too many terrible things that happen."

Her uncle sipped his tea. "Are there good things in the world?"

Images began flooding into Wen-shan's mind: the picnic with her friends, her grandfather's paintings, Mrs. Yang's bulletin board, riding in the delivery truck with Mr. Pierpont, and Master Quan's smile. "Yes, there are many good things."

"So, does God exist because there are good things, or does He not exist because there are bad things?"

"You're making my brain hurt."

"Good, that means you are thinking."

"But, if there is a God, why does He let so many bad things happen?"

"Why do *men* let so many bad things happen?" He drank his tea. "Confucius taught that social or political power does not belong to a tyrant who inherits it, but to the person of right thinking who honors it."

"'If there is rightness in the heart, there will be beauty in the character.'"

Her uncle smiled. "And that will lead to?"

"'Order in the nation and peace in the world.'"

"It looks like someone has put their feet on the path of the Way."

Wen-shan blushed at the compliment. "It's . . . it's just that Jun-jai asked me about peace the other day."

"I knew I liked him."

Wen-shan poured them both more tea. "How did you start believing in God, Uncle?"

His look turned somber, and he was silent for such a long time that Wen-shan was afraid he'd gone back to his old ways of not talking to her. She was just about to tell him he didn't need to answer, when he spoke.

"What is hanging above our family shrine?"

"Grandfather's calligraphy."

"And what does it say?"

"Truth."

"This is what I owe you, Wen-shan. I owe you the truth, though it will bring pain to both of us."

Her heart beat faster as though expecting pain at any moment. "Then don't tell me, Uncle. I don't need to know." She wished she hadn't asked the question.

"No. It's time. My life has been closed for too long, and I don't want that anymore." He looked at the poem he had written out, and then back to Wen-shan. "When your great-aunt Mei-lan and I arrived in Hong Kong, we were sent to the relief workers in charge of the refugee camps. They found a shack for us to live in. It was just a couple of pieces of rusty tin and a few boards. It wasn't even half the size of this kitchen. We had two stools, a wok cooker, and our platform bed with a thin, dirty mattress."

Wen-shan's stomach churned as she thought about her aunt and uncle living in such a place.

"There was no work and very little food—just rice and sometimes cabbage. The man who lived next to us was a scientist from Shanghai. In Kowloon, he worked lashing together bamboo poles for scaffolding. I found a few jobs like that, but it was never enough. Every day we would go out looking for jobs, looking for food, hoping for a handout." His voice strangled in his throat, and Wen-shan knew he was fighting back his emotion. "There never was a way out."

"Oh, Uncle."

"I could not support us. My Mei-lan . . . Mei-lan was forced to beg just to keep us alive." The tears flowed freely now. "We lived like that for six years."

Wen-shan cried with him.

"Then we were told we were being evicted from our shack because we couldn't pay . . . we couldn't pay. I was ashamed." He looked directly at her, and Wen-shan saw years of anguish on his face. "I could not take care of us. I was so ashamed, I tried to take my life."

"Oh, Uncle." Wen-shan moaned, taking his hands. "Oh, Uncle."

He couldn't talk for several minutes, but finally he calmed. He wiped the tears on his sleeve and stilled his breathing. "Mei-lan found me. I was still alive. She ran out into the alley screaming for help, but no one came. No one would help her. Then at the end of the alley, she saw two young men and they were running to her. They were missionaries for the Mormon Church."

Wen-shan stared at him. She couldn't find any words to express her astonishment.

"They bound up my wrists and took me to where I could get help. They saved my life." He wiped his eyes on a napkin. "At the hospital, Mei-lan kept saying over and over that it was a miracle . . . a miracle."

Wen-shan's heart could find no other explanation. It *was* a miracle. No wonder her uncle didn't question the healing of the Heaton's little boy.

"I'm sorry, Wen-shan. I should have had more courage."

"Please, Uncle, don't. No one can judge you. How can anyone know what your life was like?"

"Do you mean that?"

"Yes."

Tears leaked from his eyes again, and he took her hand. "I'm sorry for not treating you better. So many years I was distant from you. After Mei-lan died, I shut off from everyone. I'm sorry. So sorry."

Wen-shan could only nod.

● ● ●

They didn't go to work or school that day. They took the ferry to Kowloon where they walked the streets, looked in store windows, and talked about trivial things. They ate snake soup and wandered through an antique furniture store. Her uncle bought her a small porcelain statue of a French farm girl carrying a big basket of fruit. Wen-shan knew exactly the shelf in her bedroom where she would place it.

There were times when her uncle became quiet, and Wen-shan worried that he was reliving that horrible day, but then his expression would relax and he'd make a comment about the price of something or ask her opinion about a Western product with which he was unfamiliar.

She also spent quiet moments thinking about miracles and missionaries, of Red Guards smashing art and tearing up books, of the Heaton boy running to his mother. She thought about her mother and grandfather in Guilin. If there was a God, she hoped He would watch out for them.

On the ferry back to Hong Kong Island, even though the wind had picked up and the water was rough, Wen-shan and her uncle stood out on the deck watching the boats navigate the whitecaps. Her hair whipped about her face, and they both clung to the railing, but neither of them moved from their spots until the ferry docked at Central.

NOTE

Farm girl statue: The basket of fruit that the porcelain statue of the farm girl is holding is a lucky symbol meaning prosperity.

第二十二章

Chapter 22

1966

M RS. LIN HAS JUMPED *from Fubo Hill.*
Her broken body lies like a discarded rag on the
rocks beneath. Her daughter Kuan-yin is my only friend.
She gave me yellow Ginkgo leaves to hold on my marriage
day. Now my husband is gone, and my friend's mother is
with her ancestors. When Kuan-yin and I were girls, we
would go to her house and her gentle mother would ask us
about school and give us almond cookies. Mrs. Lin always
asked about school because she was a great teacher. She
taught math and science at the senior school. She received
honors for her great teaching. Her students won many
awards and went on to the university.

Then the Red Guards came to the school and yelled
at the students.

"All of your teachers are four olds! You do not need
to respect them. You do not need to listen to them. They
have given some of you awards. This is not good. Our
great leader, Chairman Mao, says this only divides us.
We all must be equal! Listen to the wisdom of our great
leader. Now you must write da-zi-bao against your
misguided teachers. You must write the big posters and
hang them like laundry in the school yard for all the
world to see!"

The big poster against Mrs. Lin was written in bold
red characters and accused her of being in love with her
favorite student.

The shame of that lie took her to the hill.

Wen-shan looked over at her uncle. His gaze was fixed on
his brother's painting of the stand of bamboo. "Their world was
turned upside down."

"I wonder how many people suffered because of lies," Wen-
shan said.

"I can understand desperation and shame," her uncle said,
standing and moving to the painting. "What I cannot understand is how an entire generation can be so brainwashed in the
cult of Mao Tse-tung that they rebel against thousands of years
of culture."

"They were young." Wen-shan ran her fingers along the
characters. "Mrs. Yang said that the Communists called young
people 'useful idiots.'" She sighed. "I don't know. Maybe they
thought they were helping."

Her uncle looked over at the ink painting of the cypress
tree. "My brother has to be suffering. He is such a gentle person.

I can imagine how the Communists must hate him." He turned to Wen-shan. "Is there more to the letter?"

"Yes." She read.

Father says I must stop writing my letters.
Chairman Mao is against writers and readers and
thinkers. Mao tells us we must not read anything except
the little red book. He says the more books you read,
the more stupid you become. We hear from Secretary
Zhang that many artists and writers have been sent
to the detention centers and they never come out. It
is a warning that the same thing can happen to us.
The demon Zhang encourages the Red Guards to
bang bang bang their drums and root out all the evil
counterrevolutionaries. They are so fierce that Father
is afraid for me. I am very careful, but they are like
spiders in the night. Perhaps they can hear the paper
crackle or the sound of the brush as it slides across the
paper. To them, all art except revolutionary art is
garbage. One young man who came from Peking to
be rusticated said that over four thousand monuments
from the old culture in Peking have been crushed by the
fist of our great leader. The young guard bragged that
he and some of his gang helped destroy a thousand-year-
old Confucian temple.

Her uncle slumped into his chair. "Madness. Absolute madness."

We wonder if Mao Tse-tung wants to make
the whole world ugly. I hide another of my father's

*paintings. It is of the heavenly mountains and the
peaceful river. My father wonders if Chairman Mao
will come to Guilin and order the peaks flattened and
the river emptied. Will he command away the mist
and destroy the rainbows? I have stripped away his
mask. Yet there are people who do not see him. We all
must wear badges with Mao Tse-tung's picture. Some
wear the badge proudly. Some of the young weep with
the honor. My father, Wen-shan, and I wear it only to
survive.*

Wen-shan slowly rolled the letter and tied it with its ribbon.
"Uncle?"

"Yes?"

"I'm afraid to read the final letters. Some of the things we've
read so far have been bad, and I don't want to read something
more horrible."

He turned from the painting. "I understand. But can you
truly say you don't want to know their fate?"

She put the letter into the drawer. "I don't know if I do."

He studied her a moment. "What else is bothering you?"

Wen-shan touched the unread letters in the drawer. "I think
in one of the next letters my mother is going to talk about sending me away."

"Ah." He nodded. "I'm sure you're right. This would be the
time." He waited to continue until she looked at him. "But don't
you want to know? You have been wondering why for a long
time, Wen-shan. Her words would give you the answer."

Wen-shan nodded and shut the drawer. "Maybe." She stood.
"I'm tired. I don't want to think about it anymore tonight."

"Of course. Go get some rest."

She leaned down and kissed him on the forehead. "Good night, Uncle."

"Good night." He reached for his scriptures.

"Oh! Did you remember that tomorrow after school I'm going to Jun-jai's table tennis game?"

"Yes, I remember. Wish him good luck from me."

"I will, Uncle."

"Perhaps the two of you would like to meet me afterwards at Xiao Nan Guo for dinner?"

"Yes. That would be very nice. Except there will be three of us. Song Li-ying will be at the match too."

"She is invited as well, of course."

"Thank you, Uncle. We can celebrate Jun-jai's win."

"So, you know the future, do you?"

"No. I just know my friend."

● ● ●

"I told my uncle that Jun-jai would win." Wen-shan switched her schoolbag to her other shoulder and looked at the traffic flowing past on the street.

"He is a very good player, isn't he?" Li-ying said.

"He is."

"And he's joining us for dinner?"

Wen-shan held Li-ying back from stepping out into the street. "Yes, but he wanted to shower in the locker room first. He also said there was a surprise he wanted to show us." The traffic stopped, and the girls crossed the street.

"This is nice of your uncle to invite us all to dinner," Li-ying said, pushing her glasses up on her nose. "I love the food at Xiao Nan Guo."

"Me too."

The restaurant came into sight, and Wen-shan waved at her uncle, who was standing in front.

"Hello, girls," he said as they approached. "Where is Wei Jun-jai?"

"He'll be here soon. He's cleaning up after the match."

"Did he win?"

"Of course. He's a very good player."

Her uncle bowed to Li-ying. "I'm so glad you could come to dinner."

Li-ying bowed. "Thank you for inviting me."

Her uncle opened the door of the restaurant and the cheering sound of voices and the clatter of dishes assaulted their ears. "I think we should find a table."

Wen-shan raised her voice to be heard. "Good idea."

The three had just gotten settled and were figuring out what they wanted to order when Wen-shan looked out the restaurant window and saw Jun-jai pull up on a black motor scooter.

"Oh, my!" She stood. "It's Jun-jai! Excuse me, Uncle." She maneuvered her way quickly to the front of the restaurant and out the door.

"Jun-jai, what is that?"

"An elephant. Don't you know an elephant when you see one?"

"Don't tease me. Is it yours?"

"It belongs to my family. My brother and I share it."

"It's wonderful!"

"Thank you. I thought you might like it."

"Did you have it at the activity center tonight?"

"I did, but I hid it away so I could surprise you."

Wen-shan touched the handlebars. "Well, you certainly did that."

The door to the restaurant opened and Li-ying came out. "Jun-jai?"

"Look, Li Li! Jun-jai has a motor scooter!"

"Is it really yours?"

"My brother and I share it. And I guess anyone else in the family who's old enough can ride it."

Wen-shan laughed. "I bet your mother would ride it. She's pretty hip."

Jun-jai laughed with her. "Everybody would have to get out of her way. My mother tried to ride a bicycle once and drove it into a tree."

Li-ying put her hand over her mouth. "Oh, dear!"

Wen-shan just laughed harder. "Well, we'd better go back inside or my uncle will think we've gone somewhere else to eat."

Jun-jai secured the scooter, and the three friends walked into the restaurant. Wen-shan's uncle stood as the three approached. He gave Jun-jai a stern look, and Wen-shan's happiness vanished. What was wrong? Had they been too noisy? Was Jun-jai dressed too hip?

Jun-jai gave her uncle a deep bow, but her uncle spoke before he could say anything.

"I do not think you can ride a scooter on the Way, Wei Jun-jai."

Jun-jai hesitated, and then his face broke into a huge smile. He bowed again. "Or perhaps it might get you along the Way faster."

Wen-shan's uncle laughed. He actually laughed.

NOTES

Da-zi-bao: During the Cultural Revolution, these large, handwritten posters were used for propaganda and to criticize, denounce, and humiliate people. Often the accusations were false.

Red writing: Something written in red is considered bad luck.

Rusticated: Many young people, especially during the Cultural Revolution, were sent from the cities to the rural areas to learn the life of the peasant.

Table tennis: Also known as Ping-Pong, table tennis is a very popular sport in Asian countries.

第
二
十
三
章

Chapter 23

THE DAYS WENT BY AND WEN-SHAN concentrated on school and her friends. Her uncle concentrated on work at the furniture store and tending the garden. Wen-shan felt more peaceful than she had at any time in her life. When her thoughts turned to Guilin or the letters from her mother, she would go to the library with Li-ying or to Victoria Peak with Jun-jai; she busied herself with helping Mr. Pierpont at the furniture store, and Mrs. Yang with school projects. Once in a while, she would catch a glimpse of her grandfather's calligraphy and feel a catch in her heart, but it was never enough to make her open the drawer and take out one of the letters. *What is truth?* Wen-shan thought of rolling the calligraphy work and putting it back in the cupboard, but she figured she'd only think about it more if she did that. *What is truth?* Truth was a dragon with claws that disturbed her sleep. For the past week her nightmares had retreated. It felt good to wake up feeling rested.

Wen-shan sat at the kitchen table eating a spring onion pan-
cake.

Her uncle came in. "I have been smelling this delicious
smell all morning."

She swallowed quickly. "I can fix you a plate, Uncle."

"Thank you, Wen-shan. I can do it. You have already done
the most important job." He sat down at the table. "What made
you cook this morning?"

"I was dreaming about pancakes and fried sticky rice all night."

Her uncle looked back to the stove. "Did I miss the sticky rice?"

Wen-shan giggled. "No. I couldn't make both so I decided
on the pancakes."

Her uncle bit into the palm-sized cake and nodded. "I am
satisfied with this. It is very good."

"Thank you, Uncle."

"Pancakes are not a bad thing to dream about."

"Except you wake up very hungry."

Her uncle smiled and continued eating.

"If you'll excuse me, Uncle, I need to get ready for school."

"Of course, Wen-shan."

She stood and took her plate to the sink.

"Wen-shan?"

"Yes, Uncle?"

"Tonight, I want to read another letter."

She held her breath.

"If you don't want to read anymore, I understand. I just
need to finish the letters. I will read them by myself."

"No, no. I want to read them, but I have to study for a
chemistry test."

"This will be after I get home from work, Wen-shan, and
after dinner."

"But, I . . ."

"Like I said, you do not have to read them with me. I understand."

The spring onion pancakes sat like rocks in her stomach. She left the kitchen without saying anything else to her uncle. As she showered, she tried to tell herself it would be all right. That maybe she'd be brave enough to finish her mother's story, that maybe the ending was hopeful. She shuddered as the warm water poured over her body. She found it impossible to convince herself.

● ● ●

"Wen-shan, do you have enough money for a cheongsam dress?"

"I do, Li Li. I've been saving for a long time. Besides, not too many weeks and it will be my birthday."

Li-ying brightened. "It is a perfect gift for a sixteenth birthday!"

"Even if I have to buy it for myself?"

"Your uncle would buy it for you, wouldn't he?"

"I suppose, but then he might want to have a say in which one I choose."

"That's true. I wouldn't want my father helping me pick my dress. He'd probably pick one three sizes too big."

Wen-shan glanced at her friend, envying her slender figure. "You would look so good in one of these dresses, Li-ying. They are straight and slender, just like you."

Li-ying smiled, showing her crooked teeth. She held up a white dress. "This one is pretty."

Wen-shan shook her head. "Too white. I'm not going to a funeral."

Li-ying quickly put it back. "Sorry. You're right. It did have little blue butterflies all over it, though. I thought you might like that."

Wen-shan continued to move down the racks, looking at all the beautiful, shiny dresses. She had chosen several favorites: a black one that looked very sophisticated, a yellow one with small pearls around the stand-up collar, a turquoise one with white embroidered lotus blossoms, and a red one with dragons. She had the saleswoman secure those four in her size and went to the fitting room to try them on. The turquoise one was a little too snug and there wasn't another in a larger size, the side slit on the yellow dress went too high on her leg, and the black dress made her look like a little girl playing dress up. She was feeling a bit discouraged until she put on the red dress with the glorious dragons. It fit her perfectly, and Wen-shan thought it even made her look taller. When she went out to show Li-ying, her friend's eyes flew open in surprise.

"Oh, Wen-shan, it's perfect!"

"Really?"

"Yes! It's beautiful!"

"And it's a good price. I can afford it." She turned to look at herself in the mirror and words floated into her head: *This one looks like her mother.* She stared at her face in the mirror as Master Quan's words repeated. *This one looks like her mother.*

"Are you all right, Wen-shan?"

Wen-shan nodded. "I'm fine. I was just a little dizzy for a minute."

"Well, it's stuffy in that dressing room."

"I'm sure that's it." She looked again at the dress and her head cleared. "I'm going to buy this one."

Li-ying clapped, and Wen-shan gave a little curtsy. The dress was so formfitting, a little curtsy was all she could manage.

After leaving the dress shop, Wen-shan walked Li-ying to her house so she could show Li-ying's mother her purchase. Mrs. Song was very impressed with Wen-shan's choice.

"Oh, this is very lucky dress. Red is celebration color. And dragon is powerful. You will always feel very confident in this dress."

In her heart, Wen-shan felt that was true.

"Would you like to stay for dinner?" Mrs. Song asked. "We are having Poon Choi."

Wen-shan hesitated. She had only had Poon Choi once and it had been the most amazing meal she'd ever had. It was a few years after she'd come from Guilin. Mr. Pierpont had given one of his employees a wedding dinner, and the feast was served big-bowl style, with meat, fish, lobster, vegetables, and noodles overflowing in a huge pot. The guests simply came up with their individual bowls and helped themselves. She remembered being shy and unable to tell her uncle what she wanted. He carefully put a little of every kind of food in her bowl, and she crawled under the draped table and ate until she fell asleep. It was a good memory.

"I'm sorry, Mrs. Song. I would love to stay, but I have to go home and cook dinner for my uncle."

"Oh, you are a good girl. Maybe next time, then."

"I would love to. Thank you for inviting me."

It was dark as Wen-shan walked home with only a thin silver crescent moon peeking now and again through the trees. She walked slowly, listening to the distant sound of traffic and the closer sound of a mother's voice calling children home to dinner. She looked down at her feet and tried to think of her baby feet kicking dust in the courtyard, of rice served by slender fingers, of mist and green bamboo, of padded jackets, and a thick braid of hair falling down her back. She tried to remember a world of floating mountains and silver rivers, a land where her feet walked but her memory could not penetrate.

Wen-shan reached the gate and shifted the store package so she could unhook the latch. She knew she could not show her dress to her uncle right away because she was supposed to have been home studying for a chemistry test. On the other hand, if he was going to insist on reading a letter, wearing the dress might give her dragon strength.

● ● ●

1966

Secretary Zhang gathered our neighborhood group to the government building courtyard. It was muggy and rain clouds clung to the tops of the peaks. Sweat poured from our faces as we listened to the demon Zhang tell us that Chairman Mao had determined that at least ten percent of all the people are counterrevolutionaries and must be dealt with.

Zhang walked about the yard with a stack of papers in his hand. We knew these were the names of people he had determined would fill his quota. We trembled as he riffled through the pages. There were police standing by with guns. A truck waited to take people away to the detention center. Most of the people who went into the detention center came out with broken souls, or did not come out at all.

Wen-shan tugged on my work pants and said she

wanted to go home. "Too hot," she whined. I told her to
be quiet and she started to cry. Zhang looked our way
and I panicked. I clamped my hand over her mouth,
which frightened her. She began to struggle and kick. The
secretary walked toward us, and my father stepped in his
path. Zhang yelled at him to get out of his way, but my
father would not listen. The demon ordered his guards to
take my father to the center of the courtyard and to put
him in the jet plane position. People moved away from us.
As Zhang continued his walk, he pulled three papers from
his stack. One was for me, one for my father, and one for
Wen-shan. These were our death sentences.

"Uncle."

Her uncle moved over and sat beside her. "I'm right here,
Wen-shan. I'm right here beside you."

"They were going to kill us? What had we done?" Desperation colored her words. "I was five years old!"

"But look, here you are, and your mother has written more
letters, so something happened to save your lives, right?"

Wen-shan pressed her palms to her eyes. "Why can't I remember this?"

"It is a kindness, isn't it, that you cannot remember?" She
looked at him but could not answer. "Would you like me to finish the letter?"

She nodded.

Her uncle took the scroll and read.

Suddenly Ming-mei ran to us. Her voice was shrill
and angry. She shoved me and Wen-shan to our knees.
She stood in front of her husband and waved a silk scroll.

"Look! Look what I have found from the house of the artist Zhao Tai-lang! It is a painting against our Great Leader!"

Zhang took the scroll and opened it. It was father's painting of bamboo. What could be wrong with that? Bamboo is a symbol of strength. Father had even glued an official picture of Chairman Mao at the top.

"See!" Ming-mei screamed. "See how the clever artist paints the yellow leaves behind? He paints the bamboo dying because he wishes our Great Leader to fail. He wishes our Great Leader to die."

Zhang took out his pistol and walked toward my father.

I stood. I had to stop him, but Ming-mei pushed me back to the ground. "Stay down."

She ran to her husband and stood in front of the gun. "There is a worse punishment than death for the clever artist. I say you break his fingers."

"No!" The anguished cry from her uncle made Wen-shan jump. He stood and paced the floor. "No! No! They can't. . . . They can't!" He ran his hands over his brother's masterful paintings. "They can't. It's not possible. Why? Why? Why would they do that? They can't break his fingers. They can't!"

"I think Ming-mei was trying to save their lives," Wen-shan cried out.

Her uncle stared at her blankly. "What? What did you say?"

"I think Ming-mei was trying to save their lives."

"By breaking his fingers?"

Tears washed down her face. "Yes." She picked up the letter. Her voice trembled as she read her mother's words.

I grabbed Wen-shan and ran. I would not let this be a memory for her. In the night, as the rain fell, Ming-mei came to our house. She pounded on the door until I let her in. Wen-shan came shivering into my arms as Ming-mei gave me my father's painting of the bamboo and told me that my father was alive and in the hospital. She went to the door and stood there for the longest time.

"Remember that things change," she said. "One day soon I may fly like a crane over the misty mountains. If I can help you, I will."

I heard the next day that six people had been shot on Zhang's orders. Ming-mei saved our lives.

NOTES

Cheongsam dress: A one-piece straight dress with a Mandarin collar, a side-slash neck opening, and hemline slits on both sides. These dresses are usually made of colorful silk fabric.

The color red: The color red stands for luck, happiness, and celebration, though if it is used in writing, it is considered bad luck.

Death warrants: Mao did not tolerate conscience in his party officials. He said, "You'd better have less conscience. Some of our comrades have too much mercy, not enough brutality, which means they are not so Marxist. On this matter we indeed have no conscience! Marxism is that brutal." The communist regime of Mao Tse-tung was one of the most brutal in recorded history. Statistics show that between 58 million to 70 million Chinese people died of starvation, hard labor, suicide, torture, or execution during the twenty-seven years Chairman Mao was in power.

Jet plane position: This form of torture was usually performed on a counterrevolutionary at a struggle meeting. A person's arms were pulled straight behind the back at a severe angle, and the head shoved down. Often Red Guards would be so merciless in performing this action that the person's shoulders would become dislocated.

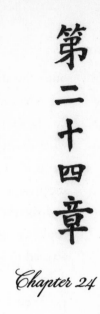

Chapter 24

WEN-SHAN DID NOT WANT to get out of bed. She felt as though a weight pressed on her chest and made it hard to breathe.

A light tap came to her bedroom door. "Wen-shan?"

"Yes, Uncle?"

"Are you getting up?"

"Yes."

"I have to leave for the store early this morning, so I may not see you."

"All right, Uncle."

"Have a good day."

"Thank you. You too."

Wen-shan stayed in bed until she heard the front door close and her uncle's footsteps leave the porch. She peeked out her bedroom window and saw him pass through the gate and out onto the sidewalk. She grinned as she slipped back into bed, snuggled her head into her pillow, and closed her eyes. She *was* nearly sixteen. She could make some decisions for herself: like what to eat for breakfast, or what clothes to wear, or whether or not to go to school. She felt a twinge of guilt, but immediately suppressed it. It had been a hard night. She hadn't slept well, and she did have a small headache right behind her eyes. How could she do schoolwork with a headache? Besides, someone had wanted to kill her once when she was five years old. Surely that deserved a day off.

Wen-shan stayed in bed until after the time for the start of school, and then she got up and went to the bathroom. She ran a brush through her hair and splashed cold water on her face. She put on a pair of comfortable pants and an old shirt. Then she snuck into her uncle's room and borrowed his transistor radio. For the next hour, she listened to rock-and-roll music, danced around the house, and ate cornflakes.

Suddenly a knock came at the door and Wen-shan's heart raced. She ran to the radio and turned it off.

Knock. Knock. Knock.

"Is somebody in there?" came a voice from outside.

Mrs. Tuan.

Wen-shan knew it was no good trying to ignore her. She went to the door and opened it a crack. "Yes?" she said in her best sick voice.

Mrs. Tuan was startled when the door opened. "Oh! Wen-shan, what are you doing home? I thought I heard music."

"I'm not feeling well today, Mrs. Tuan."

Her eyes narrowed. "But I heard music."

Wen-shan made her voice even weaker. "Oh, that must have

been my television. I was trying to distract myself. I'm sorry if it was too noisy."

"Does your uncle know you're home?"

"Hmm. He talked with me this morning before he left for work."

"Well, okay then. You get some rest. No more television."

"Yes, ma'am." She went to close the door but Mrs. Tuan stopped it with her hand.

"You need something, you let me know."

The magic of the paintings must still be working on Mrs. Tuan, Wen-shan thought.

"Thank you, Mrs. Tuan. That's very nice of you." She shut the door. Her heart rate slowed and she took a breath. Maybe she should call her uncle at the furniture store and let him know she was home. Better than having Mrs. Tuan report the juicy news when her uncle came home from work. She trudged to the phone and dialed the number. She waited for the secretary to answer, but instead the cheery voice of Mr. Pierpont came on the line.

"Good morning! Pierpont and Pierpont Limited! How may I assist you?"

"Good morning, Mr. Pierpont!"

"Mrs. Chen? Well, this is a surprise. Are you calling to order furniture?" Wen-shan giggled. "Wait a jingle—it is mid-morning. What are you doing out of school? Is everything all right, Wen-shan?"

"Yes, Mr. Pierpont. Everything's fine. I'm just at home because I wasn't feeling very well this morning."

"Oh, I'm so sorry to hear that. Is it the flu, do you think?"

"No, just a headache. Is my uncle there?"

"I'm sorry, he isn't. He's gone to the Kowloon store for the day. Would you like that number?"

"No, thank you. Will you be speaking with him?"

"I'm sure I will."

"Well, if you could just tell him I'm home for the day and not feeling well, that would help me."

"I would be glad to. Are you sure you don't need anything?"

"I'll be fine, Mr. Pierpont, thank you. I'm going to rest most of the day."

"That's the ticket. Call me if you do need anything."

"I will. Good-bye, Mr. Pierpont."

"Good day, Mrs. Chen."

Wen-shan hung up, smiling, and then felt immediately guilty for fibbing to Mr. Pierpont. Her fun time at home was getting rather complicated. She spent the next two hours cleaning the house. When she finished, she went into the front room and pulled out the jade dragon box. She set it carefully on the coffee table and wiped it down with a soft cloth. She spent time cleaning and admiring the jade carving. She lifted the lid and the faint aroma of incense surrounded her. How had her mother managed to sneak to the family shrine undetected and hide away the precious letters and paintings? How had her mother and grandfather managed to survive through all the brutality? And how had she herself ended up in Hong Kong with her great-uncle?

Wen-shan looked down at the drawer in the coffee table. She opened it and saw the unread letters. She knew one of those remaining letters held the story of her abandonment. She picked up the next scroll to be read and rubbed her fingers along the ribbon. *If I read it now, I'll know what to expect.* Slowly she untied the ribbon, debating with herself all the time whether or not she should read it. She unrolled the scroll.

1966

Someone snuck into the government building and slit Zhang's throat as he slept in his office. His wife, Ming-mei, found the body the next morning and went mad. Now a ghost roams our village and all the children scream and run when they see her. She wears a flowing gray costume from her days in the theater and a wig of straight white hair that reaches to her waist. No one will go near her, not even the police or the Red Guards. In the middle of the night, we hear her howling and snarling like a trapped animal.

All seems to be madness, but my father is home from the hospital and I shut the door to our home and bring my family close. Chairman Mao says that we are not to care about our families or have motherly affection for our children. He says that affection only diverts us from the ideals of the revolution. But my heart does not know revolution. I have tried, but my heart goes back to the sweet smile on my daughter's lips, to her funny, stumbling walk when she was a baby, to the way she squats down to look at a worm in the garden. I see the sunlight on her ebony hair, her funny faces, and even her tantrums—all are encased in my heart.

The letter crumpled in her fist as Wen-shan leaned forward and laid her arms on the jade dragon box. Those simple words released years of anger and sadness, and she cried. They included tears of loss and acceptance. She had been away from her mother for ten years, yet she knew she was tied to her across distance and time.

Wen-shan sat up and fished a tissue out of her pants pocket. She steadied her breathing and dried her tears. She still wasn't sure if she was ready for what was coming next, but she knew there was no turning back.

This is the story of the night my heart left Guilin, left the Guan Di Peak and the Flower Bridge. The night it flew away over the Li River and beyond the heavenly mountains. The heavy rains had arrived. The water that gushed off the tile roof turned the courtyard into a pool of mud. Lightning, like dragon's claws, ripped the black sky, and the thunder cracked. You wanted to climb into bed with your grandfather, but his hands were full of splints and bandages, and he could not hold you. No one slept for the pounding of the rain on the roof. In the darkest part of the night, the thunder pounded on our door. I went to press my hands against the wood so the storm spirit could not enter.

"Open the door!" the spirit commanded.

"Leave us alone!"

"I'm trying to save your life. Open the door!"

"Kai-ying, open the door," my father said in a voice that sounded like death.

I opened the door and the ghost Ming-mei pushed her way into our house. You screamed and scrambled under the bed.

A band of pain locked itself around Wen-shan's chest. She remembered! She remembered the long white hair dripping with water, the ghost's pale face. This was the night that her mother sent her away!

> *Ming-mei grabbed my wrists and forced me to look at her.*
>
> *"Kai-ying, listen to me. I am not mad. I have been acting mad so that they would leave me alone. I was giving myself time for my father to come for me. He is one of the top doctors in the Communist Party."*
>
> *I tried to look away. She shook me and made me look into her eyes. Her whispered voice was fierce.*
>
> *"My father has found a way to get me and my brother to Hong Kong. You must come with us. There are threats against you. Some people are saying you were the one who killed Zhang to revenge your father. There will surely be a struggle meeting against you and your family. And I heard the man they are sending to replace Zhang is even more brutal than my husband was. Your family will suffer terrible pain. You must all come with me."*
>
> *I looked over and you were peeking out from under the bed. You scurried back like a little mouse, and I made a decision. Father was too ill to travel, and I would not go without him, but I did not have to let you suffer torture and death.*
>
> *I dragged you out from under the bed. You were kicking and screaming. I told Ming-mei about my uncle in Hong Kong—Zhao Tai-lu. Zhao Tai-lu. I*

said his name over and over. I dressed you in your padded blue jacket and your shoes. You tried to run to your grandfather, and I pulled you back. I put a packet of cooked rice into your hand, opened the door, and shoved you out. I pushed you out into the rain. You tried to turn back, but I pushed you out into the muddy courtyard.

Ming-mei grabbed you around the waist and you were gone.

Wen-shan ran. She dropped the letter on the floor and ran—down the steps, across the garden, and out the front gate. This was her nightmare, and she remembered. She ran up the slope of Victoria Peak, past the British cottages, and into the park.

She was so focused on the white pagoda that she tripped over some of the old rotted boards and fell onto a pile of rubble. Sharp chunks of brick ripped her pants and cut into her knees. She crawled forward until she could regain her footing. She lurched to the sagging door and shoved it to the side. The wood grated on the stone floor, causing a screeching sound that made her cry out. She went up the stairs. Sobs racked her body, but she pushed forward, unaware of how high she'd climbed. She stumbled onto the balcony and fell against the railing. She reached out her arms to the west, to China, to her home.

"Mother, mother, mother, my mother! I remember you! I remember you braiding my hair. I remember us walking on the Flower Bridge. I remember! I remember!" She laid her head on the railing and cried. Only a few slivers of memory crossed the years, but they were enough to deepen the misery of separation. She wanted all those years back. She wanted to run along the Li

River and have her grandfather teach her how to make the fisherman's boats from sticks of bamboo. She wanted to watch him write her name in his beautiful calligraphy. She wanted to plant vegetables with her mother and watch the blue butterflies. She wanted to see the mist dance among the heavenly mountains. Anger and grief churned inside her and more tears came. She had spent years fighting weak emotion, transforming it into sullenness and indifference, but over this torrent of pain, she had no control.

Finally grief drained her strength, and Wen-shan sat back against the side of the pagoda. She felt the warmth of the sun on her face as it crept around the side of the old building. She thought how nice it would be to follow its westward path to Guilin. A few tears leaked from the corner of her eye, and she brushed them away. Would it be too much to ask the God her uncle believed in to give her a miracle like He had given the little Heaton boy? A miracle that she would see her mother and grandfather again? She shook her head. She didn't know Him well enough to ask.

Wen-shan closed her eyes and kept her thoughts on the warm sunlight and the sound of rustling leaves and birdsong. Slowly she became aware of the sound of an approaching motor scooter. She sat up. Who could be coming to the pagoda? No one ever came here. Had she fallen asleep? She crawled to the railing and peered over. *Wei Jun-jai? What is he doing here?* She pulled back her head as the motor stopped.

Jun-jai called out in a loud voice. "Wen-shan?"

Now what was she going to do? She was too embarrassed to answer him, but she knew he would probably come searching for her, and then when he found her, she would look foolish for not answering. What was he doing here, anyway?

"Wen-shan, are you here?"

She peeked back over the railing and called down. "I'm here, Jun-jai." She saw a look of relief wash his face, and he started forward. "Don't come up! I'm coming down." She stood and stretched her back. How long had she been sitting? She ran her fingers through her hair. She knew she looked awful, but there wasn't anything she could do about it. She hoped Jun-jai was a true friend.

He met her at the doorway.

"What are you doing here, Jun-jai?"

"Looking for you." He stepped toward her. "Are you all right?"

"How did you get here?"

He looked toward his scooter.

"No, I mean what are you doing here?"

"Your uncle called me. He wanted me to look for you."

"What? Why?"

"He's worried about you."

"But . . . but he's not even home from work yet."

"He came home early when he heard you were sick."

Wen-shan looked at the sun and noticed that it had dropped toward the western horizon. "What time is it?"

"After four."

"But how did you know I'd be here?"

"Li-ying said you two like to come up here sometimes."

"So, she's in on this too?"

"Wen-shan, she said you weren't at school today."

"Can't a person take a day off without everyone going crazy?"

He put his hand gently on her shoulder. "Wen-shan, are you all right?"

She didn't answer.

"Your uncle said that one of your mother's letters was lying on the floor when he got to the house."

She turned away. "I don't want to talk about it, Jun-jai."

"Of course. It's none of my business," he said in an even tone.

Wen-shan softened. "It is your business, Jun-jai. You're my friend. I just can't talk about it right now."

"Fair enough."

She smiled at his Western slang. "Thank you for understanding."

"I'd better get you home before your uncle sends out the police." He pulled her toward the scooter.

She pulled back. "On that? My uncle would never let me ride that."

"Actually, he said if I found you, I had his permission."

"Really?" Wen-shan was shocked. She figured her uncle would be so angry with her that she'd have her privileges taken away for a month, but instead he was letting her ride on a scooter?

"And I'm a very good driver, so you don't have to be afraid."

"I'm not afraid." Actually, she was—a little.

He showed her where to sit and then got on in front of her. "Be careful of your bare feet. Keep them up on the floorboard."

She was glad she didn't have to walk home. Her feet were raw and tender. Running for so long without shoes had not been a good idea.

Jun-jai started the engine. "You'll have to hold on to me around the waist."

Wen-shan felt heat rise into her face and was glad Jun-jai was turned forward so he couldn't see her foolish embarrassment.

She placed her hands lightly on either side of his rib cage, but when he put the bike in gear and started off, she quickly wrapped her arms around him.

● ● ●

Five minutes later, he dropped her off at her front gate.

"I'll find Li-ying and tell her you're safe."

"What a big bother I am," Wen-shan said.

Jun-jai turned off the engine. "No, you're not."

She glanced at the house then back at him. "Thank you for bringing me home, Jun-jai."

"Of course. Are you going to be all right?"

"I don't know. I think my uncle is going to be upset with me."

"I think he's worried more than anything."

"Wen-shan?" Her uncle stood a moment on the porch before moving down into the garden.

"Oh, dear, he's coming over." She called out, "I'm here, Uncle. I'm fine. Jun-jai brought me home."

Her uncle came to the gate. "Thank you, Jun-jai."

"I was glad to help."

"And you drove carefully?"

"I did."

"He did, Uncle."

"Good."

Jun-jai started the engine and smiled. "And now I must find Li-ying."

"Please, tell her I'll see her at school tomorrow."

"I will. Good-bye, Mr. Zhao."

Her uncle bowed. "Good-bye, Wei Jun-jai."

Wen-shan shaded her eyes and watched the black scooter as it moved down the street and turned the corner. She wished that Jun-jai could have stayed longer; she was not eager to face her uncle alone. She took a breath and turned to him.

He was looking at her with great tenderness and holding open the gate.

第
二
十
五
章

Chapter 25

H ER UNCLE MADE HER ICED PEPPERMINT tea and
offered her good-fortune buns for dinner. She was not
really hungry, so she only ate two. He also gave her some soothing ointment to put on the soles of her feet. He talked very little,
and whereas before Wen-shan would have found that irritating,
now she found it soothing to her jangled nerves.

She sat with her legs stretched out on the sofa and a pillow
behind her back. She read a magazine while her uncle read his
scriptures. She didn't want to break the peaceful feeling, but
there were questions bothering her—questions that needed answers.

"Uncle?"

He put his finger on the verse he was reading. "Yes?"

"Why didn't you tell me about Ming-mei?"

"What do you mean?"

"When you met her at the orphanage."

"I didn't meet her."

"Then how did they know to call you to pick me up?"

"I've told you this story."

"I don't remember anything except that you picked me up at the Catholic orphanage. How old was I when you told me the story?"

"Eight or nine."

"And that was the last time you told it to me?"

"Yes. You were not one to ask questions."

She gave him a frustrated look.

"I know, Wen-shan, I'm sorry. I did not know anything about children."

"So tell me now. I'm asking."

He closed his book. "There is not much to tell. The orphanage called and told me that they had my niece's little girl in their care and that I was to come and pick you up."

"Just like that?"

"Well, they said I had to bring documents to prove that I was Zhao Tai-lu, and some sort of stuffed animal to give to you when we met."

"My toy rabbit."

"Yes." He set his scriptures to the side. "You were born during the year of the Rat, but I didn't think that would be a very happy toy."

Wen-shan chuckled. "If I'd been a boy, I probably would have loved it." She adjusted her pillow. "Go on with the story."

"I arrived at the orphanage and went to the office to fill out the papers. The Mother Superior was very thorough in her questioning."

"Did she say anything about Ming-mei?"

Her uncle gave her a look. "Who's telling the story?"

245

"Sorry."

"She told me how you were dropped off."

Wen-shan felt her uncle could have used different words other than *dropped off* to explain how she came to the orphanage, but she wasn't about to correct him at this point.

"The Mother Superior said that early one morning a woman came to the orphanage with a little girl. The woman would not leave her name, but told the story of their escape from Guilin and conveyed the wishes of the girl's mother that she be taken to Hong Kong and left in the care of her great-uncle, Zhao Tai-lu."

"Ming-mei was as good as her word," Wen-shan said.

"Yes."

"Did the Mother Superior say what the woman looked like?"

"She did, because I asked her. She said she was a tall, slender woman with her hair put up into a bun at the back of her neck. She wore a simple skirt and a white blouse." He hesitated. "I can't remember if there was anything else. Oh, wait! The Mother Superior said she could tell that the woman had once been beautiful, but that a hard life had robbed her of her good looks."

"That's so sad, isn't it?"

Her uncle nodded.

"Why do you think Ming-mei didn't want to stay and meet you? You know, to make sure you came for me and that you were a nice person."

"I don't know. Maybe she didn't want anyone to be able to find her. Maybe once she reached Hong Kong, she wanted to disappear."

"That makes sense."

"And I think she knew the nuns would make sure you were going to the right person."

Wen-shan took a drink of peppermint tea. "I think I've remembered some things about the escape and the trip to Hong Kong. There was this big truck, and one time I think the ghost woman and I hid under these smelly burlap sacks." She shook her head. "I don't know. That could be a dream too. Most of it is a blank."

"It's understandable."

"Were you nerveous to meet me?"

"The Mother Superior warned me that you were traumatized and would not say a word to anyone. When the assistant brought you out in the secondhand dress the nuns had given you, you looked like a sad little doll."

"I remember that dress. Pale yellow with ducks on it."

"You wore it for days until I got around to buying you some new clothes." He looked into her face. "I remember the nuns were shocked because as soon as you saw me, you came right over and stood next to me."

Wen-shan smiled at him. "I thought you were my grandfather."

"I suppose we looked enough alike." He let out a breath. "And then they handed me a box with all your old clothes, blessed us to have a good life, and sent us out the door."

"That wasn't very kind."

"Oh, they were very kind, Wen-shan. You have to remember that they had many children to care for. Once they knew a child was with a family member, they could focus on the ones not so fortunate."

"You're right." She took another sip of tea. "Uncle?"

"Yes?"

"Do you still have that box of old clothes?"

He stood. "I do." He moved to the hall closet and retrieved a worn cardboard box. He handed it to Wen-shan.

She fought the tight feeling in her throat. "I used to look at these all the time."

"When you were little. You haven't looked at them for seven or eight years now."

She opened the lid of the box and removed her threadbare padded jacket. She put it to her face and breathed in the smell. "It used to smell like the soap the nuns used to clean it, but that's gone now." She held up the jacket. "Look how small I was."

"You were small."

She brought out the black cloth shoes. "I know now that Ming-mei was the ghost in my rain nightmares."

"And now you know why."

"Yes." She folded the jacket and put the articles back in the box. "Uncle?"

"Yes?"

"May we open another painting?"

"Of course. Are you up to it?"

"I think I am." Wen-shan put her feet on the floor in preparation to stand.

Her uncle stood and patted her shoulder. "Stay, stay. I'll get it." He went to the cupboard and brought out one of the two remaining scrolls. When he sat in his chair, Wen-shan noticed that he'd chosen the painting not done on silk. This one was a piece of paper much like the cheap stuff used for writing the big criticism posters. The paper had been folded in half and then rolled into a scroll. Her uncle unrolled and unfolded the paper.

Two young communists stood in front of a large picture of

Chairman Mao. The man wore a washed-out green uniform, while the girl wore a ragged blue jacket and a pair of loose-fitting pants. They were smiling the forced smile of Communism, and the girl held yellow Ginkgo leaves in her hand.

This one looks like her mother.

Finally Wen-shan spoke, her voice unsteady. "It's my mother and my father on their marriage day."

"Yes."

She leaned closer. "I don't remember her," she said slowly. "She . . . she does look like me, doesn't she?"

Her uncle laid the painting out on the coffee table and studied it carefully. "Yes. And you look like her . . . and a little like your father."

"Do you think so?" Wen-shan stared at his face. "He's not bad-looking, but grandfather made him look a bit scared."

"He probably was."

"My mother too."

"I think everyone was afraid—waiting for the next campaign, or struggle meeting, or trip to the detention center. Their lives were in constant turmoil."

"I wish I could remember her." Wen-shan touched the yellow Ginkgo leaves. "I wish she could have had her dream to be a doctor."

● ● ●

After saying good-night to her uncle, Wen-shan gathered paper, pencils, and pens and took them to her bedroom. She threw all the articles onto her bed and went to the bathroom to brush her teeth. She was exhausted, but there was one thing she was going to do before she slept—she was going to write a letter to her mother.

She slipped into bed and went through the different kinds of paper and writing utensils until she found what suited her—a parchment-type stationery and a black pen. She was not the best at writing characters, but she hoped her mother could decipher the message.

She took a deep breath and wrote.

> *To my mother,*
>
> *Master Quan has brought us the jade dragon box, and Uncle Zhao and I have been reading your letters. Grandfather's paintings are hanging around the walls in our front room, and they bring us close to you. We also feel close to you because of your letters. We are so sorry for the sadness you have had to go through. I am glad that you wrote of the night I left Guilin with Wu Ming-mei. I have had bad dreams of that night for a long time, but I am much better now. I want to know how you are. Have you eaten today? Are you still in Grandfather's house? Are you still working in the fields? Have you heard from my father?*
>
> *I go to senior school, and one of my teachers, Mrs. Yang, is a very good teacher. It made me angry to think that anyone would write horrible big posters against their teachers. I have two very good friends, Song Li-ying and Wei Jun-jai. Uncle takes very good care of me. Sometimes I eat cornflakes for breakfast and Uncle says I'm too Western. You probably don't even know what cornflakes are.*
>
> *There is so much I want to tell you. I hope this*

letter gets to you. Are things better for you now that
Mao Tse-tung is dead? I probably should not ask that,
should I? I am sorry. Things are just very different here.
We can ask as many questions as we want.

I will send this letter through Mr. and Mrs.
Smythe. They are the people who helped Master Quan
escape from Guilin. I hope somehow they can get this
letter to you.

Your daughter,

Chen Wen-shan

Wen-shan read the letter over several times and made sure
the ink was dry before she folded the paper and put it into the
envelope. She put the address on the outside, and her name and
address too. She laid the envelope on her side table and turned
out the light. She drifted away in the enfolding darkness imagining scenes of her mother receiving the letter. In one scene,
she watched as the postman stopped at Grandfather's house
and rang the bell at the front gate. Her mother would be pick-
ing peppers in the garden. She would look at the postman and
frown, thinking that they never got mail. Then she would take
the envelope into her hand, and when she saw the name and the
return address, she would smile and laugh, shake the letter in
the air, and run to tell her father!

That was a good dream.

● ● ●

Wen-shan, Jun-jai, and Li-ying stood on the stoop at Mr.
George Riley Smythe's mansion. Li-ying kept looking around
at the well-manicured yard and the huge banyan tree hung with

lanterns, while Wen-shan and Jun-jai focused on the wooden front door. Wen-shan smiled at Li-ying's curiosity and thought of herself the first time she had been here with her uncle.

"Li Li, pay attention."

"Sorry, Wen-shan. It's just such a huge yard."

"And house," Jun-jai added.

"Well, he's an important person," Wen-shan said, smiling at them. "But I'm more impressed by all that he and his wife have done for other people."

Jun-jai nodded. "'To be able under all circumstances to practice five things constitutes perfect virtue. These five things are gravity, generosity of soul, sincerity, earnestness, and kindness.'"

Wen-shan shifted her schoolbag. "I think Mr. and Mrs. Smythe and Confucius would have been good friends."

Just then the door opened and Mrs. Smythe stood smiling at them. Li-ying jumped and Wen-shan stepped back. Mrs. Smythe was an imposing person. She was quite tall—almost as tall as Jun-jai—and she wore what looked like a safari outfit with a bright red, flowered scarf around her neck. Besides her clothes, there was a forceful energy about her. She thrust out her hand to Jun-jai.

"Mr. Wei, is it? Welcome! And which one of you is Chen Wen-shan?" Wen-shan stepped forward and received the same handshake. She turned to Li-ying. "And this is Miss Song?" Li-ying nodded and Mrs. Smythe bowed. "Welcome! Welcome! Come in."

She led them into the foyer where they left their shoes, and then on through the sitting room and back into her husband's office. Wen-shan, having been to the mansion previously, did not do as much staring at things as Jun-jai and Li-ying. She sighed as they walked into Mr. Smythe's tranquil office with its pale walls and sunlit window.

"Sit everyone, and I'll fetch my husband. I'll bring some biscuits and sodas, too."

"Thank you, Mrs. Smythe, that's very kind," Wen-shan said.

As soon as Mrs. Smythe was out of the room, the three began talking.

"That is a woman who can get things done," Jun-jai said.

Wen-shan nodded. "Can you imagine her driving their jeep off to the New Territories to pick up a refugee?"

Jun-jai smiled. "I can."

"Did you see all the art treasures in their living room?" Li-ying asked.

Wen-shan turned to her. "Master Quan told us they were wealthy art dealers in London."

"I can believe it."

They heard footsteps coming down the hallway, and they all stopped talking and sat up straighter. Mr. Smythe entered, and Wen-shan saw Li-ying take a deep breath.

"Miss Chen! I'm delighted to see you again. And these are the friends you said would be accompanying you?"

"Yes, sir. This is Wei Jun-jai and Song Li-ying."

Mr. Smythe smiled at them. "Welcome, both of you."

"Thank you, sir," Jun-jai replied.

Li-ying only nodded.

"Mrs. Smythe will be in shortly. I believe she is bringing us a treat." He sat in his chair on the other side of the large desk. "Now, what can I do for you?"

"First, Mr. Smythe, I want to thank you for rescuing Master Quan," Wen-shan said. "He is a dear man, and I can't tell you what my mother's letters have meant to me . . . us . . . to my uncle and me." She stopped, feeling momentarily flustered.

"It is my wife's and my pleasure, Miss Chen."

"And my grandfather's paintings and the jade dragon box." She ran short of breath. "Thank you."

"Someday I would love to see your grandfather's paintings."

"You and Mrs. Smythe are welcome anytime," Wen-shan replied, though she couldn't actually imagine the elegant couple visiting in her little bungalow.

At that moment the door opened, and Mrs. Smythe came in with a tin of biscuits, followed by Mrs. Delany carrying a tray of crystal glasses filled with soda. Mr. Smythe and Jun-jai stood.

"Such the gentlemen," Mrs. Smythe said, setting down the tin. "I hope I didn't miss much. Just put the tray right here, Edith," she instructed, patting at a place on her husband's desk. He quickly moved some papers. The cook turned to leave. "Thank you, Edith." Mrs. Smythe pulled up a chair next to her husband's, and the men sat. "So, to what do we owe this delightful visit?"

Wen-shan started again. "I came to say thank you to you and your husband for rescuing Master Quan."

"Well, how sweet of you. He was high on our list of treasures to save, wasn't he, George?" Mrs. Smythe playfully batted her husband's arm to hand around the sodas.

"Indeed."

Mrs. Smythe opened the tin of biscuits. "He would have loved to have been here to see you, Miss Chen, but he's off playing mah-jongg with some of his newfound friends." Wen-shan smiled at the thought. "He certainly did love dinner at your home the other night."

Wen-shan was flustered again. "Really? Well, it was a small payment for the jade dragon box he brought us."

Mrs. Smythe raised her glass. "The jade dragon box . . . My, my, my! Filled with precious letters and paintings—so fascinating!"

Wen-shan raised her glass and looked over at Li-ying who raised her glass and her eyebrows.

Mr. Smythe raised his glass. "Here! Here!"

Jun-jai joined in the impromptu toast.

Wen-shan set her glass on a side table and rummaged in her schoolbag. "There is another reason I came to see you." She pulled out the letter and stared at it a moment before looking up. "I wrote a letter to my mother in Guilin, and I wondered if there was any way you might get it to her."

Mrs. Smythe reached out for it. "Oh, my dear . . . how tender."

Wen-shan relinquished the envleope.

Mr. Smythe leaned over to study the address. "Is this a new or an old address?"

"What do you mean? It's the address my uncle remembered."

"From before the Communists took over?"

"I think so. He left Guilin in 1949."

"Then this probably is not a valid address. When the Communists took control, they changed many of the street names and store names to sound less Chinese and more revolutionary."

"I don't understand."

"Well, say a restaurant was called the Lotus Flower. The Communists would change the name to something like the Red Sun. The same thing went for street signs."

Wen-shan felt dispirited. "Oh."

Mrs. Smythe chided her husband. "Now, Mr. Smythe, don't be so pessimistic. We have our ways." Wen-shan looked up, and Mrs. Smythe smiled at her. "What say we give it a try?"

"Of course! I wasn't saying we wouldn't try," Mr. Smythe defended.

"Thank you. Thank you very much," Wen-shan said, knowing that if Mr. and Mrs. Smythe said they would try, then they would. She felt a wave of emotion and worried that tears would follow. She turned to her friends. "Li-ying, Jun-jai, are you ready to leave?"

Li-ying quickly shoved the last of her biscuit into her mouth and nodded.

Mrs. Smythe's brow furrowed. "Are you leaving us so soon?"

"Yes . . . yes. I just wanted to thank you and drop off the letter. You are very kind."

Jun-jai stood with Wen-shan. He bowed to Mr. and Mrs. Smythe. "It was very nice to meet you."

They bowed in return, and Mr. Smythe fixed Jun-jai with a knowing grin. "It was a pleasure to meet you, Mr. Wei. When Miss Chen called the other day, she made introductions of her friends who would be attending with her. She told me that you, Miss Song, are tops in your class." Li-ying blushed. "And that you, Mr. Wei, are a scholar of Confucius."

"It is a lifelong study, Mr. Smythe."

"Indeed."

"Would you be so kind as to favor us with some of the teacher's wisdom?" Mrs. Smythe inquired.

Jun-jai was silent for a moment. "The teacher says, 'Men's natures are alike, it is their habits that carry them far apart.'"

Mrs. Smythe nodded. "Perfect."

Wen-shan moved toward the door. "Thank you again, Mr. and Mrs. Smythe. I will hope, but I won't expect."

Mrs. Smythe led them out into the hallway. "We will do our best."

Wen-shan nodded. "Thank you."

At the door, Mrs. Smythe issued them a hearty farewell and told Wen-shan that a thought had just popped into her head about hosting a showing for her grandfather's paintings.

"I'll telephone in a fortnight with all the details!"

After Mrs. Smythe shut the door, the friends looked at each other with expressions of amazement. Jun-jai was the first to speak as they walked through the garden to the front gate.

"I like her. If anyone can get your letter to your mother, Wen-shan, it will be her."

"That's what I think, too."

As the three friends walked their way to the ferry station, Jun-jai and Li-ying chatted about the curios they'd seen at the Smythes' mansion, and Wen-shan imagined scenes of Mrs. Smythe poling down the Li River on one of the fishermen's flatboats with the precious letter safely tucked inside the pocket of her safari jacket. The thought made her smile.

NOTES

Chinese astrology: In this discipline, there are twelve signs named after twelve animals: Rat, Ox, Tiger, Rabbit, Dragon, Snake, Horse, Goat, Monkey, Rooster, Dog, and Pig. Legend says that the Buddha honored these animals by deciding that those people born during that year would inherit some of the personality of that animal.

Marriage in Communist China: Since religion played no part in the communist society, marriages were simply contracts of the State and were normally performed at the party offices with a picture of Chairman Mao overseeing the marriage agreement.

Changing street names: From the beginning of communist rule in China in 1949, many of the names of businesses and streets were changed to reflect the new revolutionary spirit. This was especially true during the time of the Great Proletariat Cultural Revolution.

第二十六章

Chapter 26

I AM SURROUNDED BY PEOPLE, *but I am alone in my work unit. No one will come near me because they fear that madness touched my life when the ghost woman stole my child and vanished. An old man said he saw the ghost woman walking into the Li River, dragging my daughter with her. He has spread the rumor through-out the neighborhood, and many people have put mirrors and scissors over their doorways.*

My father is also alone. No one will come near him because they fear the new secretary will think they have sympathy for the counterrevolutionary artist with his twisted fingers and shuffling walk. But at home, Father and I are content to be alone. It is as though we have become invisible. It is easier to grieve when one is invisible. We have not had to worry about the new

*man, Secretary Luo. He is very cautious. He does not
want to offend the party, but he also does not want his
throat cut. I am using the last of the paper. I will place
a few more letters in the box and one more of father's
paintings that I have hidden. I will instruct Master
Quan that he can then do what he thinks best.*

*The cold days will arrive soon. I will hardly feel
them.*

Wen-shan's mind was thinking of many things as she rolled
the scroll. "I think it's good for them to be invisible. If they're
invisible, then no one will bother them."

"Yes," her uncle concurred. "I also think that Secretary Luo
is more than just cautious—I think he is afraid."

"I would be if I were him." She placed the letter in the
drawer. "Do you think grandfather will ever paint again?"

Her uncle lowered his head. "I do not know." He looked at
his watch. "Ah, you'd better get ready for school."

Wen-shan shut the drawer and stood. She hesitated.
"Uncle?"

"Yes?"

"Do you think Ming-mei actually dragged me into the
river?"

Her uncle looked at her with understanding. "Maybe she
did. It would have been easy for her father to hide a small boat
in the rain and darkness."

"Maybe that's why I'm such a coward when it comes to
water."

"You are not a coward, Wen-shan. Look how many times
you ride the ferry across the deep water of Victoria Harbor."

"Well, I have a big boat under me, don't I?"

Her uncle chuckled. "Off you go, or you'll be late for school. And remember to be home early this afternoon."

She brightened. "Of course! I can't leave you alone to get ready for the party."

"Is Mrs. Yang coming?"

"I think she is. I'll check with her at school."

"Yes. Yes. Off you go now. I'll get breakfast ready."

Wen-shan headed for the bathroom. "Just cornflakes this morning," she called back.

"So Western," she heard her uncle mumble.

She smiled.

●　●　●

Mrs. Wong from the Golden Door Bakery came along with the delivery boy to drop off the dim sum order at the Zhao home. She stood at the gate, beaming when Wen-shan approached to let them in.

"Mrs. Wong? This is quite an honor." Wen-shan undid the latch and swung the gate wide.

"Oh, this great honor for me to bring order for your party."

A big order, Wen-shan thought.

Mrs. Wong swatted the arm of the delivery boy who carried a stack of bamboo steaming baskets. "Get in there, you lazy boy! And be careful!" She followed the young man's progress and gave advice at every step. When they reached the porch, she sighed as though she'd carried the baskets by herself up Victoria Peak and back. "So difficult to get good help these days."

Wen-shan tried to look serious as her uncle opened the door. "Ah, Mrs. Wong, what a nice surprise! Come in."

The advice started again until all the baskets were safely

deposited in the kitchen. Mrs. Wong looked around proudly. "You have all the ones you ordered, plus a few extra-special ones I added. Everything from shrimp and chive dumpling to char siu bao. I have cooks make everything bite-sized for party. Your guests will like."

"I'm sure they'll love everything." Wen-shan breathed deeply. "It smells wonderful, Mrs. Wong."

Mrs. Wong tried to look humble. "You keep steam under baskets just right, yes? That way dim sum will be warm, but not overcooked."

"I promise to be careful."

"Good girl."

Her uncle brought out his wallet. "What is the total, Mrs. Wong?"

"Total?"

"The cost for the dim sum?"

Mrs. Wong looked confused. "No cost."

Wen-shan was shocked. All this food had to be two-day's pay! Obviously her uncle was just as staggered, as he stood there with his hand on his wallet, not speaking.

Mrs. Wong chuckled. "Already paid for."

"By whom?"

"Some British gentleman who said not to tell you."

"Some British gentleman?" He looked at Wen-shan. "Hmm, I wonder who that could be?"

"I will not tell you, so do not try to make me. Confucius say, 'Do not look gift horse in face.'"

Wen-shan burst out in giggles. "That's a good one, Mrs. Wong." She turned to her uncle, who was also smiling. "You'll have to remember that one, Uncle."

Mrs. Wong tapped the side of her head. "Ah, I know more

than just bakery." She looked around. "Now where is that lazy delivery boy?" She walked into the front room and found him staring at the painting of the heavenly mountains. "What you doing?" she snapped.

"I'm looking," he said. He reached out to touch the path disappearing into the stand of bamboo.

"Ah! Don't touch that!" Mrs. Wong barked. "What are you thinking?"

Wen-shan stepped forward. "It's all right, Mrs. Wong. I know how he feels. These are my grandfather's paintings. Please, take some time to look."

"Your grandfather?" Mrs. Wong glanced around. "You do not mind?"

Uncle Zhao stepped forward. "No, of course not. Please."

Mrs. Wong swatted the boy's arm. "Just look! No touching!"

The bell rang at the gate, and Wen-shan hurried to look out the front window. "It's Jun-jai and Li-ying!"

Her uncle frowned. "They are early."

"I asked them to come early in case I needed help." She went out onto the porch and waved to her friends at the gate. They waved back. As she started down the steps, Yan and Ya Ya popped out from behind the garden shed.

Wen-shan jumped. "You two!"

Yan stepped forward, giggling. "We scared you!"

Wen-shan kept walking and they followed.

"We get to go to your house for the party."

"I know, we invited you. Now go away; the party hasn't started yet."

"My father isn't going to come," Yan said in a snickering voice. "He says he doesn't want to look at silly art."

Wen-shan stopped and glared at the two tagalongs. "Well, that's his loss."

Ya Ya piped up. "That's what my mother said."

"You need to go home now until the party starts. I have to meet my friends. They're going to help me get things ready."

"Can we help?" Ya Ya asked.

"No. No, thank you." Wen-shan turned and walked to her friends. "Hello! I'm so glad to see you. Thank you for coming early to help." She opened the gate, and her friends came into the garden.

Jun-jai smiled. "It looks like you have lots of helpers."

Wen-shan turned around to see Yan and Ya Ya staring at them. She was about to scold them when Mrs. Tuan's voice punctuated the air.

"Yan! Ya Ya! You leave Miss Chen alone and come home. You have to get ready for party."

Yan kicked at the dirt. "I'm not going to dress up," he grumbled, turning dejectedly toward his house.

Ya Ya followed. "I want to dress up. I know just the dress I'm going to wear."

"See you soon!" Mrs. Tuan called cheerily. She waved and Wen-shan waved back.

"Those children sound like my brothers and sisters," Li-ying said.

"Maybe I'm glad I'm an only child," Wen-shan answered. "I hope they behave at the party." She headed back to the house. "Come on, you can help me set out the dishes."

"Who's coming again?" Li-ying asked.

"The Tuans—minus Mr. Tuan—our other neighbor, Mr. Yee, Mr. Pierpont, and Mrs. Yang."

"It will be odd to see our teacher somewhere other than school," Li-ying said. "What about Mr. and Mrs. Smythe?"

"We invited them, but they had a previous engagement. Master Quan, too."

"Is anyone here yet?" Jun-jai asked as they climbed the steps to the porch.

"Just Mrs. Wong and her delivery boy." Wen-shan opened the front door and the savory smells of dim sum assaulted the three.

"Oh," Li-ying sighed. "This is going to be a wonderful party."

• • •

Wen-shan thought her uncle looked nervous as he stood before their guests holding the final silk scroll, but maybe he was just emotional. She had been proud of him accommodating so many people in his house, and as the night progressed, it seemed as though he was actually having a good time. He greeted Mrs. Tuan in her red, flowered hat without looking too shocked, he complimented Yan and Ya Ya, who were both dressed up for the occasion, and he even invited Mrs. Wong and the delivery boy to stay—which they did. Her uncle was most at ease with Mr. Pierpont, of course, but surprisingly spent a good deal of time talking with Mrs. Yang. Wen-shan figured they had many similar stories to tell of their lives in China. Mr. Yee and Mr. Pierpont talked business, Mrs. Tuan and Mrs. Wong talked food, and both ladies were amazed when Mr. Pierpont spoke to both of them in flawless Cantonese.

Wen-shan enjoyed herself too. It was fun to play a waiter

with Li-ying and Jun-jai. Everyone loved the food and complimented Mrs. Wong over and over.

Now the group was closely assembled in the front room,
waiting for the purpose of the gathering—the opening of the
final painting. Throughout the evening, Wen-shan watched
people as they stood in front of her grandfather's paintings looking mesmerized, moved, or enchanted. Wen-shan saw the emotions play on their faces, and even caught the delivery boy muttering to himself as he stared at the calligraphy of Truth.

Her uncle's words brought her to the present.

"Wen-shan and I are glad that you could be here to share
this with us." People turned to look at her and she lowered her
head. Her uncle continued. "This has been a journey for us.
We could not have imagined where the treasures inside the jade
dragon box would take us. And now, we have come to this." He
held out the painting, and surprisingly, people clapped. "The
final painting." He motioned to Wen-shan. "Wen-shan?"

"Yes, Uncle?"

"Would you come up and unroll the final scroll?"

She stood and moved to her uncle's side. She was trembling,
and she willed herself to be calm, but to no avail. Her uncle
handed her the scroll, and she untied the ribbon and opened
it. She held it out for everyone to see. Her grandfather had
painted a large man—a party official—in his Mao jacket and
hat, scowling down at a petite girl with a round moon face. The
girl had long braids and wore a blue padded jacket—the same
blue padded jacket which sat in a box in the closet. The girl's
face was guileless as she held up a picture of Chairman Mao to
the irascible official.

Many were fascinated by the subject matter, and everyone

commented on her grandfather's undeniable skill, but it was Jun-jai who discovered the heart of the painting.

"That little girl is you, isn't it, Wen-shan?" he asked tenderly.

Wen-shan nodded. She didn't see people's reactions because she was staring at the painting, the way her grandfather's brilliance had captured not only her features, but her feelings. She remembered. She remembered the smell of the canteen, the sound of murmuring voices, the look on her mother's face when she went to give back the photograph. Her mother's face. She remembered. Tears came. Wen-shan handed the scroll to her uncle, and ran to her bedroom.

● ● ●

Wen-shan waited until the house was silent before she came out of her room. Her uncle was asleep in his chair, his scriptures open on his lap. She crept to the kitchen to get herself a drink of water and momentarily felt guilty for not being available to help with the cleanup. The dim sum baskets were gone, and the plates cleaned and stacked nicely; even the floor was mopped. Li-ying and Jun-jai had probably pitched in and helped. Even Mr. Pierpont might have picked up a plate or two. It had been such a nice evening. Why did she have to ruin it with silly emotions? Wen-shan chided herself because she knew it would have been impossible to control her feelings once she'd seen that painting. And it wasn't just the few additional memories it conjured; she saw her grandfather's love for her in every brushstroke. She saw the truth of the painting.

Wen-shan secured her glass of water, checked the kitchen one more time, turned off the light, and headed for bed. As she stepped into the front room, she saw that her uncle was awake. She walked over and stood by his chair.

"I'm sorry, Uncle, for ruining the evening."

"You did not ruin anything, Wen-shan. It was a wonderful evening." He took her hand. "Are you all right?"

She sat on the sofa. "I'm sorry I wasn't around to help clean up."

"I don't care about that. I want to know how you are."

She sat for a long time looking at the water in her glass. "I feel sad. Sad because that was the last painting. Sad because I miss them so much." She put down her glass. "Does that make sense?"

"Of course. I feel the same."

"Really?"

"Yes."

A band of pain tightened across her chest. "I just want to know if they're all right. I just don't want to be so sad."

Her uncle set his scriptures on the side table. "Would you like to have a prayer together?"

"A prayer? Will that help?"

"I think it might."

"Will you say it? I mean I've been to church a couple of times and I know to bow my head and everything, but I don't know if I could say it."

"Of course." He gave her a slight grin. "I need the practice."

Wen-shan felt embarrassed as she bowed her head, and it seemed like it took her uncle a long time to begin, but when the words came, they were quiet and simple, and she felt warmth surround her. She also felt her fear being pushed back. It was like someone was standing between her and the anxious thoughts about her mother and grandfather. The band of pain eased, and she took a deep breath. When her uncle said "Amen," she repeated the word easily.

Wen-shan looked up at the same time as her uncle. "Thank you, Uncle. I do feel better."

He nodded. "Do you think you can sleep now?"

"Yes."

"Good. Get a good rest, because tomorrow is yard work and you will be very busy."

"To make up for not helping tonight?"

"It's only fair, don't you think?"

"Yes, Uncle." She picked up her glass of water and stood. "Good night, Uncle."

"Good night, Wen-shan."

She headed for bed. "Would you like me to make breakfast in the morning?"

"It's only fair, don't you think?"

Notes

Mirrors and scissors: Superstitions were prevalent in the lives of peasants in rural China. One such superstition was that if you place a mirror and some open scissors over your doorway, it would protect the house from wandering ghosts. The ghosts would be frightened away by their own reflection, but if that didn't work, the scissors would fall and cut any ghost that tried to enter.

Dim sum: Dim sum are baked or steamed dumplings filled with a variety of savory and sweet fillings.

Chapter 27

WHEN WEN-SHAN WALKED into the kitchen the next morning, she found her uncle already there, eating a bowl of cornflakes. She stood staring at him, unable to speak. He held out the bowl to her and shook his head.

"Too Western. You make breakfast while I get dressed. Heat up the leftover dim sum. I will need good food to get rid of that taste."

He passed by her, and she burst out laughing. Her heart felt light as she puttered around the kitchen, setting the table, and steaming some of the leftover dim sum. When her uncle returned to the kitchen, she had everything ready. Her uncle said the blessing on the food, and Wen-shan's mouth watered as she smelled the savory little dumplings.

Her uncle smiled. "See, much better than cornflakes."

"I'm just hungry this morning," Wen-shan defended.

"Well, you had better eat a good breakfast. You will need your strength today."

Wen-shan gave him a half smile and ate another dumpling. Actually, she was looking forward to working in the garden. The days were cooling, so it would be nice to be out in the fresh air and exercising her body.

The telephone rang and her uncle went to answer it. She heard a few words but most of the conversation was muffled. She thought it might be Mr. Pierpont asking her uncle to come in to work, but when her uncle returned to the kitchen, the puzzled look on his face indicated something much more interesting.

"What is it, Uncle?"

"I have something to tell you that might cheer you up for the entire day."

"What?"

"That was a telephone call from Mrs. Smythe. It seems that the function they attended last night was a dinner with the board of directors of the Hong Kong Museum of Art and Antiquities."

"What does that have to do with us?"

"Be patient and you'll see." He cleared his throat. "It was an important dinner because they were honoring Master Quan."

"Oh, how wonderful!"

"But that is not all."

"Oh?"

"It seems that during the evening, Mrs. Smythe suggested that the museum host an exhibit of your grandfather's paintings at the museum next month."

"An exhibit?"

Her uncle nodded. "And the board said yes."

Wen-shan was dumbfounded. "But they haven't even seen grandfather's paintings."

"It seems the board of directors has a very high opinion of Mr. and Mrs. Smythe's art expertise."

Wen-shan thought of all the priceless art treasures in the Smythes' home, and smiled. "Oh, Uncle, don't you think it's a great honor?"

"I do."

Wen-shan sat with her chopsticks poised over a dumpling. She was thinking of the reactions of the people who would see her grandfather's work: how they would wander on the pathway through the bamboo, find the strength in the cypress tree, and laugh at the silly rooster. She stopped. "Uncle?"

"Yes?"

"Do we have to show the painting of me and the Communist official?"

"No. I'm sure we can decide which paintings to send." He pointed with his chopsticks to the dim sum on her plate. "Eat up now. Work is waiting for us."

● ● ●

Wen-shan did not want to see another pair of garden clippers for as long as she lived. She stood under the warm water of the shower and let it wash away the dirt and ease her sore muscles. If she was feeling this sore and tired, she couldn't imagine what her great-uncle was feeling. She turned and let the water patter onto her face. And what did her mother feel like when she came in from the rice fields? Suddenly Wen-shan saw her complaints as petulant and trivial. She picked up the soap and finished her shower quickly.

Her uncle had fixed long noodles and pork for dinner. Long noodles for a long life. The two workers sat and ate and talked about their day. Sore muscles aside, it was an admirable accomplishment. The garden was now ready for the change of season, and even though in Hong Kong that wasn't as drastic as in some parts of the world, the weather would be drier and cooler.

Wen-shan finished her noodles and took her bowl to the sink.

"I'd like to read another letter tonight, if you're not too tired," she said.

"I'm not too tired."

After the kitchen was cleaned, Wen-shan and her uncle took their accustomed places for letter reading and Wen-shan opened the drawer. She brought out the two remaining letters.

"We only have two left," she said.

"But we can read them over and over."

"That's true."

"Little pieces of their lives."

Wen-shan nodded and untied the ribbon. As the scroll opened, she realized there were two pieces of paper. The one was like the other parchments on which her mother had written, but the second piece was coarse and yellowed by age.

"Ah! Careful!" her uncle cautioned when she reached for the second paper. Wen-shan gingerly took the roll and handed it to her uncle.

"Clear the table," he instructed.

She moved off the magazines and he gently laid down the scroll and began to unroll it.

"Do you know what it is?"

"I think I do."

As the characters emerged, her uncle's hand began to

tremble. The scroll was the length of her arm, and Wen-shan helped hold one end. Hundreds and hundreds of names filled the aged parchment.

"I've prayed for this," her uncle whispered.

Wen-shan was confused. "What is it?"

"Better to ask who they are." He carefully placed a magazine on his end of the scroll, and Wen-shan did the same.

"These are the names of your ancestors, Wen-shan." There was respect in his voice, and Wen-shan looked closer at the characters.

"My ancestors? Where did all these names come from?"

"They have been kept by a family scribe for generations, handed down from the head of the family to the next." He traced his fingers lightly over the characters. "This is six hundred, perhaps seven hundred, years of ancestors."

Wen-shan shook her head. "But the Communists are against honoring ancestors. Why didn't the Red Guards destroy this? They destroyed my grandfather's paintings—why not this?"

"I'm sure your mother hid this in the ancestral shrine, Wen-shan, and then placed it in the box when things got worse."

"She thought the names would be safer with us?"

"Yes."

"She put a lot of trust in Master Quan, didn't she?"

"Yes. Your mother was very brave."

"You said you prayed for this. Did you mean that you prayed the names would come to us?"

"Yes. I have always honored my ancestors, and when Mei-lan and I were studying about the Church, we were taught the principle of eternal sealing. It spoke powerfully to us."

"What does that mean?"

"It means that by priesthood power families can be tied to-gether forever."

"Forever? You mean in heaven?"

"Yes."

"Me to my mother?"

"Yes. And your mother to your father, and they to their parents."

"To my grandmother who wove the blue cloth and had her feet bound?"

"Yes."

"And you to Mei-lan?"

Her uncle lowered his head. "Yes."

She laid her hand on his.

"And great-nieces to great-uncles?"

He gripped her fingers as tears rolled down his cheeks. "Yes."

"It is a wonderful principle!"

"It is."

Wen-shan felt a thrill race through her body from the top of her head to her feet. "How? How do we do this great tying together?"

Her uncle chuckled and wiped away the tears. "Tomorrow at church we will ask Mr. Pierpont. I think he is a master at genealogy."

"Genealogy?"

"The study of ancestors." He looked back to the parchment. "Mr. Pierpont will be thrilled with our good fortune."

Wen-shan unrolled the letter. "I wonder what my mother said about the ancestor scroll."

She read.

*I am sending the ancestors' names into your hands.
My heart feels strongly that they will be safe with you.*

*I look across the table at my father and think that
there are just the two of us and that my world is very
small, but then I think of you and Uncle Zhao Tai-lu
in Hong Kong, and then I think of a thousand ancestors
in heaven, and I am changed into an empress in a royal
court.*

*Remember, you are never alone, my daughter. I
think of you every day.*

Wen-shan stopped reading and took several deep breaths to
calm her emotions.

*I think of you every day. Can you hear my voice,
little daughter? Can you see my face? Look into the
mirror. Perhaps we look the same. Perhaps your face is
round and your eyes still full of wonder. Where is your
little blue jacket? Where are your cries in the night?
Know that I think of you as I cut the rice, or when I
look at the moon, or when I see a blue butterfly. I go to
the family shrine and burn the sweet flower incense. I
pray to the ancestors to watch over you. Father says the
ancestors are very clever and very good. He says they
will guide your footsteps.*

*Do not worry for us. Father and I have planned
what we will do if the new man Luo wants to make
an example of the artist. We will go at midnight when
the moon is dark. We will walk into the mountains to
Longji, to the Dragon Back Terraces where Father lived
until he was four. We will seek out his relatives and beg*

to be taken in. I will learn to plant rice on the terraces,
and Father will do what he can. He gains strength
every day. Soon he will hold his own chopsticks again.

I feel the ancestors are glad to be with you. Watch
over them. They are country people and might be
frightened of the city.

Wen-shan and her uncle chuckled over her mother's final thought.

"I think your mother is teasing us."

"Do you? I think she actually means it." Wen-shan's gaze turned back to the ancestor scroll. "It's nice to think they're watching out for us."

"It is." He carefully rolled the scroll while Wen-shan rolled the letter. She put them both into the drawer and stood. She stretched her back and grimaced.

"Good night, Uncle."

"Good night, Wen-shan. Thank you for your work."

"You're welcome." She moved to her bedroom. "I can't wait to see Mr. Pierpont's face when we show him the scroll."

In the night, Wen-shan dreamed of her mother. She was walking the streets of Central Hong Kong. Cars honked when she tried to cross the street, and people bumped into her on the sidewalks. She was wearing her torn trousers and sweat-stained jacket. There was a dunce cap on her head and shame showed on her face. She kept asking people if they'd seen the little girl in the blue padded jacket, but no one understood her country dialect. She sat down on the curb and cried. Suddenly there were many ancestors surrounding her. They picked her up and flew away with her. They turned into a flock of white cranes who flew back over the heavenly mountains.

Wen-shan stirred awake. She took a drink of water and turned her pillow to the cool side. She would try to remember her dream. She wanted to share it with her uncle.

NOTE

Dragon Back Terraces: These terraced rice fields were built in the Yuan Dynasty (1271–1368). They cover an area of 66 square kilometers (about 16,308 acres) and are approximately 27 kilometers (about 16 miles) from the Guilin area. It is considered to be one of the most amazing sites in all of China.

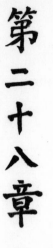

Chapter 28

T HE DISPLAY OF HER GRANDFATHER'S masterpieces in the Museum of Art and Antiquities was stunning. Someone had drawn a graphic interpretation of the heavenly mountains as a backdrop, and each painting was showcased on its own pillar. The central piece was her grandfather's calligraphy: TRUTH. Large vases of bamboo were placed throughout the exhibit so it seemed as though you were walking through a forest.

Wen-shan had been caught by the magic as soon as she'd entered the intimate exhibition hall. She was glad she had decided to wear her red cheongsam dress with the powerful dragons. She needed all the strength she could find. There was going to be a crowd of invited guests: their friends, Mr. and Mrs. Smythe and their friends, the museum's board of directors, and business and city leaders. It was even rumored that the mayor of Hong Kong might make an appearance.

Yes. She was glad she had dressed up. She was also glad that she and her uncle had this quiet time to view the exhibit by themselves before the crowds arrived.

They stood together in front of the now-framed painting of her father and mother on their wedding day.

Her uncle turned to her. "You look very nice, Wen-shan."

"Thank you, Uncle. You look nice too."

He smiled. "Are you nervous?"

"A little."

"So am I. We are not used to these fancy parties."

Wen-shan giggled. "But it is good for us to be here. It is good for people to see grandfather's paintings."

"Yes. Confucius says that the country with the most exalted culture will always yield the greatest power in the world."

Wen-shan nodded. She turned back to study the painting and to think about all the changes that had come into their lives over the past several months. In a few days, she would be sixteen, and because of her mother's letters, she would be a different sixteen. The stories of suffering were difficult, but always there was courage and endurance, a facing of the past and the future. She had learned from that.

Last night in honor of the exhibit, she and her uncle had read the final letter. It was short and written hurriedly but contained news that offered hope.

> *I must run quickly and place this last letter in the jade dragon box. Father and I enclose pieces of our hearts within. We do not know what will happen. There are rumors that Secretary Luo is planning a purge of some dangerous counterrevolutionaries, but*

Father and I will stay together and hope we remain invisible.

I have heard from Han-lie. He will be coming home after the rainy season. The CCCP has noted his good work and will send him back to his family. I hope he will understand why I had to send you away.

The bamboo still bends in the storm.

"Wen-shan?"

Wen-shan blinked and looked up into the face of Wei Jun-jai.

"Jun-jai, what are you doing here?" She glanced around. "Are they starting to let people in?"

"No, I snuck in early to see how you were doing. I'm sorry. I'll go back out."

She caught his arm. "Don't be silly. I'm glad you're here."

The embarrassment slid from his face. "Oh, good." He bowed to Wen-shan's uncle. "Good-evening, Mr. Zhao. The exhibit is beautiful."

"Yes, they have done a good job, haven't they?" Wen-shan could not read the expression on her uncle's face, but it seemed that a slight grin touched the corner of his mouth. "If you two will excuse me, I'd like to check the lighting on the cypress painting." He bowed to Jun-jai, who bowed back. When he was gone, Jun-jai seemed a bit nervous.

"I like your dress. You look very nice."

"Thank you, Jun-jai. Would you like to see the exhibit before everyone comes in?"

"Yes. I would love to."

The two walked through the stands of bamboo discovering the sparrow painting, the Yellow Cloth Shoal, and the comical rooster. Just as they reached the painting of the plum blossoms, the door to the exhibition hall was opened, and people started drifting in.

Song Li-ying found her immediately. "Oh, Wen-shan, this is magical."

"It is, isn't it?"

"Hello, Wei Jun-jai."

"Good evening, Song Li-ying."

Li-ying stared around the room. "Look at all the people."

"I know, let's move off to the side," Wen-shan suggested.

The three went to stand by a wall on the far side of the room. Wen-shan liked this vantage point. She could watch the people without them being aware of her. Among the guests, she picked out Mrs. and Mr. Tuan, Mr. Yee, Mrs. Yang, and Master Quan with her uncle. The two were walking toward her—the scholar in his long scholar's dress.

"Would you like to see one of China's great treasures?" Wen-shan asked her friends.

"Of course," they chorused.

Master Quan came to her and bowed. "Miss Chen, what a perfect night, yes?"

"Yes, Master Quan." She motioned her friends forward. "Master Quan, I would like you to meet my friends, Song Li-ying and Wei Jun-jai."

He bowed to both, and they bowed back. "These are friends that do good. I can tell."

Jun-jai smiled. "It is easy to be a good friend when one has a good friend."

"Ah, Jun-jai has now become a teacher," her uncle said.

Jun-jai took the teasing good-naturedly.

"I am taking Master Quan to see the exhibit. Do you want to join us?" her uncle asked.

Jun-jai and Li-ying accepted immediately, but Wen-shan declined.

"I'll stay with you," Jun-jai offered.

"That's very kind of you, Jun-jai, but I think I'd like a few minutes by myself."

He smiled at her. "I understand. We'll see you later." He and Li-ying went with the elders, matching their stride to Master Quan's shuffle.

It was just as she imagined it: people standing in awe of her grandfather's skill, reaching out toward something that touched their heart, discussing some aspect with a partner. She had decided to join the crowd when she noticed Mr. and Mrs. Smythe enter the hall. They both looked elegant. He wore a tuxedo, and Mrs. Smythe wore a blue silk gown and diamond accessories. Wen-shan saw them glance around the room. When they spotted her, they split up. Mr. Smythe went one direction, and Mrs. Smythe headed to her.

"My dear! Don't you look stunning!" Mrs. Smythe said as she approached.

"So do you," Wen-shan returned. "And this exhibit is stunning."

"It is, isn't it?" she answered, perusing the venue. "There are a few visionaries on the board, thank heavens."

"Didn't you want to view the paintings with your husband?"

"Oh, all in good time. He's actually gone to retrieve your great-uncle. There's something we need to share with you. Ah! Here they come now."

The two men came up and Mr. Smythe bowed to Wen-shan. "My, my, my, Miss Chen. You look lovely."

She blushed. "Thank you, Mr. Smythe." She looked to her uncle, noting that his expression had become one of concern. "Are you all right, Uncle?"

"Mr. Smythe said they had something to share with us."

Wen-shan shrugged. Did her uncle think they were going to charge them for the exhibition?

"Oh, please, Mr. Zhao, not to worry. The news we have is good news," Mrs. Smythe said. "George, would you like to do the honors?"

Mr. Smythe nodded, and his voice took on a calm and assured tone. "Miss Chen, do you believe in miracles?"

Wen-shan was so shocked by the unexpected question that she almost forgot her manners and said *What?* Instead she stammered, "I . . . I beg your pardon?"

"Miracles. Do you believe in miracles?"

"I think maybe I do, Mr. Smythe."

He reached into his pocket. "I'm very glad you do." He brought out a letter and handed it to her.

She looked at the characters on the front, and her vision blurred with tears. "From my mother? You found my mother?"

Mrs. Smythe's voice took on a tender timbre. "We did, Miss Chen. She was still living in the same house in Guilin."

Her uncle's arm was around her. "Here. Sit here on this bench, Wen-shan."

She was grateful for his help because the room was suddenly spinning and her legs didn't have any strength.

"Oh, my word, George, we should have thought a little bit more about the possible reaction! That was dreadfully shallow of us, Miss Chen."

Her uncle sat next to her on the bench. "I am not feeling very steady myself."

"Rock of Gibraltar, George! Go find a doctor!"

Wen-shan started to giggle. "No. No, Mrs. Smythe, I'm fine. We'll be fine. We're just a little . . ." She began to cry. "Overwhelmed."

Mrs. Smythe sat on the other side of her. "Well, George and I are nincompoops, that's all there is to it."

Now Wen-shan was laughing and crying at the same time. "You are both wonderful," she stuttered. "Wonderful. Look at what you did. It *is* a miracle. Thank you." Impulsively she threw her arms around Mrs. Smythe's neck and hugged her. "You brought my mother to me." She pushed away and saw Mrs. Smythe flick a tear from the corner of her eye.

"Don't you dare make me spoil my makeup."

Mr. Smythe stepped forward. "Are you sure you're all right, Mr. Zhao? We'll get you whatever help you need."

"We are fine, Mr. Smythe. It is just very emotional."

"Of course. We should have had you come to the house."

Mrs. Smythe spoke up. "But we just received the letter today, and I guess we lost our wits."

At the mention of the letter, Wen-shan held it in front of her to get a better look. It was her name and her mother's name, right in front of her, on the same envelope.

Mrs. Smythe stood. "All right, George, we've made enough blunders for one day. Let's go look at this exquisite art and leave these two to their letter."

Wen-shan caught her hand. "I will never be able to repay you for what you've done."

Mrs. Smythe put her gloved hand under Wen-shan's chin. "Your happiness is payment enough." She turned to go, then turned back. "Oh, there is something you can do."

Wen-shan swallowed. "Anything."

"You and your friends must come again for another round of tin biscuits and sodas. And you must stay longer for a proper visit."

"Yes, ma'am."

The couple left, and Wen-shan turned to her uncle. "I know it is not the best time and place, but I have to open this letter. I have to see what it says."

"I understand. I want to know too."

Wen-shan didn't hesitate. She ran her finger along the glued portion of the flap and took out the letter.

She unfolded it and read.

When your letter came, my father, your father, and I wet the sleeves of our jackets with tears.

Her uncle hugged her. "Alive, Wen-shan! They are all alive! It is such a miracle." He let her go. "Sorry, sorry. Read on."

You and Uncle Zhao are safe in Hong Kong, and you, my daughter, have become a young woman with words, and friends, and schooling. I tell everyone in my neighborhood about my daughter in Hong Kong. Your father would like a picture if you can send one. I think with the new leaders things will be easier.

The big news for you is that you have a brother, Huan-bai, and a sister, Wen-lan. Perhaps someday they can meet their big sister.

Wen-shan stopped reading and stared at the paper. "I have a brother and sister?" She was having a hard time working through all the new information. Just knowing her mother was alive was overwhelming, but she knew she had to read to the end.

> *Father is doing well. He has retrained his fingers to paint.*

Her uncle put his head in his hands and wept. Wen-shan's voice grew husky as she continued reading.

> *I no longer work in the fields. I take care of my family, grow a large garden, and sell some of the extra at the village market. I will not try to tell you everything in one letter. Now that we are tied together, other letters will come.*
> *I saw a blue butterfly in the garden today and thought of you. I think of you every day.*
> *Mother*

Wen-shan slowly folded the letter. "Alive, Uncle. They're alive."

Her uncle nodded, unable to speak.

She stood. "May I share this with Li-ying and Jun-jai?"

"Of course."

She went off to share the unbelievable news with her friends and with Mr. Pierpont, Mrs. Yang, and Master Quan. The happiness seemed to swell with each telling and in the end, the evening became not only a tribute, but a joyous celebration.

● ● ●

Much later that evening, Wen-shan stood at the front gate looking toward the twinkling lights of the city and the shimmer of moonlight on the water. Most people had settled in for the night and all was quiet. A cool breeze blew her hair back from her face, and she breathed in the tangy air of salt water. She still wore her dragon dress but had abandoned her shoes to the front porch. She now stood barefooted on the cool stones of the path.

Wen-shan looked up at the half-moon, wondering if the other half was with her mother, shining over the heavenly mountains and the Li River. She closed her eyes and thought about God and miracles. She said a silent prayer of thanks. She smiled to herself as she walked through the forest of bamboo to her grandfather's house, as she watched the fishing birds dive for fish, and as she stood with her mother on the Hundred Flower Bridge.

Someday. Someday.

NOTES

Based on a true story: The character of Wen-shan's uncle, Zhao Tai-lu, is based on an actual person. His name and family configuration have been changed to fit the needs of the story and to protect his anonymity, but his military background, his life in the refugee camp, his rescue by LDS missionaries, his membership in the Church, and his running of a noodle factory are all actual events.

Confucian teaching on the arts: Confucius looked upon music, art, and poetry as powerful instruments for moral education. He taught that the country which develops the finest music, the grandest poetry, and the noblest moral ideals—that is, the country with the most exalted culture—will always yield the greatest power in the world.

Although Chen Wen-shan is a fictional character, she represents thousands of citizens from mainland China whose lives were disrupted during the reign of Mao Tse-tung.

Following Mao's death in 1976, the Communist government under the leadership of Deng Xiaoping brought the worst of the party criminals to justice, including Mao's fourth wife, Jiang Qing, and her ruthless Gang of Four. Also under Deng's administration the stranglehold on communication and travel was loosened slightly, and it became easier to move about the country. Although there were strict regulations on travel, those who could afford the fees were able to visit family members living outside of China. Educational reforms were also instituted and a few of the brightest college students went abroad to pursue advanced degrees in science and technology. The classic Communist Party position calling for prolonged class struggle was exchanged for the attainment of economic goals, and

Deng's ideological position of "seeking truth from facts" began the formation of a new system of laws and judicial organization.

These changes allowed the Church to make significant progress in China. On October 1, 1992, President Gordon B. Hinckley announced the Hong Kong Temple; a mere seventy years after apostle David O. McKay had stood in the Forbidden City in Peking on January 9, 1921, and dedicated the land of China for the preaching of the gospel. The Church of Jesus Christ of Latter-day Saints would build a temple on British soil—soil that would soon belong to Communist China.

Hong Kong became a British colony in 1898 with the signing of a ninety-nine-year lease, which would expire June 30, 1997. In December 1984, British and Chinese authorities signed a declaration confirming that the British government would hand over Hong Kong to the People's Republic of China on July 1, 1997.

The Hong Kong Temple was dedicated in May 1996.

When young mission president H. Grant Heaton purchased the property in Kowloon for the mission home and church offices in the 1950s, could he have envisioned that someday a unique and beautiful temple would stand upon the site to bless the lives of the Saints in Hong Kong?

President Gordon B. Hinckley made this statement to the *Ensign* just prior to the dedication of the temple: "I almost weep every time I think of having a temple in the great Chinese realm [wherein live one-fourth of the inhabitants of the earth]. It will be a different kind of temple. I want to say that if I ever felt the inspiration of the Lord in my life, it was on the occasion of going over there to find a place to build a temple" (in Kallene Ricks Adams, "A Dream Come True in Hong Kong," *Ensign,* June 1996, 47).

To me, the blessing of the gospel taking root in China is yet another miracle of the Lord.

Appendix

China Dedicatory Prayer

David O. McKay
January 9, 1921
Forbidden City, Peking

"Our Heavenly Father: In deep humility and gratitude, we thy servants approach thee in prayer and supplication on this most solemn and momentous occasion. We pray thee to draw near unto us, to grant us the peace asked for in the opening prayer by Brother Cannon; and to let the channel of communication between thee and us be open, that thy word may be spoken, and thy will be done. We pray for forgiveness of any folly, weakness, or lightmindedness that it may not stand between us and the rich outpouring of thy Holy Spirit. Holy Father, grant us thy peace and thy inspiration, and may we not be disturbed during this solemn service.

"For thy kind protection and watchful care over us in our

travels by land and by sea, we render our sincere gratitude. We are grateful, too, for the fellowship and brotherly love we have one for the other, that our hearts beat as one, and that we stand before thee this holy Sabbath day with clean hands, pure hearts, and with our minds free from all worldly cares.

"Though keenly aware of the great responsibility this special mission entails, yet we are thankful that thou hast called us to perform it. Heavenly Father, make us equal, we beseech thee, to every duty and task. As we visit thy Missions in the various parts of the world, give us keen insight into the conditions and needs of each, and bestow upon us in rich abundance the gift of discernment.

"With grateful hearts, we acknowledge thy guiding influence in our travels to this great land of China, and particularly to this quiet and secluded spot in the heart of this ancient and crowded city. We pray that the petition setting this spot apart as a place of prayer and dedication may be granted by thee and that it may be held sacred in thy sight.

"Holy Father, we rejoice in the knowledge of the truth, and in the restoration of the Gospel of the Redeemer. We praise thy name for having revealed thyself and thine Only Begotten Son to thy servant, Joseph the Prophet, and that through thy revelations the Church, in its purity and perfection, was established in these last days for the happiness and eternal salvation of the human family. We thank thee for the Priesthood, which gives men authority to officiate in thy holy name.

"In this land there are millions who know not thee nor thy work, who are bound by the fetters of superstition and false doctrine, and who have never been given the opportunity even of hearing the true message of their Redeemer. Countless millions have died in ignorance of thy plan of life and salvation. We feel deeply impressed with the realization that the time has come when the light of the glorious Gospel should begin to shine through the dense darkness that has enshrouded this nation for ages.

"To this end, therefore, by the authority of the Holy Apostleship, I dedicate and consecrate and set apart the Chinese Realm for the preaching of the Gospel of Jesus Christ as restored in this dispensation through the Prophet Joseph Smith. By this act shall the key be turned that unlocks the door through which thy chosen servants shall enter with glad tidings of great joy to this benighted and senile nation. That their message may be given in peace, we beseech thee, O God, to stabilize the Chinese government. Thou knowest how it is torn with dissension at the present time, and how faction contends against faction to the oppression of the people and the strangling of the nation's life. Holy Father, may peace and stability be established throughout this republic, if not by the present government, then through the intervention of the allied powers of the civilized world.

"Heavenly Father, manifest thy tender mercy toward thy suffering children throughout this famine-stricken realm! Stay the progress of pestilence, and may starvation and untimely death stalk no more through the land. Break the bands of superstition, and may the young men and young women come out of the darkness of the Past into the Glorious Light now shining among the children of men. Grant, our Father, that these young men and women may, through upright, virtuous lives, and prayerful study, be prepared and inclined to declare this message of salvation in their own tongue to their fellowmen. May their hearts, and the hearts of this people, be turned to their fathers that they may accept the opportunity offered them to bring salvation to the millions who have gone before.

"May the Elders and Sisters whom thou shalt call to this land as missionaries have keen insight into the mental and spiritual state of the Chinese mind. Give them special power and ability to approach this people in such a manner as will make the proper appeal to them. We beseech thee, O God, to reveal to thy servants the best methods to adopt and the best plans to follow in establishing thy work among this ancient, tradition-steeped people. May the work prove joyous, and a rich harvest of honest souls bring that peace to the workers' hearts which surpasseth all understanding.

"Remember thy servants, whom thou has chosen to preside in thy Church. We uphold and sustain before thee President Heber J. Grant, who stands at the head at this time, and his counselors, President Anthon H. Lund and President Charles W. Penrose. Bless them, we pray thee, with every needful blessing, and keep them one in all things pertaining to thy work. Likewise bless the Council of Twelve. May they continue to be one with the First Presidency. Remember the Presiding Patriarch, the First Council of Seventy, the Presiding Bishopric, and all who preside in stakes, wards, quorums, organizations, temples, Church schools, and missions. May the spirit of purity, peace, and energy characterize all thy organizations.

"Heavenly Father, be kind to our Loved Ones from whom we are now separated. Let thy Holy Spirit abide in our homes, that sickness, disease, and death may not enter therein.

"Hear us, O kind and Heavenly Father, we implore thee, and open the door for the preaching of thy Gospel from one end of this realm to the other, and may thy servants who declare this message be especially blest and directed by thee. May thy kingdom come, and thy will be done speedily here on earth among all peoples, kindreds, and tongues preparatory to the winding up scenes of these latter days!

"And while we behold thy guiding hand through it all, we shall ascribe unto thee the praise, the glory, and the honor, through Jesus Christ our Lord and Redeemer, Amen."

Bibliography

Analects of Confucius. Translated by D. C. Lau. Harmondsworth,
Middlesex, England: Penguin Books, Ltd., 1979.

Becker, Jasper. *Hungry Ghosts—Mao's Secret Famine*. New York:
Henry Holt and Company, 1998.

Buck, Pearl S. *The Good Earth*. New York: Washington Square
Press, 2004.

Cannon, Hugh J. *David O. McKay around the World: An
Apostolic Mission*. Provo, Utah: Spring Creek Book
Company, 2005.

Chang, Jung. *Wild Swans: Three Daughters of China*. New York:
Simon & Schuster, 2003.

Chang, Jung, and Jon Halliday. *Mao: The Unknown Story*. New
York: Alfred A. Knopf, 2005.

Cheng, Nien. *Life and Death in Shanghai*. New York: Grove
Press, 1986.

The Communist Manifesto and Other Revolutionary Writings.

BIBLIOGRAPHY

Marx, Marat, Paine, Mao, Gandhi, and Others. Edited by Bob Blaisdell. New York: Dover Publications, Inc., 2003.

Compestine, Ying Chang. *A Banquet for Hungry Ghosts—A Collection of Deliciously Frightening Tales.* New York: Henry Holt and Company, 2009.

———. *Revolution Is Not a Dinner Party.* New York: Henry Holt and Company, 2007.

Ebrey, Patricia Buckley. *Cambridge Illustrated History: China.* New York: Cambridge University Press, 2003.

Heaton, H. Grant, and Luana C. Heaton, comp. *Southern Far East Mission, 1949–1959.* Salt Lake City, Utah, 1999.

Jiang, Ji-Li. *Red Scarf Girl: A Memoir of the Cultural Revolution.* New York: HarperCollins Publishers Inc., 1977.

Liang, Jian. *Guilin's Landscape.* Guilin, China: Fairyland, 2006.

———. *The Scenery of Li River.* Guilin, China: Fairyland, 2006.

Mao, Tse-tung. *Quotations from Chairman Mao Tse-tung.* Peking: Foreign Languages Press, 1966.

Marx, Karl, and Friedrich Engels. *The Communist Manifesto.* New York: Penguin Books, 1967.

Somerville, Neil. *Your Chinese Horoscope 2007.* New York: Barnes & Noble, 2006.

Tan, Amy. *The Opposite of Fate.* New York: Penguin Books, 2004.